BUZZARD HOUSE

JONAH GREENE MYSTERIES BOOK 2

GRAHAM H MILLER

THE WELSH LANGUAGE

Don't be alarmed, but there are a few Welsh words in this novel. In Welsh the letter W can be a vowel with a short U sound. So, the Welsh name of Buzzard House is Tŷ Bwncath, which is pronounced Tee Buncath (or even B'ncath). The word cofiwch is pronounced covi-uch (F sounds like a V). The bike gang are the Riders of Annwn, so that's pronounced Annun. Finally Welsh is a language where the first letter of some words changes in some situations. So the phrase 'Cofiwch Dŷ Bwncath' is correct even though the T has changed to a D.

PART ONE

CHAPTER 1

Jonah Greene picked up his mobile – 6:37 in the morning – this call was not going to be good news. He got some small reassurance from seeing a work number rather than a family one.

"Uh? Hello?"

"Is this DS Greene? Jonah?" The voice sounded familiar and Jonah scrambled in his memory for a name.

"Yes. Dave? What's up?" He nearly added that it had been over six months since they last spoke but bit it back. Even in his hungover state he knew he didn't want to go back over that history.

"Yeah." There was a pause. "Thing is, we need a hand. CID, I mean."

"Okay, what's up?" He checked to see if his wife, Alex, was being disturbed by the call. She pulled the duvet closer and rolled away so Jonah stayed where he was.

"Well, I pulled the overnight duty manning the phones, and we had someone fall under a train at Pontyclun this morning. Dozy 999 operator put it through to us."

"Isn't that a British Transport Police matter though?"

"Yeah, it should be. Is there any way you could swing it as a matter that the coroner needs to investigate?" There was a pause as Dave got to the point. "Last time we got into a head to head with the BTP we lost out. We'd like to even the score."

Jonah tried to swallow but his mouth was dry and tasted horrible. His head throbbed and his eyes felt gritty. Slowly he marshalled his thoughts and tried to work through the logic of what David Jones, DC Jones in fact, was saying.

"Pontyclun is definitely in our area. And it counts as a sudden death." His thoughts were sluggish, so he felt his way along, thinking as he spoke. "So, I can certainly start my investigation before the BTP call me in."

"Definitely. And, of course, if it is complex you can always call in CID for extra support."

Jonah's emotions were slower than his thoughts, but they caught up. CID and BTP were fighting. He was a way round the problem, a way to get CID onto BTP turf. But the important thing wasn't the politics – it was that they'd called on him. For so long he had been a pariah but now he had a way to mend fences with his old team. He was even able to overlook the fact that DC Jones was treating him as an equal even though Jonah now outranked him as a sergeant. As his head cleared, he knew he had to find a way to call in CID support. He didn't want to waste this chance to prove to his former colleagues that he could be trusted again.

"So, you'll do it?"

"Yeah, sorry, yeah. Of course. I'll call ahead and tell them not to move anything until I get there. It's the other side of Cardiff but I should only be thirty minutes or so at this time of morning."

"And you'll keep CID in the loop?" And show BTP who's in charge, was the unspoken message.

"Of course," Jonah said with a smile. Usually he hated all the politics but the chance to get one up on another force and win points with CID lifted his mood.

The fog of Jonah's headache was lifting and a quick shower got him back into work mode. By the time he had finished, Alex had given up trying to sleep and was getting up for work.

"You're not normally up before me?" Alex frowned at Jonah.

"Yeah, sudden death. But it'll get me back in CID's good books so I'm willing to help."

With that, he got dressed, and within forty minutes of getting the phone call from CID, Jonah was on the platform of Pontyclun Station. It was a small, commuter station, and was more or less deserted. It had just two platforms, a bridge connecting them, and two basic shelters. Everyone who was there was official: station employees, rail workers, British Transport Police. Jonah looked around and couldn't see any passengers.

On the Cardiff bound side of the tracks was the standard white scene of crimes tent. Further back, just off the platform, the train was parked. Everything was eerily quiet – no train noise, announcements, or passengers talking. Jonah moved towards the tent, trying to work out who to ask if it was safe to go onto the tracks.

A short man in glasses approached, wearing what looked at first glance to be a regular police hi-vis vest. But Jonah knew better – he saw the chequered stripe and the words 'British Transport' above the police patch.

The man held his hands out and attempted to shoo Jonah back down the platform. "I don't know how much you bribed that plod who's meant to be stopping journalists, but I'll have his job and you won't get your story! There's nothing to see here, we haven't even informed the relatives, so scuttle back..." His monologue stopped when Jonah refused to move. Slowly the other man looked at his warrant card.

"Police. Here to have a quick look over the scene."

"South Wales? CID?" He shook his head. "Fuck's sake! How many times do I have to tell them? This isn't your jurisdiction." He gestured around, then spoke slowly as if Jonah was deaf or stupid. "This is a railway. Tracks. Platform. Train. Buildings. All of it's legally railway. That means it's British Transport Police jurisdiction. If this place had sidings and sheds, then they would be mine too. Now piss off back to your station!"

"You have a dead body?"

"You know we do."

"Right. I'm DS Greene, the coroner's officer. This is a sudden death. So, I'm investigating on the coroner's behalf, under his jurisdiction."

The man gave a grim laugh. "It was sudden all right! Have you looked in the tent?" When Jonah shook his head, he continued. "Well I wouldn't if you want to keep your breakfast." There was an awkward pause. "You're the coroner's what? Which station?"

"Officer... from Cardiff Central." Jonah decided he'd pushed the other man far enough and adopted a more conciliatory tone. "I'm not CID – I answer direct to the coroner."

There was a pause as the two men stared at each other. Jonah felt a sudden twinge of doubt. What if this was a careful set-up by CID to make him look stupid?

But no, he thought, Dave had sounded like he didn't

want to talk to Jonah. He knew from his CID days that Dave didn't have any great imagination or flair for practical jokes. He felt sure that calling him had been a last resort.

He was also certain that cases like this should be cooperative between BTP and South Wales Police, but he knew it wouldn't be. Whoever this officer was, he was clearly aware of whatever dispute had happened in the past between CID and BTP.

"Wait here while I phone my boss." This sounded like an admission of weakness from the BTP man, who turned his back to make the phone call.

With nothing better to do, Jonah looked around. He had no desire to look inside the forensic tent, even before the warning from Mr BTP. He could only imagine what happened when hundreds of tons of moving train hit a human body.

He looked past it to the train which was stationary. He wondered if there were flecks of blood on the cab, but from this distance he couldn't tell which marks were dirt and rust, and which were evidence.

It was warm, even early in the morning. The combination of feeling gritty and tired at a station in the building heat cast Jonah's mind back to when he'd been a commuter. He imagined all those people packed onto trains, the different scents of deodorants and body odours mingling. He was glad he'd left it all behind, nearly twenty years ago now.

One of the train workers, in grubby overalls and hi-vis jacket waved to him. "You can come down if you want. It's not electric yet. They keep promising, but..." He shrugged.

Jonah jumped down awkwardly. It was further than he'd realised. He had an uneasy feeling. Since his school days the message 'stay off the tracks' had been drilled into him.

He walked slowly towards the tent, allowing his eyes to sweep left and right across the tracks.

"Hey! What you doing down there?" BTP was back.

"The maintenance guy said I could," Jonah said.

"Well I didn't authorise it. I told you to wait while I phoned my boss."

"And, what did he say?"

"Apparently, we're to cooperate and share our findings," he said grudgingly.

"There you are, this is me, cooperating," Jonah said. As there seemed to be nothing else to say, he turned around and continued walking up the tracks, still scanning for anything that the BTP had missed.

At first, there was nothing of interest, just the usual litter of cigarette packets and fast food wrappers, all covered with a thin film of grease and dirt. Then something brighter caught his eye.

Trapped under one edge of the scene-of-crime tent was a crumpled photograph. Jonah pulled on a latex glove and carefully picked it up by one corner. It was still bright, not dirty like everything else down on the tracks. The subject was a boy, grinning awkwardly into the camera, slightly out of focus, and badly framed. It looked faded as if it was an old photo.

Jonah flipped it over and sagged. On the back was written 'Cofiwch Dŷ Bwncath'. Welsh. He hadn't been taught the language at school and had only learnt the basics since to get by. In this part of Wales, it wasn't necessary. With a sense of resignation, he slipped it into an evidence bag.

"Oi!" Jonah looked up to the platform, BTP was glaring at him. "What are you doing down there?"

The man was short but being on the platform he loomed over Jonah.

"I'm just doing my job, checking for evidence. Second pair of eyes and all that."

BTP man moved down the platform to get closer to Jonah. "What did you pick up?"

"Just an old photo," Jonah admitted, holding it up in its bag.

"Hmmm, well, like I said, cooperate and share," he said grudgingly. "Make sure you let us know if it's significant. There's so much crap on the tracks though, it's going to be nothing." He looked awkward as if making a confession. "I suppose with a high-profile case like this we'll have to bring in some CID officers to help us. When they're on board, I'll tell them to set up an evidence officer and you can show him your photo."

Jonah smiled to himself and nodded curtly. He had to turn away before the other man saw him smiling. He was imagining the reaction when the BTP officer tried issuing orders to CID.

"How high profile exactly?" Jonah asked. "Have you identified the body?"

The BTP officer looked around as if seeking a way out. He couldn't find one. "According to his driving license he was one Leo Davidson, aged fifty-seven." Jonah got his pocketbook out to make his own notes. "He lived near here, so he was probably commuting up to London. Obviously, we can't check if he looks like his photo but there's nothing to indicate he's not."

"Occupation?"

"He was a big name in sport, football and stuff, then he

sat on committees. Probably lived near here because it's close to Ninian Park. He was on the board of directors for Cardiff FC and various charities."

Jonah looked around again. "Any witnesses? Did you take names?"

"No, as soon as it happened most of the commuters bolted for the car park. We cleared the train, got buses to take them onward. They won't have seen anything either."

"So, no witnesses then. What about CCTV?" Jonah looked up and down the platform for cameras.

"Only in the ticket office and the car park." He jerked a thumb at the end of the platform. "That one was busted last week. Kids messing around."

"Kids? Are you sure?" Jonah looked up at the camera. It was a good ten metres above the platform on a thin pole. "What happened to it?"

"Plastic cover over the lens shattered. Like I said, it'll be kids with catapults or an air rifle or something. It's down on the list to be repaired."

"You don't think it's odd? The week before our victim goes under a train?"

"No." There was a firmness in his voice. "This is a railway. Kids always vandalise railways, it's what they do. We have thousands of miles of track, buildings, bridges, tunnels, machinery. You name it, they'll have a go. It's like they know we can't watch it all at once. If you went up and down here, you'd find graffiti, broken windows, stuff chucked on the tracks, anything and everything. And none of it would be connected with this case, it happens all the time."

Jonah thought around the problem. He came to one uncomfortable conclusion. "The driver, he must've seen what happened?"

"He'll be in the system now. We have a process to

follow, some time off and mandatory counselling. When or if he feels able to tell his counsellor what happened, we have an arrangement. The details of what he saw, whatever he feels able to say, will get passed to me." He stopped there, and Jonah waited for the rest of the process.

"You'll let me know when that happens." Jonah filled in the gap. "I'll need to determine whether it's suicide, accident, or murder."

The BTP officer stomped off without a word. Jonah would've preferred a chance to interview the driver himself, but he knew he would get no further. He also acknowledged that the driver had witnessed something horrific and should be dealt with professionally.

Jonah shrugged and slipped the photograph into his pocket. As he left the scene, he phoned in to CID to let them know that he'd done what they wanted. Now, he would have to start a full investigation into the life of Leo Davidson and determine how he came to die under a train.

———

LATER THAT MORNING, Jonah sifted through a folder full of paper and tried to put together a picture of Leo Davidson's life. In the past he'd tended to pigeon-hole people and define them by their occupation, such as a librarian, or a retired property developer, but Leo's life was more complicated. He had been a football player in his youth – he'd never broken into the higher leagues of the sport as a player, but after he left the pitch, he'd moved first to coaching, then to management. Recently his time had been split between sitting on the boards of several local teams, and various charity committees, all of them based around promoting sport among the young. Jonah picked up a brochure and phrases leapt out at him. 'Legacy of the Olympics', 'obesity time bomb', and 'timely intervention to create a lifelong passion for sport'.

The door opened, and DS Farida Philips came in, holding two coffees. She was wearing her official dark blue hijab. They had become friends over the last few months and she'd saved his life earlier in the year. "I brought coffee." She looked closely at him. "Looks like you need it."

"I'm fine, just got woken up early by this case. The victim was a commuter on an early start."

Farida's eyes narrowed. "Still looks like you're not sleeping."

Jonah took the coffee and pointedly didn't answer.

"So, what have we got then?" Farida changed tack.

"Well, a lot of passengers who may or may not be witnesses left the station as soon as they realised they wouldn't be able to get the train into work that morning."

"Brilliant," Farida said sarcastically.

"And as soon as the track was closed, station staff set up a replacement bus service which took the remaining passengers off to the next station."

"So, no witnesses?"

"Well the driver should make a statement in the next couple of days. But that'll be made to a counsellor and funnelled through the BTP, so God only knows when we'll see it."

Farida frowned and reached for a folder. "So, what are you doing here then?"

"Well, he was some big shot in the world of sport. Professional footballer when he was young, moved on to various boards and charities. Ate lunches on expenses and drank champagne with councillors, Assembly Members, and MPs. So, however he died, it's going to be high profile.

"What we need to do is look into our victim's life. What was he like, what happened to him? Was there any event recently that might lead him to commit suicide? Was he depressed? Or did he have enemies?"

"Even you can't be thinking murder at this early stage?"

"I don't know. I can't see why he would have simply fallen off a flat platform, so it's either murder or suicide."

"He could've had another problem, like a stroke or something."

"That is possible, but it'd be a one in a million chance if he had an event like that at precisely the moment the train was coming in." Jonah stopped to think. "I really doubt the post-mortem would pick it up."

"So," Farida said, "murder or suicide, with no witnesses?"

"It's not as if we can't track down the witnesses. He was waiting for the six twenty-two into Cardiff Central, where you can change for a train to London, stopping at Bristol." When Farida looked blank, he continued. "That's a commuter train. I can go down there tomorrow at the same time, and most of the same people will be there. They'll be waiting at the same spot on the platform so they can get on their usual seat on the train, every day."

"You'd better catch up on sleep then. It looks like the next early morning will finish you off!" Farida's tone was light, but Jonah ignored the jibe again. "Is there any CCTV?"

"Yes, but only the ticket office and car park. Should be emailed through later today. If you have time, you could help me go through it? We can see who was on the platform this morning. Then tick them off and see who doesn't turn up again tomorrow."

"Anyway, what am I doing here?" Farida asked. Jonah frowned at her. "I mean, no disrespect, but you could do this. It's your bread and butter now to go through the details and build a profile. And he's a public figure so there's plenty of information out there."

Jonah gave a wry smile. "I think this is part of my rehabilitation back into the murky world of CID office politics. At some point, BTP stood on South Wales Police's toes and they've been at odds ever since. Because I answer to the coroner, I have a foot in the door of this investigation which will upset the BTP and therefore make CID happy."

"So, I'm your reward then?" Farida had an amused half-smile.

"Kind of. Also, you're in CID, so you can report straight back to them and keep tabs on what me and the BTP are up to."

Farida shook her head despairingly.

"Damn! I almost forgot, what do you make of this?" Jonah took the photo out of his pocket and passed it over to Farida.

She took the evidence bag and turned it over to study both sides. "Don't know. Looks old. It's a proper photo, not a digital one. No website address or anything on the back. Is it from the scene?"

"Yes. But no way of telling how long it was there. That on the back looks like a blood spot."

"And it's fairly clean and dry." She frowned for a minute. "It rained last week so at most it's been on the tracks a few days. Have you translated the Welsh yet?"

"No." Jonah shook his head. "I didn't do it in school, and I haven't picked up that much since."

"It means, 'remember house something'. Hold on, there's an app you can get." She fished out her mobile phone. "Remember Buzzard House," she said triumphantly after a few seconds.

Jonah frowned. "Buzzard House? Where is that?"

"No idea. But I do have Google." They fell silent as she tapped away on her phone. Then she pushed the phone away from her as if she'd been burned.

"Shit!"

Now Jonah was worried – Farida hardly ever swore.

He looked at the screen and saw the result. It was a site for survivors of child abuse to tell their stories. And there was a whole page just for Tŷ Bwncath. He read the first paragraph out loud.

"From 1981 to 1994 Tŷ Bwncath operated as an outdoor activity centre. Specialising in giving holidays in the countryside to looked after children from inner-city areas, thousands of children stayed there on residential courses. However, rumours have circulated for decades about the abuse some of them allegedly suffered." Jonah frowned at the screen. "What are looked after children?"

"Children in care," Farida explained. "It's the new term for it, but official bodies use both."

Jonah nodded and handed the phone back to Farida. They looked at each other, unsure of what to say.

"This is not good," Farida finally said. "This could end our careers."

"What do you mean? Surely if this man was involved, people should know?"

"Not necessarily. It closed twenty-four years ago. At the moment, the only link we've got between Leo Davidson and that place is this one photograph." She stopped and rubbed her eyes, then got up to stand by the window. "How did you collect the photo, has it been logged yet?"

"I did it properly," Jonah said, hurt. "Rubber glove, by the edges, into the bag."

"Good. This is a nightmare. I say we get it a full work

over from documents. We need to know the age, subject, everything. Is that Leo's blood? How long was it on the tracks? Are there any fingerprints?"

Jonah came over to stand next to her. "Are you sure? It's only one photo?"

"After Savile and Operation Yewtree there is only one way forward, and that's by the book. Actually, it wasn't Operation Yewtree, it's what happened beforehand. People reported Jimmy Savile several times. Reports were made, police forces opened cases, and nothing happened."

"Nothing?"

"No, the reports all just disappeared. Savile was canny and had friends in high places who could make all the trouble go away." Farida stopped to make sure that Jonah was listening. "Now that's happened once, we need to be super careful. There's only two ways this can go – either we ruin the reputation of someone who was innocent but had political connections, or we prove that he was a paedophile. I'm not sure which would be worse."

Jonah went back to the desk and opened a file. "You're right. The thing about Savile was that he was a loner. And everyone thought he was a creep. I mean no one heard the news and said, 'What him? I don't believe it!' Everyone kind of expected it. The reports must have been floating around for decades. It was only when he died that the victims came forward."

"Is there any family for Davidson?"

"We haven't had a chance to work out anything detailed yet. Next of kin was his wife, now his widow, so we'll need to be careful."

Farida left the window and walked to the board. Miraculously she found a pen that worked. "Right. We have one photo that may or may not be linked to Leo." She wrote 'photo' and 'Davidson' on the board with a dotted line between them. "That photo itself may or may not be linked to a place called Tŷ Bwncath. Which in turn may or may not have been the site of historic child abuse." She added these to the board.

"Can you do the document forensics?" Jonah asked, looking at the square of dotted lines that Farida had now drawn on the board.

"Yes. If I tell them it's sticking it to BTP, then the budget will be okay."

"Great, and I'll tackle Tŷ Bwncath." He picked up her phone and scrolled down a bit. "It says here it's north of Merthyr, so the first thing is to see if it's in our area or Dyfed Powys. Then I'll go through this website, see if it's real or not. Check for any outstanding investigations. I'll do it on the quiet, not raise any expenses. I can also check and see if there's any legitimate connection between Davidson and Tŷ Bwncath."

"Legitimate?"

"Well, he was a professional footballer, then he moved into management, and ended up getting onto the board of directors of several clubs. Tŷ Bwncath was an outdoor activity centre. It's just the sort of thing he'd have supported, been on the board of, or maybe coached at. That kind of thing. I have to build up a profile anyway, so I can keep an eye out to see if he had any connection to this place."

"And who do we tell?" Farida asked the one question that had hung in the room since that Google search.

"No one, yet. You're right – this is a time bomb. It could be nothing. Or mistaken identity."

"Or someone could've pushed a paedophile under a train," Farida said darkly.

"Which is still a crime," Jonah reminded her.

CHAPTER 2

"You LOOK BEAT," Alex said by way of greeting.

"Yeah, all afternoon staring at CCTV will do that to you." Jonah hung his coat in the hallway of their home.

The minute the files had arrived from the station cameras, he and Farida had pored over them. They weren't perfect; that early in the morning the sun was low, causing flares and there were marks from dirt on the camera lens. Worse than all the quality issues was the fact that they didn't know what they were looking for.

Between them they'd worked through a week's worth of CCTV to draw up a list of regular commuters who'd arrived from 6:15 onward. They were called things like 'Spiky-haired Young Man' and 'Smart Business Woman'. The plan was to check them off a list as they came in. Anyone who didn't show up the next morning would immediately be of interest. Not necessarily as a suspect, but worth having a word with.

They already had one such person, 'Green Coat Man'. Even though the days had been hot and sticky recently, he'd worn a heavy army-surplus coat with the hood up and he never turned to face the camera. Jonah thought it was suspicious behaviour while Farida thought that with only two cameras it could be accidental.

"You look miles away," Alex commented.

"Yeah, planning strategy for tomorrow. Another early start, try to catch some creatures of habit and find out what they saw."

"Really? You'll need to find a better way than the bottle to catch up on your sleep if you're going back to early starts."

Jonah's shoulders stiffened, and he froze. He thought he'd done a good job of pretending to be okay. These occasional comments punctured his bubble and made him realise how perceptive his wife was.

Jonah waited without turning around, one hand frozen on his coat. He couldn't deal with Alex right now. When he heard her sigh, followed by retreating footsteps, he relaxed.

Later that evening, he felt the need to make some sort of amends. Once they were eating a Chinese takeaway, he launched into his explanation.

"It's quite common, you know. With police and firemen." Alex turned to look at him, wondering what he was talking about. One minute they'd been eating chow mein, the next he'd made this pronouncement from nowhere. "You know, the post-traumatic stress thing. Not sleeping, funny dreams, and all that."

"You are going to the counsellor though, aren't you?"

"Well, they have signed me off." He had the good grace to look a bit sheepish. He'd been around the track with counselling before, so he had known the right things to say. Yes, he had bad dreams, but they were reducing in frequency and intensity. He had made some comments about panic and how he was gradually improving.

"Hmmm," was all that Alex said.

"Yeah, no, it was fine. It's normal to have a few bad dreams and trouble sleeping." He wondered if Alex had seen through his lies. She very pointedly didn't reply and instead went back to eating.

The rest of the evening passed without any further comment from Alex on Jonah's state of mind. He really wanted something strong to drink before bed, but he made do with a single beer with his meal. He felt that Alex was watching him and somehow, he needed to prove – either to her or to himself – that he could cope without the crutch of alcohol.

Predictably, he slept fitfully and woke at five am., tangled in the sheets. Alex was still asleep, but he had arranged to meet Farida at the station to catch the commuters, so it was time to get up. His mind was still full of fragments of dreams. His sleep had been broken by the familiar motifs of the family in peril but this time they were mixed up with the events of the previous day.

In his dreams he was sat at the CCTV console watching grainy, black and white images. Unlike real life, his view was of the platform and tracks.

Instead of Davidson, this time he saw his grown-up children, Gareth and Emily on the platform. The mysterious man in the green coat loped across the screen towards his family. Jonah knew what would happen when he reached his target but was powerless to stop him. In the background, he could see the train moving into view. It was slowing, but he knew for certain that Green Coat Man would push his children under the moving train.

At first, he clicked frantically on the mouse, trying to pause the image, to rewind the tape. When nothing happened, he resorted to brute force, hammering on the screen to rescue them. But nothing worked. He was power-less to prevent the tragedy.

Before the inevitable disaster he jolted awake. He sat up, breathing hard. He didn't feel like he'd slept at all and headed, on autopilot, to shower and get dressed.

———————

ALL TOO SOON, Jonah was stood in the ticket hall with Farida. They were waiting to catch the morning tide of commuters. She gave him a quick once-over and he could tell by her face that he looked rough after his disturbed night. He idly wondered what the protocol was around mental health and PTSD. Did he just nonchalantly say that he'd had a flare up with bad dreams and wasn't getting enough sleep? Or, would work allow him to go back to bed and come into the office at 10:30? But his job was to be here at six in the morning so that wouldn't work. His thoughts chased each other around in a circle.

Jonah decided to do what police officers had always done – he drank coffee, said nothing, and tried to get on with his day to the best of his ability. He wished he could ask the witnesses if Davidson was pushed or if he jumped. But a sudden death under a train was a traumatic event, so they needed to go softly-softly. They would have to walk the witnesses through it step by step. They would establish if they were present yesterday morning, then if they'd seen anything suspicious.

"What do you think our strategy should be then?" Farida asked, puncturing his thoughts and bringing him back to the case.

"Remember what we discussed yesterday," Jonah said. "This could go nuclear. We need to prove that we've ticked all the boxes. And interviewing potential witnesses is a key part of that."

"We'll soon find out – here comes the first one. We can tick off number four, young blonde business woman."

The questions and answers fell into a pattern over the next twenty minutes.

"No, I was playing Candy Crush. Only looked up when I heard a scream."

"It is awful though, isn't it?"

"I've never seen the man in the green coat before, he's not one of the regulars."

"I couldn't describe him, really. He kept his head down and hood up."

"He was quite tall but with a stoop."

In a break between witnesses, Jonah stretched, gazing across to the opposite platform. A man was watching him and Farida work their way down the platform. He had a perfect view and was obviously fascinated by what was going on.

"I'll interview the other platform!" Jonah didn't wait for an answer before jogging up the footbridge stairs. Halfway up, his breath caught, and a stitch started. His left leg gave a warning twinge, and he felt sweat breaking out on his forehead. He slowed and cursed his lack of fitness. Walking over the top he took some deep breaths and by the time he came down the other side he had enough breath to ask questions. He heard Farida running behind him.

They spread along the platform showing their warrant cards and asking the same questions as they had been for the last twenty minutes. Jonah had just drawn level with where Leo had died when the train arrived at his platform.

"Excuse me, police." He showed his warrant card to a

woman about his own age. She had short hair and was dressed respectably.

"This is my train," she replied.

"It's very quick, about the incident that took place here yesterday."

"Oh. That man who died?" She looked at Jonah, then back at her train, indecisive.

"Did you see anything?"

"Yes. I'd rather watch people than play with my phone. But I can't talk now, this is my train."

Jonah made a snap decision. He turned to wave at Farida and point at the train. Then he followed the woman on board, wondering if he was going to start another feud with BTP by fare dodging.

They found themselves standing by the doors, Jonah leaning against the glass partition, the woman hanging on to the pole. Luckily there was no one else there so Jonah decided to start the interview. When he had her name and address, he asked her what she'd seen.

"It was quite weird, really. I mean, most mornings you see a bunch of commuters, you know men in suits or business casual, women in smart clothes." She looked shifty as she glanced around the carriage. She lowered her voice. "I like to make up stories. Like if one of the regulars is late, I imagine she's had a row with her husband, or her car wouldn't start." She looked at Jonah for approval.

"That's fine. I used to commute, you've got to do something for the boredom. About yesterday though?"

"Well, this younger man came up, wrapped up in this big green army style coat. Scruffy jeans too. So obviously I started watching him. Most people are in business suits on their way to work. He made his way down the platform towards the far end."

"The far end? To your right?"

"Yeah, that's it, he seemed like he knew where he was going. But there was only this older guy down there, in his fifties, wearing a suit. He made a beeline for him. Very odd."

"What happened then?"

"Then my train arrived, and I couldn't see any more. But if everything's on time, the other train is only a minute or two behind ours, so that must have been just before, well, you know." She faltered as she realised she'd come up to the awful truth of what happened. She took a moment to stare out of the window with a handkerchief pressed to her face. "Oh. It wasn't him was it? That man in the suit on his own down the end? I must have seen him moments before."

"Yes. I'm so sorry. The person involved in the incident was at the Cardiff end of the opposite platform." Jonah left a suitable pause for her to regain her composure. "Do you think you'd recognise the man in the green coat?"

"No, he was a bit further down and turned towards the man in the suit, so he was side on to me. With his hood up, I couldn't see anything."

Jonah slumped against the partition. He could feel the train slowing down. His hunch was right. He thanked the woman and hopped off before the conductor could check his ticket.

Soon he had summoned Farida to give him a lift back to Pontyclun.

"Did you learn anything useful with your fare dodging?"

"I made a strategic decision based on the situation on the ground," Jonah said with mock pompousness and Farida laughed. He quickly recounted what he'd learnt. "I'm not sure we're much further forward, although Green Coat Man is now our main suspect. I wonder if we could link him to the photograph?"

"It'd be nice," Farida said. "But I think you're reaching a bit, trying to link it all together."

"Probably." Jonah paused to think. "It's not brilliant though, is it? We have a suspect whose name we don't know. He may or may not be linked to the photograph. And without a name we have no idea why or if he's linked to Leo Davidson. For all we know he might just go around pushing people off platforms for kicks! But I still think Green Coat Man is the best suspect we've got."

"Might not be him," Farida argued. "He could have a good, legal reason for being there that day."

"It wasn't raining so why did he have his hood up?" Jonah was tired and aware that he sounded truculent.

"You're just being pessimistic," Farida chastised him. "Your witness said he made straight for our victim, Davidson, so there must be a connection. Even if he's a nutter, he picked his victim for a reason. Why don't you go back to the CCTV and see how far you can follow Green Coat Man? With a bit of luck, he might have got into a car with a readable number plate."

"By now, I really doubt it'll be that simple. This whole case is all held together by possiblies, maybes and tenuous connections."

Back at his desk, Jonah took two co-codamol with coffee. The lack of sleep the previous night combined with the early start had given him a terrible headache. He was back to looking at the CCTV, but couldn't concentrate. The slightly fuzzy black and white images made his head throb even through the pills.

Green Coat Man walked straight across the car park. He weaved through the cars but seemed to focus on something just beyond the edge of the camera's range. He stopped at the gate, reached out to get something from someone who was unseen and then he disappeared.

Jonah switched the footage off. He'd watched it three times over and still couldn't see who he was meeting or what he took.

He rubbed his eyes and left them closed. There was something about the man's gait – the way he slouched across the car park with that big green coat and his hands stuffed in his pockets. Had he seen that person before? He thought he was familiar. But he couldn't decide if it was because he'd just watched him over and over on the screen or if something deeper was trying to surface from his memory. He'd seen someone walk like that before, but his name was right on the edge of his grasp. And the harder he tried, the further it slipped away from him.

"Jonah?" The bubble burst and the thought fled from his mind.

"Yes?" He opened his eyes and saw the coroner, Timothy Carlton, standing in his doorway. As usual he looked immaculate.

"You okay?"

"Just resting my eyes after too much CCTV. What's up?"

"This Leo Davidson case. I'm getting some pressure from on high. How's it shaping up?"

Jonah gave him a quick recap of progress on the hunt for Green Coat Man. While he was talking, he was deciding whether to mention the photograph. He remembered the chart with the dotted lines. All he had was three things that might be linked. If one of them proved a firm link to Davidson, then he'd tell the coroner about it.

"So, this witness, how good is she? Would she be convincing on the stand?"

"Yes, professional and calm. Obviously upset by what she nearly saw but she'll do well if you want her for the inquest."

"Good. Good. Do we have anyone who actually saw what happened?"

"Well, we can imagine the driver did. But he's been whisked away by the BTP and has mandatory counselling. Apparently, anything he says of value will be passed through the BTP to us."

"Hmmm. Well I'll make sure I keep on top of the BTP. This unidentified person is a real problem though. We need to find out who this man is and what he was doing there. The one thing I don't want in this case is unknowns."

Jonah nodded, wondering about the photograph. Had Green Coat Man brought it to the station or did Davidson already have it?

"What are the next steps then?"

"Well, I need to see if there's any CCTV in the roads around the station. Our suspect is quite distinctive, we might be able to follow him, certainly learn more about him."

"I can arrange that. I'll phone ahead to the council control room and tell them to expect you. You set out now. With a bit of luck, we can track him down by the end of the day."

Timothy then stood pointedly in the doorway until Jonah got up and fetched his coat.

Before long, he was parked on an anonymous industrial estate on the outskirts of Cardiff. All around were low modern buildings, the usual mix of small businesses. But the place he was interested in had higher than usual security. It had no sign outside, but he knew it was the centre for all the council run CCTV in Cardiff.

Once he had completed the visitor's sign in, he was escorted to a dark room with a young technician. He explained what he wanted and showed them the video from the car park on a tablet.

"Right so, Pontyclun Station." The man had a west Wales accent and pronounced it Ponty-clean. He pulled up a computerised map and expertly zoomed into the right area. "Okay. Nothing on Station Approach, that's a shame. Let's hope he's not too savvy and cut up through the foot-paths into the residential area. First off though let's check both ways on Cowbridge Road. Six twenty did you say?"

"Yeah, but I want to watch for about ten minutes? The incident was about six twenty-two so he'd need a bit of time to leave the platform, cross the car park, and get down to Cowbridge Road."

They spent the next few minutes in silence, watching the figures flickering past in black and white at double speed. Just as he felt his headache returning, a motorbike went past. The pillion was wearing a big heavy coat.

"That's it!" Jonah said. "He was being handed a helmet. That must be him!"

The technician froze the frame and backed up a bit until the motorbike, rider, and pillion were centre frame. More importantly, the number plate was clear.

"What are those markings on the rider's jacket? Any way to get them clearer?"

The technician went back and forth on the video, from the point they turned out of Station Approach until they vanished from the camera range. But because he had a pillion, there were no clear shots of the jacket. Jonah could see it had curved white patches with orange writing, but not much else.

The technician went backwards and forwards until he

got a shot of the rider looking into the camera as he checked left and right at a junction. He had a black open-face helmet and sunglasses and the image was grainy. The quality would be useless in a court case. But it would be useful to establish who the rider was. If the registered owner was the same race, build, and roughly the right age as the man on the CCTV, then he could assume that they had the right person. Unfortunately, the suspect he was interested in had added a full-face white helmet to his green coat.

Soon enough the motorbike turned off the main road onto side streets with no cameras. Jonah stood up and stretched. He thanked the technician and made his way back outside.

He winced when he got to his car. The light was now so bright after the darkened CCTV offices that it lanced into his head and lodged painfully behind his eyes. Grimly he threw the few printouts onto the passenger seat. The top one was a photo of the motorbike rider looking straight into the camera and underneath was one showing his number plate. The pillion was hidden behind his big coat and full-face helmet, but Jonah was sure he could reveal his identity.

CHAPTER 3

When Jonah got back to his desk, it was past his lunchtime, but he was itching to log onto the PNC, track down the number plate and see who was giving Green Coat Man a lift. Maybe he'd even be able to give him a name and finally find out what had happened on the platform.

But he was stopped on his way to his office by Denise, the coroner's secretary. "Did you put a call in to Dyfed Powys Police?" Something about a property just outside Merthyr?"

"Yes," Jonah said warily. He glanced at the door to the coroner's office. "Does Timothy know anything about this?"

"No, should he?"

"Not necessarily. I'm just fishing at the moment, making sure I cover the angles. Don't want anything coming out of left field. But the coroner said he didn't want any unknowns in this case so there's no point in worrying him about it just yet."

Before Denise could reply, Timothy's door opened. A tall thin man came out, older than either of them, with iron grey hair, clipped close around the back of a large bald patch. He had half-moon glasses and looked like either a retired accountant, or an undertaker.

"You must be DS Greene," he said in a low gravelly voice. Seeing Jonah's confusion, he continued. "Albert Mayweather. I was a friend of Mr Davidson. The whole family actually. Just keeping an eye on the case. I'm offering what comfort I can to his wife. As I'm sure you can understand everyone wants a swift resolution to this whole affair."

Before Jonah could say anything, he swept from the office as if he owned the place.

Jonah looked round and for a second caught a strange expression on Timothy's face. He was usually not only very well dressed, but almost old-fashioned in his formal manners. He certainly always maintained a professional image. But just now he had looked annoyed with Mayweather's interference.

"Mayweather?" Jonah said. "Where do I know that name?"

"If I said ACC Mayweather?" Denise asked.

"Yes, of course. Isn't he retired though? What's he doing here?"

"Throwing his weight around," Timothy said from his doorway. "He thinks his personal connection to the case means he has the right to come in here whenever he likes." He paused for a minute to regain his composure. "I'm sure he's just concerned for the family and wants to be kept in the loop." There was an awkward pause. Having retired senior police officers interested in a case never ended well. "How is it going? I gave him the usual platitudes about lines of enquiry and so forth. He might be a retired senior officer, but he can still be handled."

"We might have a lead on Green Coat Man," Jonah admitted. "I'm just going to follow it up now."

"Good, good." Timothy wandered back into his office looking distracted. Denise and Jonah exchanged a glance. He understood that she'd keep his secret about Dyfed Powys for now, but he didn't have long to sort it out.

Jonah went into his office, closed the door, and sat behind his desk. He needed to work out a plan of action, to eliminate some uncertainties. The stills from the CCTV of the two men on the motorbike were on his desk, begging to be dealt with.

But next to it was the Post-it note from Denise. At any minute Dyfed Powys Police could call. Or worse, get in touch with the coroner. Jonah thought he'd better close off that avenue first.

He made the phone call, explained who he was and was put through to a young sounding DC Dan Price.

"What's your interest in Tŷ Bwncath then?"

"Well, it came up in an enquiry. I checked online and as far as I can tell, it's just over the border into your area."

"You've been online, have you? So, you've seen the accusations then?"

"Of abuse when it was a children's centre? Yes. Are you actively investigating them, in Dyfed Powys?"

"I wouldn't say actively. But there have been some official complaints made. Trouble is it's so long ago, it's proving very hard to make any headway. It's been punted over to the historic abuse team in Builth Wells and that's probably where it'll die. It's a tricky case."

"Why?"

"Well, Tŷ Bwncath was a centre where kids went for holidays. They took looked after children from all over the country, usually inner-city or town kids. So to even find records to prove who was there and when, you would have to fight with social services from all over – the London boroughs, Birmingham, Liverpool, Manchester, Cardiff, and even Glasgow and Edinburgh. All from well over twenty years ago and based on some fairly hazy memories. As far as I know, none of the complaints even had specific dates on them."

"But there must be some records somewhere?"

"Not necessarily. It was privately owned and run."

"And if I was looking for records of who they might have employed?"

"Well, as far as I know it was just one bloke who ran it and when he died, the place shut down. He lived and ran it from the same site so that might be where the records are. If there are any."

"But that was over twenty years ago, surely the records won't still be there? Who owns it now?"

"As far as the locals know, it was just boarded up and left when the owner died. Apparently inherited by someone in London."

"Would I be stepping on any toes if I tried to trace the owner, get access, stuff like that?"

"To be honest, as long as you told us what you were doing, you'd be doing us a favour. We're overstretched here already so if you want to go digging around, that saves us a job."

"Thanks!"

Jonah put his head down on the desk to think. He hadn't replaced any of his maybes with anything concrete. He still had no firm link between Tŷ Bwncath and Leo Davidson. He raised his head and reached for his keyboard. There was something easy that he could do. He went onto the Land Registry and put in a search for Tŷ Bwncath. Knowing who owned it now would be one step further forward.

Then he did what he'd been waiting to do since he was sat in the darkened room looking at the CCTV. He called up the PNC and learnt that the motorbike was owned by Jeremy White. The address was on the other side of Cardiff, in Grangetown. He reached down his battered A to Z and found that it was tucked under the railway line into Cardiff Central. Not ten minutes away was Ninian Park, traditional home of football in Cardiff.

He rubbed his temples. Leo Davidson had planned to get on the train in Pontyclun and ride straight through Ninian Park station, past the road where White lived and into Cardiff. He would've looked out at the stadium where he had built his career. Instead, his life ended under that same train.

There had to be some link between the train line, football, Leo Davidson, and Green Coat Man. He shook his head and went back to the screen to see what he could learn about Jeremy White.

He had a fairly decent list of offences to his name, a couple for possession of cannabis and some theft of motor vehicles. He had spent a few months in prison. But recently he seemed to have either gone straight or got better at avoiding the police. Well, up to now, Jonah thought grimly.

There was a final note on Jeremy White's record. 'All queries should go through DC Brian Shaw in Cardiff Central.' Jonah frowned but couldn't place the name. He supposed it was another item on his ever-growing to-do list connected to this case.

He put a call through and got hold of someone who took a message asking Shaw to call back. Having set everything in motion he called Farida to see if she wanted to meet in the canteen for coffee. Thankfully, she not only agreed but also said that she had some preliminary findings from the lab about the photo.

First, Jonah filled Farida in on the patchy details about Tŷ Bwncath. Then she pulled out her pocketbook and gave him the run-down on the photo.

"Well, I pulled some strings and sweet-talked the lab boys a bit. This is only preliminary based on an initial look and their experience. The photo itself is old, like thirty something years, original film stock. It is just about possible that someone kept film that long and took it more recently, but highly unlikely. Also, if it had been developed recently, there'd be a website or something on the back. And, the clothes look about right for the eighties, maybe even the late seventies.

"The writing on the back however looks like a more modern marker pen and therefore probably recent. There are corner marks where it's been taken from an album."

There was only one question that Jonah really wanted an answer to. "What about fingerprints? It's a good, smooth surface?"

"That's the rub. There is a half print there. It's a bit smudged, probably from when it was screwed up. I sweet-talked the pathologist and got a set of Davidson's to compare. It might match, but there's not enough data there to stand up in court. It could be his right thumb, there are no features that rule it out."

"But not enough to rule it in?"

Jonah suddenly felt weary. There was still nothing but a big bag of ifs, buts, and maybes and very little else.

"Look at it the other way around," Farida argued. "We know, through a credible witness, that Leo Davidson and Green Coat Man met just before the accident. You found the photograph, the only clean, dry piece of paper there.

Reasonably, the photo is connected. None of the evidence contradicts this story."

Jonah nodded as she laid it out. He took a long drink of his coffee. "So, what's the next move?"

"I think you have to sit down with the coroner. We need to throw resources at this. You need to get up to Tŷ Bwncath and have a poke around, get a feel for it. With your record you can't go off on your own, tilting at windmills."

"Yeah, I think you're right. Unfortunately, it's already getting political."

"How's that?"

"Retired ACC Mayweather has been in to see the coroner."

"Mayweather? What does he want?"

"Well, he has a personal connection to the family, and he's taking an interest the case." Jonah shook his head.

"Definitely go to the coroner then." Farida sounded sharp which made Jonah look up. "Do you have a better working theory than he was somehow mixed up in the rumours of abuse up at Tŷ Bwncath?" Jonah thought for a moment, then shook his head. "So, we don't want to be on our own if we're dragging a friend of the ex-assistant chief constable into the next Jimmy Savile scandal."

"Damn!" Jonah stared out of the window. There were trees out there in the sunshine, but he wasn't seeing them. He was mulling over the case, the involvement of Mayweather, the obvious inference that this case important enough to warrant his intrusion, and the many unanswered questions. There was something very wrong about the whole case. He knew in his gut that he'd follow it through. It didn't matter who Davidson had been friends with, he needed to know who had been on that platform that morning and what had happened.

"Listen, Farida, you don't have to carry on. I've nearly derailed your career once already. You can transfer all the results over to me. I can take this forward with the coroner."

Farida pursed her lips and thought. Then she shook her head. "No. No, I trust your intuition. And there are too many unanswered questions in this. The more we look, the less we see. Anyway, it beats rounding up the same drunks and drug users day in and day out."

"Okay." Jonah still wasn't completely sure that he should put it all in front of the coroner. He wished he could get a clear story before presenting it to his boss.

IN THE END, Jonah didn't get to make the decision. When he got back to his desk, he had a message summoning him to a meeting with the coroner.

As soon as he walked in, he saw another person in the meeting, a woman who wasn't in uniform.

"Ah. Here's DS Greene – our coroner's officer. This is Ms Houghton, she's the force's press officer, been seconded to us just while we cover the Leo Davidson case. Jonah, Debbie."

"Pleased to meet you," Jonah said automatically, sizing her up. Mid-thirties, shoulder-length hair, very dark auburn. As he'd expect of a PR person, she was immaculately made-up, with smart business clothes – dark suit and white blouse. She nodded and let the coroner take the lead.

"We need to know where we are on the Davidson case."

Jonah took a deep breath then outlined what he'd found out so far. He emphasised the reliability of the only witness.

He briefly mentioned the photo, but more as a way of identifying Green Coat Man. Then he asked, "Why are the press office involved? It looks fairly cut and dried. Once we've got the train driver's statement and an identity for Green Coat Man, then we'll be able to move forward and establish precisely what happened."

Debbie Houghton nodded slowly, a tactic to marshal her thoughts before speaking. Her eyes slid sideways to check with Timothy Carlton who nodded slightly.

"He was well connected. His family have already approached us to make sure this goes smoothly."

"Smoothly?" Jonah fought to keep his voice calm and even. "But we have to find out what happened on that platform. Like I said, once we have those two pieces of information then we'll know where we stand."

"I would like to move this to a quick conclusion. I was thinking misadventure?" The coroner glanced sideways at Ms Houghton for confirmation.

"We can't rule yet!" Jonah failed to keep his outrage in check. "Until we know what happened on the platform, we can't make a verdict. If this man pushed Davidson, then we might have unlawful killing and then it'll be up to the CPS to choose between murder or manslaughter. Or it still might be an accident. Or a suicide."

Debbie Houghton said, "The one thing that we don't want is this hanging around and rumours starting. The longer it takes to resolve this case, the more the press will dig around and the more stories will surface. And that's the last thing that his widow and the rest of the family want." There was an awkward pause before she picked up the conversation again. "What did you say was written on the back of the photograph?"

Jonah told her and was dismayed when she asked him to spell the words and translate them for her.

Debbie went quiet for a moment and Jonah felt that she was making a decision. Finally, she said, "The one thing we don't want is another Savile, only this time on our patch. Have you looked into it at all? What have you found?"

"I've made some preliminary enquiries," Jonah said. He spoke slowly to give him time to decide how much he should say. He was still shaken that Debbie had made the leap straight from Tŷ Bwncath to a potential scandal. "There are unconfirmed reports of historic child abuse connected with it. It's something I'm working on at the moment. I've put some preliminary enquiries out and I'm just waiting to see what comes back."

"Shit!" Jonah's eyes widened as Mrs Houghton swore. "Please tell me that you didn't mention Leo Davidson in any of these enquiries." She emphasised the last word as if it was something distasteful.

"No, I've not told anyone what I'm working on or why I'm interested. Like I said, just general enquiries, tangential to an ongoing enquiry, that kind of thing." He immediately thought of Farida but discounted mentioning her. He didn't want to drag her into this much political trouble.

Debbie Houghton sprang up from her chair and went to the window. Jonah wondered what inspiration she was getting from the view of flat roofs, air conditioning units, and other office windows. He was also fascinated that her slick, professional demeanour seemed to be falling away.

"Right." She turned and leant against the sill, trying to look nonchalant. Jonah wasn't fooled. "This story is out already – the three of us in this room know about it. We can presume that the suspect in the green coat has at least seen the photograph." She focused on Jonah. "We need you to, very quietly, investigate this.

"First, we need to know if this is all smoke without fire. What's the current status of any official investigation into this Buzzard House? We need to know how credible these claims are. Then see if you can find any provable link between Davidson and Tŷ Bwncath.

"Once we know all these things, we'll have the ammunition to deal with any potential story ahead of the press." She turned back to the coroner. "Can you provide support and liaise with the police side of it? We need DS Greene to be free to pursue this without people asking why he's spending time on it."

Timothy Carlton nodded but didn't speak, his expression a mixture of horror and calculating how much damage this would do his career.

Jonah had had his fill of politics and pussyfooting around the question. "What's really going on here?" When he was met with blank looks, he thought he'd better expand. "Retired ACC Mayweather is creeping around the building, you're rushing to a verdict before I've completed my enquiries and we've got a cloud hanging over everything that we're not even looking at."

Before Timothy could say anything, Debbie spoke. "Welcome to the real world. Davidson wasn't just anybody. He was on the board of charities that did outreach work in deprived communities. You know, using sport to turn people away from crime. That means he sat in committee meetings with senior officers. His nephew is an Assembly Member. I'm still waiting to find out, but there's a good chance he has a say in police funding and works with the commissioner. I don't particularly care which way it goes.

Leo Davidson could be innocent or guilty, makes no difference to me.

"What I do care about though is this force. I won't have it either accused of a cover-up or a witch-hunt. We need to have the facts first so if the story breaks, we have enough time to make decisions. It's as simple as that."

Jonah noticed that she hadn't said what those decisions would be. He wondered what would happen if not only Davidson was found to be a paedophile, but the net of suspicion spread over senior officers. He hoped to never find out. More than that, he wondered how he would react if he had to decide whether or not to expose a paedophile on the force.

CHAPTER 4

I⊤ was one of those annoying days where it was too hot and sticky. Jonah couldn't find a parking space within a hundred yards of Jeremy White's house. He decided to walk down in shirt sleeves and stopped opposite a dark red door. A motor-bike was parked in the road right outside.

Jonah stopped to have a good look. Since his wife Alex had started riding a few months ago, he had taken more of an interest and was quickly learning there was a lot more to it than two wheels and an engine. He compared this bike both to the CCTV footage and to his wife's machine.

It was totally different, far more exposed than Alex's BMW. Hers was all plastic casings and fairings. This was all exposed chrome and metal with high swept handlebars.

It was also, without a doubt, the bike he had last seen taking the green coated man away from the station. He turned to knock on the door, only to find that it was now open. The man standing in the doorway stared at him with a strange expression. He was a couple of inches shorter than Jonah, stockily built, with a shock of black hair and heavy brows. He was wearing jeans and a rock T-shirt. His arms were covered in tattoos.

"Good job you didn't touch it," he said by way of greeting.

Jonah was a bit taken aback. "Are you Jeremy White?"

"Depends who's asking. What are you selling?"

"Not selling, I just need to ask a few questions," Jonah said holding out his warrant card.

"It's Chalky and I don't talk to police. Article eight."

"Article eight?" Jonah said, feeling stupid.

"Article eight of the rules by which a member of the Riders of Annwn must conduct themselves. 'No member shall in any way knowingly assist or communicate with any representative of the police force.'"

"And you're a member of this," Jonah paused trying to remember the words. Chalky had a rolling Welsh accent and had no trouble with the Welsh words. "This Riders of Annwn?"

"Fuck's sake, man! You lot get stupider every year!" He reached behind into the house and brought out a leather waistcoat. He held it out so that Jonah could see the back. Riders of Annwn arched over the top in ornate orange letters. A stylised dog's head was in the middle and Cardiff across the bottom. Other smaller patches with symbols and letters were dotted around the waistcoat. He slipped it on with practised ease. Jonah noted that it gave him confidence. "You caught me in a good mood so I'll spell it out. I've been a member since they'd have me. We don't talk to police. Goodbye!"

He turned and slammed the door.

Jonah stood there for a second. The last thing he had seen was Jeremy, or Chalky, White's highly-decorated back. As he walked back to his car he had a small smile to himself.

He had certainly learned one thing today. Not only was the bike the same as the one seen leaving the station, Jonah was more certain that he'd just met the rider. The few letters that had been visible on the edge of the rider's jacket on the CCTV were the same colour and style as Chalky's. He took the photo from his pocket and compared it to the man he'd just met. Clean shaven, same nose, maybe even a hint of eyebrows above the sunglasses.

Although the quality on the CCTV was too poor to stand up in court, he was confident that Chalky was riding that morning. Jonah knew in his gut that White had picked up his mystery man just after Davidson had gone under the train.

All he had to do now was get him to talk.

WHEN JONAH WAS BACK at the station, he fetched a coffee and returned to the safety of his office. There was a Post-it note on his desk informing him that DC Shaw had returned his call. He checked with Farida, and she confirmed that DC Shaw was in charge of bike gangs in the South Wales Police area.

Jonah returned the call and finally got through to the officer from Cardiff Central. Once they'd exchanged details, Jonah got down to business.

"I've got a Jeremy White come up in an enquiry over here. Apparently he's part of something called The Riders of Annwn? I've asked around and you seem to be the best person to tell me what the score is."

"Chalky? You're welcome to go and have a chat. Won't tell you anything though, that's the Riders of Annwn for you." He pronounced it Ann-un. When the silence stretched, making it clear Jonah had no idea what he was talking about, he explained. "They're one of the old-school bike gangs around here. Relatively small in numbers but there's enough of them that they have chapters all over Wales. They formed in the seventies and liked it so much they stayed there." He chuckled at his own joke. "But they have a club rule that they don't talk to the police."

"What, not at all?"

"Nope. You might get one or two to slip up. But they won't discuss club business or anything." There was the slightest of pauses. "What do you want with Chalky anyway?"

Jonah briefly explained about Davidson and the man in the green coat and where Chalky fit in.

"Like an army style coat? So no colours then?"

"Colours?" Jonah felt that he'd wandered into a new country where he didn't speak the language.

"The patches sewn on to a waistcoat, normally called a cut. You said the pillion was wearing an army surplus coat."

"No, he wasn't wearing any patches or anything. Is that significant?"

"The club scene is very isolated. They live by the whole 'us and them' mentality. If you've got one giving a pillion to someone who isn't in the club..." He stopped to think. "It's not unheard of, but it is, well, a bit strange. Your mystery man must either be a friend of the club or a personal friend of Chalky."

"Couldn't it just be that he's in the club but not wearing his colours? You know, so we wouldn't recognise him?"

"That's extremely unlikely, almost impossible. A member on a bike, on his home turf must wear his colours. It'd be in the rules somewhere."

"The rules? You mean that stuff about article eight was all true?"

"Oh yes. Not only rules, but also a sergeant-at-arms who can enforce them and hand out fines. We hear article eight all the time, it's their standard answer to all our questions."

"So, how bad are they? Are you part of the police response?"

"Not really. They aren't bad lads at the end of the day. I just get their cases as I graduated from the motorcycle division of traffic to CID. They like to think they're all hard men not talking to the police but they aren't too bad. They actually do a lot of charity work. Of course, they keep to themselves. The properly nasty gangs are national, like the Hells Angels and the Outlaws. They've been killing each other for years. And they've got their own department in Serious and Organised.

"But the Riders of Annwn are local to Wales. You could probably raid one of their rallies on a Saturday night and round up some uninsured bikes and some drugs, possibly a few weapons. But as long as they don't bother anyone, we just keep an eye.

"If you want to find this mystery man, look into Chalky's past. You wouldn't find any of the Hell Hounds giving a lift to a random stranger. It'll be someone close to him. Family, old school friend, something like that."

"Right, thanks for that." Jonah said goodbye and leaned back to think. Somehow he'd succeeded in identifying the rider and had still failed to put a name to Green Coat Man.

JONAH UPDATED the case file with the details on Jeremy 'Chalky' White and linked it in to the scant details on his criminal record. While he was doing that, the Land Registry search came back.

When he opened the email, the mysterious cousin in London became Simon Collingsworth of Islington. No time like the present, Jonah thought. Hoping for a quick and easy result, he picked up the phone.

Mr Collingsworth answered the phone and introduced himself.

"I understand you're the owner of a house in the Brecon Beacons called Tŷ Bwncath?"

"More's the pity. I inherited it and then couldn't sell the damn place!"

"Why not? I'd have thought property up in the Beacons would be worth a fortune."

"Ha! Shows what you know! My uncle died over twenty years ago. Left me his outdoor activity centre. At first I thought I was minted, nice big place, lots of land with it, established business. But no. Bloody bureaucrats got in the way didn't they. Apparently the whole thing was some kind of nod-and-a-wink system with people in councils all over the country. As soon as old Bryn died, they didn't want to send their children there any more.

"I tried to sell it, first as a going concern, then as a development property. You know, someone could knock it down and put a new fancy house there. Everything fell through, then before I knew it 1996 rolled around."

"1996?" Jonah was struggling to follow Mr Collingsworth, but thought it best to keep listening and making notes.

"Yeah. Passed some Act of Parliament or something. Meant that the way national parks are run was changed. Suddenly there was planning for this and for that. Turns out the road to Tŷ Bwncath is too narrow. So it couldn't be run as any sort of activity centre or other commercial business. Apparently, the access is insufficient and it wouldn't be safe with minibuses or any level of traffic.

"Bloody bonkers! Bryn had run that place as long as I can remember. Every week a minibus full of disadvantaged kids would roll up there and back down again. Never any accidents. Suddenly they pass a law and it's not safe any more?"

"So, what did you do with it?" Jonah was getting frustrated.

"Well, I looked into residential planning, but that wasn't going to fly on account of the conservation aspect. Again, it's really stupid. They want to preserve it, even though it's a Victorian farmhouse, that was knocked about and extended in Edwardian times. Between the wars, they more or less Jerry-built extra buildings out the back. Some of them were no more than shacks built out of tar paper. But now, they're part of the heritage of the place and need to be preserved!" This time Jonah decided that silence was probably the best way to make him keep talking. "Anyway, I was down there one day in 1998, chatting to one of the estate agents and we realised that the biggest value was in the land around it. Over twenty acres. We split it up into four parcels, and sold it off to the farmers whose land already adjoined Tŷ Bwncath. All they had to do was move some fences. I even persuaded one of them to be keyholder for the house."

"It really is the house I'm interested in Mr Collingsworth."

"Yes, well what about it? I paid to have security shutters put up and like I said one of the farmers agreed to be keyholder for the padlocks. You know, in case there's any trouble. Can't say I've been there, or even thought about the place for the last fifteen years."

"Did you remove any of the records from there?"

"What, for the business? No interest in them. Like I said, it pretty much collapsed when Bryn died. The solicitor who did the will paid the last of the tax out of the estate and transferred what was left to me. I can tell you once everything was paid for, there wasn't a whole lot left over."

"So, they would still be there?"

"The records? I suppose so. Last time I was up there, there were filing cabinets and box files and all sorts in the office. No idea what state they'll be in, but they should've stayed dry." A note of suspicion crept into his voice. "Why are you so focused on the records? Are they important?"

"It's just something that's come up in our enquiries. We need to have a look at those records." Jonah clearly remembered the warnings from the meeting. He was not to mention Leo Davidson. He thought even a mention of the train suicide could be risky. "If you could let me know the name of the keyholder and tell him we'll be coming, then we needn't bother you any further."

"Why should I do that? You won't even tell me what you're looking for! Do you know what I do for a living DS Greene?"

Jonah had to admit that he had no idea.

"I run an advocacy centre for the homeless. We advise them on their rights, and try to stop police like you from harassing or moving them on."

"We're not harassing you, Mr Collingsworth, we just need some cooperation with our enquiries." Jonah cursed silently to himself. If only he could explain to Mr Collingsworth the lengths he'd gone to in defence of the homeless of Cardiff. But he knew the other man wasn't listening by now.

"No. If you're not telling me what you're looking for, I'm not telling you who the keyholder is. And when I'm done with you I'll phone him straight away to tell him not to let you in. When you have a warrant, fax it over to me!" He cut the connection, leaving Jonah staring at the receiver.

Still puzzling over his reaction, Jonah looked closer at all the files attached to the Land Registry search. Sure enough, in late 1998, the land had been parcelled into four and sold off to the adjoining farmers. Only four names that could be keyholders, but by now Mr Collingsworth would be on the phone to one of them.

CHAPTER 5

AFTER DINNER, Alex and Jonah sat on the sofa. Once he'd dealt with Mr Collingsworth, he'd spent the rest of the afternoon clearing his stack of paperwork. While he was processing forms his mind ran around the problem. He went from Mr Davidson to the photo to Tŷ Bwncath. In his mind's eye he saw a link from the photo to Green Coat Man and from him to the bikers. None of it made any sense.

But, now he was home, he saw one opening that he'd previously ignored. He looked across at his wife. Last year she had, against Jonah's better judgement, bought a motorbike. It was nothing like the world of Chalky and the bike gangs but it might be a start. "You know those biker pubs you go out to?"

"It's not like a chain thing, they don't put a big sign outside and all have the same menu!" She looked at Jonah to make sure he got the joke. "They're just regular pubs where people who ride motorbikes choose to meet up. You pretty soon get to know if a landlord is going to be welcoming or not if you turn up in leathers and a helmet."

"Yeah, whatever, you know what I mean." Jonah waved

his hand as if to dismiss her concerns. "Have you ever come across a group called the Riders of Annwn?"

"The Hell Hounds? Yes, of course. They pop up at shows, take part in charity runs. Keep to themselves pretty well though, that's because they're an MC though."

"MC?"

"Yeah, you know." She could see that Jonah really didn't know. "There's like a progression, depending on how serious you are. I'm definitely at the lowest rung – people who just own a bike and ride out to pubs and stuff. Above us are informal groups with a name and maybe a single patch. Next come the MCC crowd – stands for Motor Cycle Club. But the Riders of Annwn are MC which stands for Motor Cyclist. They are the proper lifestyle bikers. They have a very formal system of patches, chapters, clubhouse, the whole thing. If you're not in the club, then more or less you don't exist."

"We have one on CCTV. He's giving a mate of his a lift and the pillion wasn't showing any patches."

Alex stopped and stared off into the distance, gathering her thoughts. "A bloke riding pillion but not wearing colours you mean? They might give another member a lift if they were in trouble. But they'd be more likely to stop and help fix the bike."

"No, this was at the train station. And, yeah, it was a man by all accounts. We haven't seen his face."

"No, it doesn't really happen. Lots of them don't even put pillion seats on their bikes, those that do, they're for their women."

"For the women? That's a bit sexist isn't it?"

"Listen, they're stuck in the seventies more or less. You ever see a black gang member? A woman actually riding and wearing a patch? If there are any gay bikers, they keep it really quiet and join in with the wet T-shirt and mud wrestling contests!"

Jonah burst out laughing. "Wet T-shirts! That's a blast from the past!" When he'd calmed down, he said, "So we have this CCTV of a bloke walking away from the incident. He gets to this bike, ridden by a member of the Riders of Annwn. Gets given a helmet, hops on and rides off."

"No patches?"

"Not on the pillion. We've traced the bike and the rider but--"

"He won't talk to the police," Alex interrupted. "They never do. Think it's some kind of hard-man thing."

"So, who could he be? Gang member with his patches covered up?"

"Maybe. There's probably a fine for not wearing your colours, but you'd have to see the rule book to know for sure."

"Yeah, we've got a guy at work, Brian Shaw, he keeps tabs on the club. He told me all about the rule book and the sergeant-at-arms who keeps them all in line. So, if our pillion is a club member, he should be wearing his patches?"

"But on the other hand, if a member did a crime wearing their colours, you'd be able to get down to under fifty suspects almost immediately. And if the picture was good quality you'd be certain who it was."

"That can't be right. Brian from work told me that there were several hundred members in the club spread all over Wales."

Alex sighed dramatically and pulled a sheet of paper over. She drew two curved lines like an arch. "This is your top rocker, lists the name of the club." She drew a circle below it. "Club logo, in the case of Riders of Annwn, that's the Hell Hound." She drew two more lines at the bottom, curving upwards. "And this is your bottom rocker. That indicates your chapter, basically the area they control."

"Like turf for a regular gang?"

"Yeah, that's it. So if you saw a member's back patch you'd immediately know which chapter they were in, which would give you a smaller pool of suspects. Plus, there are other patches, for a start they have to have an MC patch on there as well. Also, if they hold an office like president, vice president, road captain or whatever then that'll be on the front breast. Once all that is done, the other patches are more personalised. You might see one in memory of a dead brother, or for a run they've been on, stuff like that. A member's colours are as unique as their faces."

"Couldn't they just swap jackets to throw us off?"

"God no! Their colours are so important to them. When a new member joins they patch them in – that's what they call it. They'll be presented with their patches on their cut. After that it becomes their most important possession. There are even cases of the big gangs in America killing rival members when they refused to take their colours off." She stopped to think. "So, back to your original question. You have a guy getting a lift from a fully patched member of the Riders of Annwn and you don't know who the passenger is, but you've identified the rider?"

"That's right."

"Well, if your man is a member, then he puts a big coat over his colours to make sure he's not known, and he heads outside. No, that doesn't work. If he was in the club he'd ride his own bike. Or steal one. Or borrow it. He wouldn't get a lift from anyone, certainly not a fellow member. Just doesn't make sense. What I said about lifestyle bikers? They're called that because they often don't even have car licenses. A lot of the clubs have a minimum number of miles you have to ride each year to stay a member and that's usually measured in tens of thousands. So they wouldn't consider anything but riding away from the scene of a crime. Probably on a stolen bike if they thought about CCTV."

"So, what are we left with?"

"Where you started, really close friend. Like a brother. Maybe even an actual brother? What do you know about your biker's family?"

"Not a huge amount, seems he was born in Liverpool but there aren't many records about him. Probably spent time in care. He went to secondary in Merthyr and has been living in Cardiff since he left there." Jonah paused, then asked, "Since when did my wife learn so much about the world of bike gangs?"

"When you hang around a biker pub and someone walks in with a patch, everyone looks. Some of the older hands explained what to look for. They like to think that they're outside society, but really they've made their own with just as many rules."

Jonah just nodded. He'd only just started learning about the world which Chalky White lived in and was starting to feel more lost than ever before.

CHAPTER 6

JONAH WOKE up with his eyes and mouth feeling gummy. He was also uncomfortable and disoriented. He blinked several times and the room came into focus. He was on his sofa. He sat up and pulled a half bottle of Scotch out from under his thigh. He held it to the light – empty.

He remembered now. Once he'd gone to bed he had been awoken by his recurring vivid dream. Frustratingly he would awake, heart thumping and body covered in sweat. As he regained consciousness however, the dream would vanish, leaving just the impression of fear and threat. Last night he didn't want to risk going back to sleep in case the dream returned.

Instead he had come downstairs thinking that if he made a complete break then he might get a sleepless night. So he'd watched TV with the volume down and intended to have a couple of nips of whisky to settle his nerves.

Although, he thought looking at the bottle, he'd had more than a few. At least he'd found a glass and hadn't slipped as far as drinking from the bottle.

He looked at the clock and mentally reviewed his day. He didn't have long to get ready.

"What happened to you last night?" Alex sat up in bed as Jonah walked in. "Wow! You look rough!"

"Thanks," Jonah said drily. "I need to have a shower and get my suit out!"

"On a Sunday?"

"Yeah, there's a big memorial service for Leo Davidson. That bloke who went under a train nearly two weeks ago. He was some big shot, so it'll be worth attending. I'll probably hang around at the back and just keep an eye on everyone."

"Sounds like a fun day out."

"Yeah, right. I should be back by lunchtime. I've got to run."

Fifteen minutes later he was crammed into his suit and feeling worse than ever. He decided to wait five minutes to have a coffee. His tongue was thick, eyes gritty and head just starting to pound.

The coffee didn't help much. It tasted bitter and swilled around his stomach. It did however do a little to banish his tiredness and push his headache back.

He tore across a very quiet Cardiff, desperate to make up some of his lost time. As he expected, with the police and press presence, there was no parking to be had anywhere near Llandaff Cathedral.

The minute he left the A48, he was into traffic and could see no spaces anywhere. He flashed his warrant card at the bored looking traffic cop and got waved through to find himself half a space. It was on double yellows and a corner, but at least he was parked.

The day was warming up slightly and at a brisk walk, he still took nearly five minutes before the cathedral came into view. It was hard to think that this was in the middle of a modern city. There were lawns separating medieval houses, and odd chunks of stone were dotted around – Jonah felt isolated from the modern world as if this place was kept apart. If he strained he could just hear the A48.

He finally cut through the gardens and approached the oak door at the end of the nave. He checked his watch – three minutes late – and looked around to see if anyone else was coming in. He thought it would be easier to arrive late if there were other people with him.

Looking towards the road, he flinched back as a flash of sunlight from chrome hit his eyes. He squinted and saw a figure astride a motorbike. The figure stopped watching him and turned forwards. The bike started and the exhaust was loud and harsh. Rather than idling, the engine sounded like it was stumbling and about to stall. The noise bounced off the surrounding stone. Jonah resisted the urge to duck and cover his head when the engine revved, shattering the silence.

He looked up as the bike left and saw the three-part patch. He couldn't read the words but didn't need to. The roaring hound's head in the middle told him all he needed to know.

Without thought, he moved. There was a set of shallow steps up the side of the grounds. He had no hope, but he went anyway. He ran with heavy steps, roiling stomach and pounding head. He cleared the steps three at a time and when he reached the top he saw enough of the motorbike to see that he was indicating left.

Knowing it was futile, he jogged on to see what else he could learn. Turning left he found more old stone walls and no traffic. Without hope he moved on, round the corner and came to the high street.

Now he was outside the cordon, there was much more traffic. The high street also had pubs, coffee shops, pedestrians. But there was no sign of the motorbike or its rider, who Jonah presumed was Chalky. He took a deep breath that made him cough and double over.

When he stood up, he saw something else that had haunted his thoughts for the last ten days. A figure in a green army coat with a slow, slouchy walk.

His target was a long way down the high street but Jonah set off at a jog, ignoring the way he felt. His vision actually doubled for a minute and he was forced to stop. He thought he saw green around a corner, and made himself walk on.

When he reached the main road that led down to the A48, he had to admit he was stumped. Roads led off up and down. Green Coat Man might have got a lift; Chalky could even have doubled back to pick him up.

He craned his head around but could see no sign whatsoever of his quarry. Defeated, he went into a Greggs to get some breakfast and a bottle of water. He considered a coffee as well but the thought made his stomach churn. By the time he was back at his car, he'd drunk the bottle of cold water and felt revived. He could see no point in going back to the service now so he perched on the boot to eat his breakfast sausage roll and wait for the mourners to leave.

Every time he went somewhere for the Leo Davidson case, Green Coat Man was there. Along with Chalky White. He needed to know more about the biker. Jonah had done some basic checking but now he needed to turn the screw a little. There was a sealed record so Chalky obviously had a youth spent on the wrong side of the law. In his early teens he had settled into a local comprehensive and seemed to calm down a little. It had not escaped Jonah's notice that the school was in Merthyr Tydfil and therefore very close to Tŷ Bwncath.

In his head he could see it as a triangle linking Chalky to Green Coat Man to Tŷ Bwncath, with Leo Davidson in the middle. If he could just understand what the links were along the sides of the triangle, then maybe he could find out what had happened on that platform.

When the service was over, he saw the congregation start to file out. As expected, it was mostly politicians and senior police officers, with a smattering of press. Jonah quickly lost track of how many dress uniforms he saw with their dark blue jackets adorned with white braid, silver badges and medals. The politicians were equally easy to spot with their dark suits, sombre expressions and black ties. The more important among them had small entourages of assistants with them. He wondered if he was seeing budgets being decided, priorities settled upon, promotions agreed. Every few minutes he'd break off from watching the crowd and scan the surrounding streets for Green Coat Man or Chalky.

Looking back at the mourners, he recognised the figure of Mayweather, working the crowd like a professional. He had said that he was a friend of the family, but as Jonah watched, he seemed to be spending more time networking with senior police and politicians than comforting the relatives.

He found himself watching Mayweather, wondering what the retired assistant chief constable was talking about. He was shaking hands and touching shoulders. Eventually he made his way to reserved parking, slipped into a bright red BMW and drove off.

Jonah stayed watching for a couple more minutes as people gradually drifted apart. Even when the crowd had dispersed and he was back in his car, he was still scanning the road for Chalky and his pillion, but to no avail.

JONAH SAT UP IN BED, suddenly awake. After missing the memorial service and chasing around Cardiff he had spent the afternoon watching sport and dozing before eating a disappointing takeaway with Alex.

Caught between sleep and waking he tried to grasp the dream that had woken him. Thankfully it hasn't been a nightmare, but a strange mixture of what he'd been through in the past few days. He was still running, searching through the close around Llandaff Cathedral. Everyone who was at the funeral was gathered there and Jonah saw Green Coat Man in the crowd. But when he started pushing through his fellow officers, he saw they had their rank and station on curved patches on their backs with the South Wales Police silver star in the centre. In his dream every time he tried to read the text, the letters moved and flowed so he never really knew who was who. The more he chased, the further away the man in green was.

Jonah shook his head, realised it was four in the morning and he was still tired so he went back to sleep. He managed to wake up on time, feeling more refreshed than he had done in a long time.

He got through his morning routine and commute without incident. However when he was climbing the stairs to the coroner's suite of offices, he heard voices coming down the stairs from the floor above – CID. He heard two voices, one much deeper than the other. With the acoustics and the fact that they were keeping their voices low, he couldn't tell what was being said or who was speaking so he slowed down to give himself more time to listen. The other voice might have been Linwood. It seemed that the deeper voice was giving orders, and the other was agreeing.

He heard a door slam, and silence fell. He had just started back up the stairs when the figure of Mayweather came around the corner.

"Greene." There was the merest hint of a nod. "Good to see you're fully recovered."

"AC..." Jonah checked himself from saying the man's rank – he was retired. "Mayweather."

Jonah was itching to know who the other person was and didn't have to wait long to find out. Once he had taken his coat off and settled behind his desk, his computer booted up and showed that he was due in a meeting, called at nine in the morning. Without even time for a coffee, he made his way to the meeting room.

When he got there, he was grateful to see a supply of coffee and biscuits even if he didn't know why the meeting merited it.

Around the table were Timothy Carlton, the coroner who as usual looked as if he'd slept deeply and woken with enough time to ensure he looked flawless; next to him was DI Linwood, his slightly dishevelled look emphasised by the coroner to his left. Unfortunately for him, the other person in the meeting room was Debbie Houghton from PR. Due to the nature of her job, she was also very smartly dressed. Between her and the coroner, both Jonah and DI Linwood, his boss looked like poor relations.

Jonah thought quickly. He was sure he'd heard two men on the stairs and that the door to CID had slammed shut. Given that Carlton worked here and usually arrived at work first, it must've been Linwood. Was his boss receiving orders or guidance from the retired ACC Mayweather?

Deciding he was both thoroughly outranked and unsure of the politics, Jonah decided to sip his coffee, eat the biscuits and attempt to keep quiet until he had more of an idea what was going on.

"Right," Timothy Carlton took charge of the meeting. "Let's get down to it. Nearly two weeks have passed since the death of Leo Davidson. How's the investigation going?"

Jonah quickly outlined what was known so far. An unknown man had walked towards Davidson just before the incident. He was certain that Chalky White had then given him a lift away from the scene but with his refusal to talk that was a dead end. Likewise all the surrounding CCTV had been checked but there seemed to be no way to identify the man in the green coat, and therefore no way to tell what role he had in Davidson's death.

"Thank you for that summary of your efforts so far. It seems that we definitely know who died, where, when and how. It also seems that the investigation has reached a dead end. With that in mind," Carlton said, looking around the assembled officers, "I'm thinking misadventure?"

"The family are keen to avoid suicide as a verdict," Debbie Houghton said, nodding to indicate her agreement.

Jonah leaned back on his metal framed chair. As if speaking to himself, he said, "What about unlawful killing?"

"That has to be beyond reasonable doubt," Carlton explained. "And with a single witness and no name for your mystery man, it doesn't reach that burden of proof. How far have you got in tracing this person? Have you put pressure on this White character?"

"In CID we have taken a close look at him." Linwood leant his elbows on the table as he spoke. "But he must know we're onto him, he doesn't even break the speed limit on his motorbike. Most weekends he drinks at the club house, then sleeps it off before riding home sober. We have intelligence that he's been involved in drugs in a minor way, but he's keeping his nose clean at the moment."

"Even if we did arrest him, he'd go to prison rather than talk to us," Jonah said resignedly. "It's part of the whole biker thing – it's the way they are. I've been trying to look into his background but that's not easy. One theory is that this man in the green coat has to be some close friend, possibly from childhood."

"And how is that panning out?" Carlton asked.

"Like I said, we're reaching a dead end." Jonah hated admitting his failure. "He's in his thirties, so he grew up before records were computerised and centralised. He was born in Liverpool, moved around, went to secondary school up in Merthyr, then joined the army. Nothing to suggest who he helped to get away from the station though."

"So, there's no realistic chance of any new information," Carlton summarised. "In which case I stand by misadventure. I've read the driver's report – he doesn't add anything to this discussion. He didn't see the man in green, but we know from CCTV and a witness that he was there. How does that sit around the table?"

Debbie Houghton nodded. "That's fine. We're monitoring the PR aspect. Now we've had the memorial service we can expect things to die down. Even more so if we get a verdict announced. It draws a line under things." Jonah looked closely at her. There was something about the set of her mouth, around her eyes. She didn't agree with what she was saying – it was definitely the party line.

"It seems like we're all in agreement." Linwood looked relieved that the meeting had passed without incident. All the way through he had kept glancing at Jonah Greene to make sure he wasn't going to disrupt things.

Jonah just nodded as if he agreed. Mentally though he was trying to decipher the meeting. He was now certain that ex-ACC Mayweather was pulling the strings. He'd obviously put the strong arm on Linwood this morning, but he suspected that the other people in the meeting were under pressure as well. On the other hand, he had done it before – carried on an investigation when it was supposed to be closed. He wondered if he now had the necessary energy to do the same thing again.

He kept half an ear listening to the other three people in the room while he tried to think of ways around Chalky White. He didn't believe in absolutes. So they had a rule that said they couldn't talk to the police. Rules could be broken, clubs could be left, loopholes could be found. His colleagues recapped the situation until the time was up and they started to disperse.

To his surprise Debbie Houghton caught his eye as she tidied the cups. She gave the tiniest of nods but Jonah got the message. He reached for a biscuit and finished his coffee as Linwood and Carlton left the room.

When they were alone, she spoke. "You looked uncomfortable there. Do you think more could be done?"

"Well, more could always be done. It depends if there's the political will to do it or not. How high up does this go?"

"Well, the nephew is an AM and he's friendly with at least one chief super. He's probably got more connections, but that's where some of the pressure's coming from. It's no secret that Davidson himself was well connected in political circles." Jonah filed this away – Mayweather obviously wasn't the only one pulling strings behind the scenes. "They want a quick verdict that doesn't cause ripples, everything swept away, business as usual."

"And you don't?"

Instead of answering, she reclaimed her seat. She rested her chin on one hand and appeared deep in thought. "You know when the whole Jimmy Savile story finally broke in the mainstream news, it sent shock waves through the PR community. It was a nightmare. Everyone knew and no one said. Then Cliff Richard – the exact opposite, months, years of being dragged through the mud for no charges to be brought.

"I believe the key to this situation is quite simple. We need to have more information than the press. We need to know before they do, and decide how we're going to react, how we will be seen."

Jonah's mind whirled. He had very carefully not mentioned Tŷ Bwncath or any possible link to historic child abuse, yet here was this woman throwing Jimmy Savile's name into the mix as if she knew about the photograph and what it implied. Further than that – she knew that he knew – he just didn't know how. He realised he'd been quiet for too long.

"What did you? I mean, not what, when or rather how?" Jonah paused. He needed to know how definite she was that Davidson was mixed up with any paedophile activity at Tŷ Bwncath. For that matter, he wasn't certain that there had been activity at that site. She was ten steps ahead of him. Maybe she was trying to draw him into an admission? In the end he decided to keep quiet. He took a deep breath. "That's not what you said in the meeting." Jonah tried not to sound hurt, but he did feel as if he was on shifting sands.

She held up her hands. "I admit I wasn't totally honest in the meeting. When you get a sudden death of someone famous, the press often don't know the name until the family have been notified. That slows down the story. The memorial service though – the press have had two weeks to work on an obituary. Plus, you've got AMs, MPs and mayors all mixing it with senior police and the odd celebrity. It'll make a much bigger splash. I read your case file before I came to this meeting, and like you, I followed the trail from the photo to looking up Tŷ Bwncath to see what the score is.

"If there's anything to this paedophile story, then this next week is when any rumours will come to the surface. We both know that this meeting was a covering exercise. Before we met, they knew that they wanted a misadventure verdict. This was just to get it on the minutes, and make sure we were all agreed. Would you have got anywhere if you'd pushed for further investigation?"

Jonah thought about how the meeting had gone. Every question he'd been asked had pushed him further into admitting that he was at a dead end.

"So, what do you want to do?"

"Well, if you had carte blanche where would you go next?"

"Seriously? Merthyr Tydfil. Poke around the school. Even if he left there over ten years ago, you know what teachers are like. Someone might remember. Or see if they'll let me have a look through the records. Even to get his mother's name and address would be a start."

"And you think that would help?" She left her seat and moved to the doorway.

"He's in a bike gang." Jonah swivelled round to follow her. "They're serious about the whole thing. I've got good information that he wouldn't offer just anyone a lift on his bike. If it's not anyone in the club then it'd be someone he's known for years, probably since school."

"That makes sense. I could get you tomorrow to go up there. I'll say you're doing deep background research for me, tell them that I need to prepare a statement on Leo Davidson. Not for release, just as a contingency in case something blows up. I'll square it with Linwood and Carlton. Just one day though, and then we'll see where we're at."

"And once I've got the information, I could take a run at Chalky White on my own," Jonah said, half to himself.

"You'd have to be careful though. There are powerful people who want to see this go away."

"I know. I won't move or do anything until I actually have proof, firm facts. That's the problem with this whole case. It's all supposition."

She went to leave, then turned back. "But, you be careful." There was a concern in her voice that made Jonah pay attention. "More than careful, suspicious of everything."

Then she left before Jonah had a chance to ask her what she meant.

CHAPTER 7

THE NEXT MORNING Jonah came in to work to find that Debbie Houghton had used her influence in his favour. He had an email, copied in to both Linwood and Carlton, telling him that he was to work for her for the day. As expected, he was to do some further research on Leo Davidson in case a statement needed to be issued.

Seeing no contradicting messages from either of his bosses, he left the office and was soon driving up the A470 out of Cardiff, north towards Merthyr Tydfil.

At first he drove through Cardiff, up wide main roads whose shops defined the different areas. In the stop-start traffic he passed through areas of Polski Sklep – Polish shops – into areas with halal butchers and Afro hairdressers. Gradually the traffic eased off and got faster. Then he came out to a belt of housing interspersed with chain pubs. Once he got past the roundabout with the M4 he was out into green countryside.

He kept on going north, feeling the ground rise. Around him was an odd mixture of Victorian industrial architecture and breathtaking scenery. Together with steep plunging hillsides, covered with dark trees, there were red brick buildings and viaducts.

In under an hour, he'd reached his destination. The town was on the edge of the Brecon Beacons and sat in a bowl, mountainsides rising up around it. However the base of the bowl was not flat – streets rose and plunged as he followed the satnav through the town.

Whereas the poorer areas of Cardiff had their own vibrancy, Merthyr seemed like the poor relation. with graffiti and boarded-up shops sharing space with e-cigarette, betting and second-hand shops.

Soon however, he was out of the town and above it, pulling in to the grounds of the high school. It was surrounded by an estate of grim grey houses. As he drove past the playing fields and looked at the long low building he realised that they might rename it as a high school, but it was a standard secondary modern, stamped out of the same mould as hundreds of others across the country.

He was lucky enough to find Mrs Williams – a woman in her fifties who'd been one of the school secretaries for many years. She had certainly been there at the same time as Jeremy White was but shook her head when asked.

"Some of them, you remember. Usually the ones who do well in sports, or otherwise succeed. Or, the really naughty ones, those who end up in trouble with you lot. But the truth is that the best part of a thousand pupils are here every day, a couple of hundred leave in July, and then another set start the next September. A lot of them just float through, get enough O levels and move on."

The picture wasn't all bleak, however. Luckily for Jonah the school kept good records. Mrs Williams led him off to a long low room. Inside it was dark and damp, but it had rows of filing cabinets.

"Born October 1979 so he would've been in the 1991 intake," Jonah said.

"White, you said." She flicked through the hanging files and tutted. "Nope, no Whites started that year."

Jonah frowned. He was sure of his information. He'd run the standard checks and he knew that he'd left in 1996. Unless he had his information wrong.

"You might not be wrong, sometimes pupils move schools, then we put them in the year they started, even if it's year eight or nine," Mrs Williams explained. She moved to the next filing cabinet her fingers flicking through expertly. "Nope, well let's try 1993 then. Only five to check and I've done two already." She hummed to herself as she worked. "Ah! One Jeremy White, born tenth October 1979, joined and went straight into class U9 – that's year nine in 1993."

"That's certainly him, right date of birth and everything. What do you know about him?"

Mrs Williams frowned. "Well, that's strange, there's no handover form from his previous school. He spent some time in remedial classes to bring him up to speed. Didn't really distinguish himself, managed to keep out of trouble, left with a few GSCEs."

"No idea of who his friends were, who he kept in touch with?" Jonah asked, more out of desperation than anything else.

"No," Mrs Williams said. "But here's the address he was registered at. You could start there? Mother was down as Gwen White, no additional emergency numbers so probably a single mum."

"Does that list if he had any brothers?"

"There's no siblings listed, but we only record older siblings who've gone through the school ahead of that student." She stopped to gesture at the ranks of filing cabinets. "There's a chance that he's listed somewhere in there as an older sibling but it's only on the written forms so there's no way to find it unless you have a name and year."

"Could we do that? Maybe only five or so years? We know the surname." Jonah knew he was grasping at straws, but Mrs Williams simply nodded.

"Of course. Won't take too long if we split up. I'll tackle 1994 to 1999 and you can take 2000 to 2004. I doubt you won't find many siblings with more than ten years between them."

The two of them worked in companionable silence. It was fairly quick work, find the drawer, flick through the Ws, pull any likely files. There were only three other Whites in the whole ten year spread. None listed Jeremy as an older sibling, two lived in Merthyr and one in a village to the south that Mrs Williams assured Jonah was miles from where Jeremy White had grown up. In all cases the mother's name was different as well.

He shrugged. "Thanks for checking anyway. It was worth a shot."

"It's not a problem, livens up the day a bit, helping the police." There was an awkward pause. "Well, I can let you have the mother's address. I've no idea if she still lives in the same house but people don't move that often around here. Even if she has moved out, the people who are there now might know where she is."

Jonah nodded glumly and noted down the name and address. He didn't share Mrs Williams' optimism. But at least he had an address even if it was over twenty years ago.

Maybe she was right and someone in – he glanced at the page – Llandavy would remember Gwen White.

He thanked Mrs Williams and went back to his car. Once he'd programmed the satnav he found he was being led further from Cardiff, north into the Brecon Beacons. He idly wondered where the South Wales Police area ended and Dyfed Powys began. But he had a trail now, faint as it might be, and he wasn't going to abandon it to check his jurisdiction.

As soon as he passed the Brecon Beacons National Park rock, the town came to an abrupt end. He was now on a road that wound its way through the unbroken countryside. Hills towered above him, their sides looking as if they'd been carved out by a giant spoon.

Llandavy turned out to be a village that straddled the main road. Jonah was amazed when he turned off to find what appeared to be a council estate, here inside the national park. If he looked at the maze of streets, small houses and cheap older cars he would think he was in an estate anywhere in the suburbs around Cardiff.

But if he raised his eyes and looked between the houses, everywhere was the vast open heathland of the Beacons. The air was noticeably colder and crisper when he stepped from his car. This was an area that attracted tourists from all over. But they flocked to the tourist towns and stayed on the main road when passing through working villages like this.

Jonah looked up at the house and immediately knew he'd have no luck. The curtains were drawn and his years of experience told him that the house was empty. Nonetheless, he went up the path and knocked sharply on the door. When he got no answer after two or three tries, he bent down to look through the letterbox.

The hallway in front of him looked worn and dated but

clean. He looked straight down and saw a drift of letters on the mat. Frowning he stepped back for a better look at the house.

The front door fitted well and the gutters were clear. He turned and had a close look at the lawn. It wasn't well kept and short, but still hadn't completely run wild yet either.

Looking back through the letterbox, he realised there weren't a huge number of letters there. Either the house had been abandoned recently, or someone was coming back every couple of weeks for basic maintenance.

Jonah spent ten minutes knocking on doors but failed to find a neighbour who was in. Given the lack of cars on drives, this did not surprise him. Finally he decided to head back to the main road where he'd seen a pub. Maybe he'd be able to get both lunch and some information from there.

The village owed more to the valleys than it did to the Beacons. It had a big agricultural showroom on the main road with an attached petrol station. Further down the road were a tatty looking corner shop and the Prince of Wales Inn. This was set back from the road, behind its car park. It in its day it had been a grand piece of Victorian architecture. Now it had been modernised and extended without any care or grace. The extensions were low, 1950s buildings to either side with peeling flat roofs. Satellite dishes and modern signs adorned the exterior.

The sign on the road had peeling paint and the car park had weeds and rubbish in the corners. The only modern car parked there was a red BMW that looked vaguely familiar. He looked up and realised that the establishment was bigger than he'd thought. Not only were there two storeys above the bar, but at least one wing stretched back away from the road.

Still, thought Jonah, he had a choice between eating a hot meal from this place or a stale sandwich from the shop down the road. He had another look and deciding the small supermarket was even more forbidding than he'd first thought, he pushed open the door to find the dim interior of a traditional, dated pub.

At the bar, he indicated a beer tap that he recognised. The barman was balding with hair only around the back and sides. He was clean shaven, small and neat, with round glasses. "Pint?"

"Please. Are you serving food?"

The barman nodded. "If you go through to the dining room, we'll take your order from the table."

Jonah looked around the bar, which was silent. A few regulars sat around with pints. Newspapers were open on tables, but most of the men in the place were studying him with undisguised curiosity. Nowhere could the twenty-first century be seen. There were no large screen TVs, juke boxes, or mobile phones on tables.

"I'm looking for someone called Gwen White who lives in the village." Jonah raised his voice slightly, not openly addressing the bar, but making sure they could hear. There was an awkward silence so he continued. "She lived in the estate on the other side of the main road."

The barman pursed his lips and considered the question as he placed the pint on the bar. "Awful common name that, Gwen White. I'd imagine there aren't many villages in Wales where you wouldn't find a White or a Gwen."

Before Jonah could process this non-answer, the man had turned and gone back through the curtain. Jonah heard a muffled conversation, the landlord's tone higher and faster than the low tones of the man he was talking to.

He was sure he wasn't imagining the stares at his back. He sipped his pint and went through to the dining room.

After a long corridor with a couple of steps, he found himself in one of the flat-roofed extensions. Its look owed more to dated village hall than fine dining. There were tables and chairs dotted around, but no diners. He chose a chair nearest the door and surveyed the menu.

Like the tablecloth, it was covered in plastic. He was a world away from Cardiff and its restaurants. Halfway through his pint, a tall younger woman came out. She seem cowed, almost deferential.

"I'll have the chicken curry, please." Jonah noted that it was just curry, not specified as korma or madras or anything in between.

"Would that be with rice, chips or half-and-half?"

"Half-and-half, please." Jonah picked up his pint glass. "And another of these. With a whisky?"

"Right you are." With that the woman scuttled away. Jonah didn't subscribe much to feelings, intuition or policemen's hunches. But there was something so wrong about this place. It was shut off. The whole place and the people in it didn't want him there. Still, he had something to drink and hot food on the way. He also felt he was closer to understanding Chalky White by being in the village where he'd grown up.

He mentally reviewed what he knew of Llandavy. Petrol station, hotel bar, convenience shop and a few bus stops. Not a very inspiring place for a young teenager to grow up. Would he have been allowed to take the bus to Merthyr? Or would he have hung around the village? Or gone up into the hills to amuse himself? It was probably a boring place for a teenager, whose main ambition would have been to leave.

Did the man in the green coat come from here too, he wondered? Had they got up to mischief here and formed a bond that had lasted a lifetime? He had no way of knowing.

His musings were disturbed when his food was brought through – a generous serving of curry with both rice and chips crowding onto the plate.

When he'd eaten and finished his drinks, he found the younger woman behind the bar with his bill.

"Was everything all right for you, sir?"

"Yes, thank you." Jonah thought about his meal. All right was the perfect description. It hadn't been either awful or outstanding, just average.

As he settled up, the woman turned to work the till. With her back to him she spoke, almost to herself. "You were asking my father about a Gwen White?"

"Yes, I was."

"Are you sure the surname was White? Do you have a photo?" She turned back to him with his change. Her eyes narrowed and she surveyed Jonah closely.

"No, but she'd be somewhere between fifty and seventy as far as we know."

The woman frowned. "So, you don't know much then?"

"She lives, or lived over on the estate," Jonah said, more in hope than anything else.

Before Jonah could get an answer, the father appeared. His daughter's back immediately stiffened.

"Are you all done then?" The barman's tone was bordering on the hostile.

"I think I am," Jonah answered, wishing he could carry on talking to the daughter. But, clearly afraid, she scuttled back through the curtain without a backwards glance.

JONAH STOPPED when he got to his car. What was the landlord hiding? More importantly, where was Gwen White? He was aware that he only had one day and he was already halfway through that. He could feel his last chance to put pressure on Chalky slipping away.

He got his phone out and checked that there was signal. A bit of data showed, then flickered off. He tried to think what he should be searching for. A woman called Gwen in a remote Welsh village? Someone who sent her children to the local comprehensive school and might have worked in the pub? It was all too vague.

When the signal bar went up a bit, he dialled through to Farida.

"Hi, where are you? I could do with meeting for lunch."

"Sorry, I'm stuck somewhere north of Merthyr. Feels like the middle of nowhere."

"What are you doing up there? Isn't that into Dyfed Powys area?"

"I haven't looked at a map yet to check who's area I'm in." Jonah was defensive – he definitely didn't want to know.

"So, if we can't meet for lunch, what can I do for you?"

"Are you busy? I need to find someone and I've no internet signal here." He paused. "And no real idea how to find them."

"I suppose so." Farida gave a heavy mock sigh. "What have you got?"

"I'm looking for a woman called Gwen White." A barely suppressed snort of laughter from Farida. "She'll be at least fifty, probably older. She's from Llandavy and it sounds like the owner of the pub might know her but maybe under another surname." He read off the address but stressed that it looked as if she was no longer living there.

"So, you're looking for a woman called Gwen who used to live in a village north of Merthyr? Although the address you have might be twenty years out of date. How does it connect to anything?"

"She's the mother of the biker who gave Green Coat Man a lift. I thought that if I spoke to her about her son, who his friends were at school, if he had any siblings, something might come out of it." He paused, staring across the roof of his car at the terraced houses over the street. "I know I've seen the man in green before. That oversized coat and his slouchy walk. I just thought if I heard the name I would remember."

"Okay! I'll have a poke around. Maybe she got married or divorced." There was a pause as she weighed her next words. "I heard that it's down as misadventure. I take it pressure was brought to bear?"

"Yes," Jonah said. He was as wary as she was. "But that's not all that's in play. I've got cover to be up here for today. I'm not going off solo on this one."

"Well, still be careful. This stank of politics from the very start."

"Oh, I will. And thanks for looking that up for me."

"No problem. If I find someone called Gwen living in Wales, I'll let you know the details!"

Jonah sat there and stared at his phone. His head was spinning and not just from the drinks with his lunch. Was he being watched from the pub? Did anyone in there know Gwen?

He nearly dropped his phone when it buzzed in his hand. Had Farida found Gwen that quickly? He answered it to the coroner, Timothy Carlton.

"Where are you at the moment, Jonah?"

"I'm just outside Merthyr, in a village." Jonah was careful not to reveal that he might have gone into Dyfed Powys area. "Debbie Houghton asked me to compile some background information for a press release about Leo Davidson. She cleared it with Linwood."

"It's all right, Jonah. You're not in trouble for bunking off school! It turns out that I need a favour." There was a pause, during which Jonah wondered why Carlton was being nice to him. "It's a bit delicate." He paused again. "Where are you exactly?"

"A village called Llandavy, somewhere north of Merthyr. Right on the edge of the Brecon Beacons." Jonah braced himself for a warning about going out of area.

"Right, right. That's good. Excellent in fact. Listen, have you heard about the reorganisation of the coroner's offices?"

"There's always something in the pipeline," Jonah said. "Last I heard they wanted to merge several areas into one."

"That's it, precisely. They want to combine South Wales, Gwent and part of Dyfed Powys into one huge coroner's area. There would be one full time coroner, supported by assistant coroners in each region. Now, if one were interested in the top job, then showing that you could cooperate with other forces would be a good thing. And, from your point of view, each of the three forces would have one coroner's officer. But because it's such a big change, you'd have to reapply for your job. Well, all of us would do really."

Jonah processed all of this, trying to work out what exactly his boss was asking for. "So, if we can demonstrate that we're cooperating, then you might become the senior coroner and then I'd be the senior coroner's officer?" Jonah had a glimmer of hope that his career might not be at a dead end.

"Yes, that's what I was getting at. It's a bit unofficial but

Dyfed Powys have a case and their coroner should be handling it. It's so close to the force area boundary that we're both poring over maps trying to decide who gets it. What's happened is that a farmer has found some bones on a farm. It might be archaeological, or it might be forensic. Either way, it'll need resources, help from a university archaeology department plus forensics and maybe pathology as well depending on what the age comes back as. Dyfed Powys could get all of that from Aberystwyth but that's well over two hours away. We could do it much easier from Cardiff."

"Right, and that would show that you are helping?"

"And it would show that you are too. This kind of cross-force cooperation has the potential to make us all look good."

"Okay then, if you send me the details I'll head up there." Jonah rubbed his eyes, trying to get used to the rapid change in direction and wondering if he'd be able to spend another half day looking for Green Coat Man when this had blown over.

"Right, it's a place called Sticklebridge Farm." Carlton read out the postcode. "Apparently your sat-nav will get you close but not exactly there. From there, head past the church, turn right, then after two hundred yards there'll be a farm track on the right. I'll tell them to send a uniform down to guide you up to where the bones are."

"What stage are they at? What exactly will my role be?"

"As far as I can tell, there's a farmer, a couple of uniforms and a detective all standing around looking at a muddy hole in the ground." He paused again. "I need you to be there to cooperate, but make sure it comes our way. You know the way these things go, the sooner we get in there and offer help, the quicker we'll be able to bring it our way.

But to answer your question, we don't even know if the bones are human and whether they're historic or recent. I'll coordinate forensics from here and make contact with the university. They're usually quite good about helping out with cases like this. I'll give them your details and then you can take over on the ground."

Jonah agreed and made some quick notes. Back in the car, he programmed the satnav and headed up onto the high moor. As predicted, the postcode only got him as far as a lonely row of farmers' cottages. He dutifully drove on towards the church, and followed the directions. He was met by a PC in Dyfed Powys uniform, standing in a farm entrance where two cars were already parked.

"This is the closest we can get, sir. The scene is just over that rise." He turned to point to a ridge several hundred yards into the field. A flock of sheep watched with disinterest.

He felt completely out of place – he was dressed for investigating in a town. His shoes had smooth leather soles and he was wearing a suit. The afternoon was building to be a hot one and his shirt stuck to his back.

His first sight of the scene was a corner of a field sectioned off with police tape. It seemed incongruous to have the blue and white tape in the countryside. The scene was quite close to a hedge and the tape was tied to fence posts, a water trough and a lone tree.

A plain-clothes policeman broke off from his conversation with the farmer and approached the newcomer. He shook Jonah's hand warmly. "Hi! I'm Dan Price. We spoke on the phone." Before Jonah could recall when he'd spoken to him, the officer continued. "You were asking what we knew about Tŷ Bwncath. And now, here we are!"

"It's good to meet you in the flesh. What have we got here?"

"This farmer, Mr Williams, was lifting some paving slabs in his field. He was worried the sheep might break a leg on them or something. Anyway, he lifted one and there was a bone sticking out so he called us."

"How sure are we that they are human? Could it be a farmer cutting corners on the disposal of farm waste regulations?"

"We've both had a look, Williams and me. We're both fairly certain they look human."

Jonah got out his phone. Strangely, up here had a good signal.

"Yeah, I know." DC Price saw him looking at his phone. "Up here, the signal is brilliant. But you come off this ridge and you might as well be on the dark side of the moon as far as signal is concerned." Dan looked carefully at Jonah to see how the land lay. "Is your boss okay to pick up the tab on this one? I know that Cardiff is closer than Aberystwyth." And I'd rather your budget than mine was the unspoken sentiment.

"Yes, my coroner sent me up here. It does make sense as Cardiff is closer. Give me ten minutes to talk to the pathologist and we'll see what we have here." Jonah used his phone to call through to the pathologist, Fiona Harrison.

"I'm about to send you some photos through, can you tell me what you think?"

"I'm not making any determination over the phone based solely on smartphone photos," she said.

"No, I don't need a definite answer. I just need your personal opinion on what the most appropriate response would be."

"I can do that as long as you recognise the limitations."

"Of course, I'll send them now."

He took a few photos with his phone and sent them off to Fiona. Once they were gone, he phoned her back.

"Hmmm. Are they definitely bone? Not plastic or anything."

Jonah gingerly scraped one with a trowel and found it was hard. He reported this back to Fiona.

"It does look bad. I keep zooming in and it doesn't look right. Have you got a pound coin in your pocket?"

"Yes, why?"

"Put it carefully near the skull and send me one more picture would you?"

When this was done, Jonah got back on the phone.

"Has the scene been controlled?" Fiona sounded brisk and businesslike now.

"Yes, just me, one from CID, one uniform and the farmer."

"Right, one of you has to wait there. Let no one near it. From the size and colour, you could be looking at a child skeleton. It could be recent enough that you have a crime on your hands. The trouble is that the colour doesn't come through well on the phone. I'll have to see it in person. I'm on my way now."

"Okay. The coroner already knows and he said he'd be in touch with the archaeology department at the university."

"That's good. But if the archaeologist gets there first, ask him to treat it like a crime scene, please."

Jonah went back to talk to Dan Price. "It looks like we're going to have a party. The pathologist is on her way up from Cardiff and we might get an archaeologist here too. Once we have it confirmed as human remains, we'll get a date and see if we need scene of crimes as well. Looks like we'll be in for a wait."

"Well, I hope your boss really is okay with the budget. Once you start getting forensics and the university involved the costs will go up and up and up."

"Yeah, like I said, he's running his own agenda and he's fine with this."

A silence settled over the pair of them. Jonah looked around at the beautiful countryside, hills in the distance, sheep closer to. There were far worse places to be stuck guarding a crime scene. He noticed over the next ridge a chimney stack and a section of slate roof.

"What's that over there?" He was only really asking to pass the time.

"That house through the trees? I thought you knew, that was why you came up here so quick." He paused for effect. "That's Tŷ Bwncath."

Jonah stared through the trees, straining to see more, to understand how it all fitted together. He thought back to his conversation with James Collingsworth about the history of Tŷ Bwncath.

"Mr Williams, where did this land come from?"

"What do you mean?"

"This part of the field, did you buy it from Mr Collingsworth in 1998?"

Mr Williams nodded slowly. "I did. Everything from that stunted tree up by there, over to the right of that gate and then down to the road. You can see it's a tidy size, I took out the fences, made this field much bigger. There's not a problem with the sale is there?"

Jonah frowned. He didn't like the coincidence; everywhere he went, Tŷ Bwncath came up. "Mr Williams, why did you decide to do this now?"

"What do you mean?"

"Well, you've had this land for nearly twenty years, why suddenly start lifting the paving slabs?"

"It's the funniest thing. I was in the Prince of Wales, down in the village, and the landlord said to me that a hiker had been in. Apparently he was complaining that he'd been walking up here, and had slipped and hurt his leg or something." Mr Williams shook his head. "I don't know what he was doing, there's no footpath across here. But these bloody ramblers, think they can go where they want. Anyway, I talked it over in the pub and the other regulars said I could be liable, you know, if it happened again." He looked annoyed. "Lawyers, with their no win, no fee. So I thought, you know, one afternoon's work, no hassle." He looked around at the two policemen and all the tape. "Now it looks like this'll drag on forever."

"Well, we'll try to get this sorted out as quickly as we can. The pathologist is already on the way."

"If you say so."

Jonah could think of nothing to say so they lapsed into silence. He started thinking about the house just over the rise then turned to talk to Dan Price, walking a few steps away from Mr Williams as he did so.

"Is there any way to get into Tŷ Bwncath? We've got some time to wait until the pathologist gets here." He spoke softly.

"Did you look into its history and access?"

Jonah looked shifty and his heart sank. "I have spoken to the owner but he was very prickly. He said he was going to contact the keyholder and tell them not to let us have access."

"The keyholder? That'd be me." Obviously Jonah had not done enough to shield his conversation from Mr Williams. The farmer actually puffed his chest out slightly.

"You are right, I spoke to Mr Collingsworth just recently. He warned me about you, how you might try to sweet-talk your way in. You're going to be needing a warrant. If I've any doubts, then I'm to call him."

"Ah, yes. You see, that was back when I was just making enquiries into a case. But now," Jonah indicated the patch of disturbed earth with a sweep of his hand. "Now, we have human remains on your land. Land that used to belong to Mr Collingsworth. And there's a world of difference between taking your legal right to privacy and obstructing the police in the course of their duties."

"I'm not doing anything without speaking to Mr Collingsworth. And I don't have his number here. I'd have to go back to the house to call him." He looked at his field and the policemen as if he expected them to run off with his sheep the minute he left.

The two men squared off for a moment before Dan Price stepped forward. "Listen, I know this area well. How about, just to make things quicker, I get on the phone to our local magistrate? I know her quite well. I'll explain to her what the situation is, and then I'll pass the phone to you." He indicated Mr Williams. "Let her tell you if she'll draw up the warrant or not." He looked hopefully between the two men.

Reluctantly Mr Williams nodded.

Within fifteen minutes, Jonah and Dan Price were walking towards Tŷ Bwncath. They came down off the moor to approach it from the lane that led past the house.

It was typical of the area, a big whitewashed building with two storeys under a slate roof. Every window was covered by metal shutters. The main house had been modified and extended – different roofs met at odd angles. Behind the house was a car park, surrounded on the other three sides by low, ramshackle buildings. There was a very small garden before the farmers' fences started.

Dan Price had found can of WD-40 in his car. With a bit of work, he managed to free the padlock on the shutter over the front door and once that was open, they had to work together to open the warped wooden front door and finally reveal the dark interior of Tŷ Bwncath.

PART TWO

CHAPTER 8

JONAH HAD BEEN CALLED BACK to the corner of the field by the imminent arrival of Fiona Harrison, the pathologist. Dan Price had come back with him and the long-suffering PC was still guarding the scene.

Fiona had a preliminary look and confirmed that they were indeed human bones, possibly recent. Before she could get properly started, an archaeologist arrived. Even though he looked young, he also looked academic and he was breathing hard by the time he got to the top of the ridge.

The police were then left feeling useless, standing around while the archaeologist knelt by the hole and carefully scraped away the soil from the bones that were already visible. Every now and then he beckoned the pathologist over, and together they studied the bones in place in the ground. Finally, when endless photographs had been taken, and sketches made, a bone was lifted and placed in a tray, surrounded by tissue paper.

Jonah and Dan had only managed to venture as far as the hallway of Tŷ Bwncath. The metal shutters had meant that the interior was in permanent twilight and they had relied on Dan's torch. Dark wallpaper and green painted wood stopped the light penetrating far into the gloom. They had seen a staircase rising ahead of them and a reception hatch at the end of a hallway which split off in both directions.

Then, the policeman who'd been left guarding the hole radioed Dan Price to say that he was just heading down to the field entrance to guide the pathologist to the scene
, so, with reluctance on Jonah's part, they had resealed Tŷ Bwncath and headed back to the open moor. After the dim interior, the sunlight seemed blinding but it was nothing more than a pleasant day in June.

The pathologist and archaeologist carried on working, slowly and methodically. Jonah eavesdropped on their quiet conversation. It was very technical but he did glean that they were concerned that the bones were recent enough to be worthy of a police investigation.

Fiona took Jonah off to one side. "There's a day or two of work here. We're going to stay until the light goes. You might want to warn your family that you'll be late back."

"Thanks. I'd better make some arrangements. If you'll be back here in the morning, I'll see if expenses can run to a Travelodge in Merthyr." Jonah remembered that the Prince of Wales offered rooms but he couldn't face the thought of staying there. One lunchtime was enough for the time being.

The next morning, having had several phone calls with Alex, a couple of really forgettable meals and a night in a perfectly average room, Jonah returned to the site. He felt refreshed and was pleased that the whole experience had been bland and corporate. He was getting fed up of the Brecon Beacons and villages where you would be an incomer for the first twenty years.

He drank coffee and watched the archaeologist and pathologist at work as they slowly revealed the skeleton of a child. Then they worked and extended test trenches to either side. By lunchtime they were talking about three skeletons and by the end of the day they were all uncovered, lying neatly side by side. Heartbreakingly, they were all young.

There was more conference between the specialists. Jonah heard words like 'fusion' and 'ossification' and the eruption of wisdom teeth was discussed. By the end of the day, he had the preliminary finding that two boys and a girl were buried in the field. They had all been in the ground anywhere from twenty to forty years. The estimated ages were spread between eight and thirteen, to be confirmed with more accuracy when the bones were taken back to the lab.

Despite the fact that there were three different disciplines in the field – police, medical and academic, they all worked together to give the remains dignity. The archaeologists were solemn when they entrusted the remains to the pathologist who treated them like any other body recovered. In his experience, it didn't matter if the scene was a road accident or a murder, whether it was fresh or decades old – once the presence of a body was confirmed, everyone present adopted a new sombre attitude.

Jonah's role was to gather what evidence he could and record the event so he could start his investigations. In his time in the police he'd been to his fair share of upsetting scenes. Parents who neglected their children to the point of death, along with the random chance that snuffed out young lives in car accidents and fires, but he'd never hardened to it and found these two days particularly hard.

He couldn't escape the thought that three children had

vanished, either died or been killed, and no one had missed them. Watching the archaeologists work, he had cast his mind back over the previous decades but he could not recall three missing children from the area. There were the occasional children who went missing but they were usually teenagers who ran away. Three school age children was unusual in the extreme, and Jonah was moved by the fact that no one mourned them.

Jonah prepared to follow the sets of remains back to Cardiff. His primary job was done now that the bones had been recovered and were in the hands of the pathologist. But if he thought that was the end of it, he was mistaken. In saying goodbye to the visibly shaken archaeologist, he learned that in the next couple of days, all sorts of machines would be carried up to the field.

He was informed that geophysics and ground penetrating radar were being brought in. The trench had been extended a metre in every direction without discovering any further remains and the archaeologist told him that although he'd found the clear edge of the grave cuts, he still wanted to be sure. In that spirit, and seemingly not to be outdone by the university, Dyfed Powys promised that they would bring in their own expert – a cadaver dog, specially trained (Jonah didn't want to think about how) to sniff out dead bodies.

When they were all done, they would be certain that they'd recovered all the bodies from the field. Jonah made an operational decision that, pending all the reports, it was time for him to return to Cardiff. On the balance of probability, they had recovered all the bodies from the scene.

CHAPTER 9

JONAH SAT at his usual desk in Cardiff Central and started ploughing through the paperwork. He was exhausted after two days of coordinating between two police forces, two coroners, the pathologist and the university archaeologists. He wouldn't admit it to himself, but he was also wrung out from the emotional toll of watching the tiny bones being lifted from the ground. The whole excavation had taken place in a solemn atmosphere once they realised what they were seeing.

Now that all the paperwork was in order, he had time to catch up on his routine work. While he worked, he let his mind wander. He knew in his gut that somehow Green Coat Man and the bike gang were connected to Tŷ Bwncath. When he'd first realised that the bodies were on land associated with Tŷ Bwncath, he'd felt a flush of excitement that he'd be able to move his private investigations onto a more official footing. He knew he'd become obsessed with trying to trace the man and also that time was running out. The train driver's statement hadn't added anything useful and there were no new witnesses. Since the verdict had come through, he had lost his only chance to connect Leo Davidson with the mystery man and the photo.

He sighed. That lack of a link meant that he'd have no reason to draw his personal crusade to find the mystery man into the overall investigation into Tŷ Bwncath. In fact, now that the three bodies on the hillside were taking up so much time, he'd have less spare time to spend tilting at windmills.

He needed some official help so he went to the one person who had cleared him before – Debbie Houghton. He didn't know exactly what her agenda was – did she want to uncover the truth behind the rumours that swirled around Tŷ Bwncath or was she just interested in managing the story?

One short phone call later and they met in a coffee shop opposite Cardiff Castle. She had been reluctant to meet in the canteen or even on police property.

"So, what's up? I haven't seen you in the office recently."

Jonah wondered if he was being watched but let it pass without comment. "I've been up near Merthyr Tydfil, helping out Dyfed Powys with a complex case." He paused, unsure of how to continue. "You know the whole Leo Davidson investigation? I found a photo at the scene that said 'Remember Buzzard House' on the back in Welsh. It might have been handled by the victim before he fell but it was all very inconclusive. In the end it was decided that it was peripheral to the investigation. I don't think it even got mentioned when we sorted out the verdict. But when we spoke afterwards, I got the distinct impression that you not only knew about the photo, but also what it implied, the rumours about abuse at Tŷ Bwncath." Debbie nodded slowly. "At the time, I got the feeling you thought that more weight should have been given to that photo. And to the implications that follow once you assume that it was dropped at the same time that Davidson died."

"I think that's fair to say."

"This case I've been investigating, it looks like there are three bodies up at Tŷ Bwncath." He stopped and back-pedalled. "There are three bodies in a field adjoining the house at Tŷ Bwncath. Preliminary enquiries suggest they were buried at a time when Tŷ Bwncath was operating as an outdoor activity centre for children and the land in question was part of their grounds."

"That is what I heard, unofficially. However, I've also heard, completely off the record that at a very high level they do not want me to issue any press release over the bones."

"Why? Surely with a case like this, it would be beneficial to ask the public? It might be our only chance of identifying the remains."

"The reasons, as I understand them, are that the bones have been in the ground at least twenty years. If no one's reported them missing yet, then there's very little chance an appeal is going to throw up any new information. They want to know what they've got first before going to the press with half a story."

"The tests are ongoing. It shouldn't be too long before we get a tighter time frame for when the bones were deposited and how old they were at time of death."

"That might cause things to change. But I have to warn you not to get your hopes up. The pressure is definitely coming down from the top that they want a lid very firmly kept on this." She stopped to look at Jonah. "What exactly do you want out of this?"

"First of all, I want Green Coat Man. He was last seen talking to Leo Davidson. He only appears on that day's

CCTV. The best guess that fits the evidence is that he, Davidson and the photo were all there and connected to his falling under a train. But they shut down that avenue by not admitting the photo into evidence for the verdict."

"If the photo has Tŷ Bwncath written on it, you could enter it as evidence in this case. That might get you back onto the search for Green Coat Man?"

"Yeah, I could do that. In the meantime though, I've got to narrow down the dates on the bones, and I've got an introduction to a specialist historic abuse team that has been set up and is working out of Builth Wells."

"That's way off your patch, isn't it?"

"Yes, but the coroner's playing a long game. Emphasising co-operation between the forces. That kind of thing. Reading between the lines, Dyfed Powys have a huge area and as Tŷ Bwncath is right on the border between us and them, they'd rather come to us for support."

"And to help their budget," she said cynically. There was a pause as she sized him up. "What do you think about all this? The bodies found up on the farm?"

"Personally, I think it's a tragedy. That three children could be killed and there not be an outcry. Not even that, there's hardly a murmur anywhere. I suppose we could find some missing person records to tie it to but it's not likely. If one child goes missing there's usually a national campaign to find them, never mind if three vanish." He stopped and took his time to study Debbie and her reaction before continuing. "What's worse is that there seems to be a desire, from all sides, to keep it quiet."

"That's a serious allegation."

"Yes, but from what you've said, it's one that you would agree with."

To his surprise, Debbie smiled. "I was just seeing what

you really thought. There is pressure coming down to make this go away and I wondered where you stood. I should've known from your history that you'd want to find the answers."

"Sometimes I wonder what the point is though. From what you've said, even if I do untangle all of this, then it'll never see the light of day because of some obscure political reason."

"Sometimes all you can do is keep your head down and keep plugging away. Don't look to the horizon, don't try to work out where it's all leading. Just do today's job well and hope the future will sort itself out."

"You should be writing motivational posters," Jonah joked.

"I do feel your frustration. Probably more so as my entire job is controlling what information gets released to the press and the public. So I'm on the inside for a lot of politics."

With this the meeting wound up. But at least Jonah now felt that he had an ally. And for all his mocking, he did take Debbie Houghton's advice.

When he got back to the evidence, he went onto the computer system to allocate the photo that was in evidence from the Davidson case over to the Tŷ Bwncath enquiry. Then he phoned Fiona Harrison, the pathologist.

"Yes, I got straight on with the bones as soon as we got them back. Poor little mites, it seems as if no one cared about them in life so I thought I'd give them priority in death.

"Our initial findings at the site were correct, we have the complete skeletons of two boys and one girl. Boy One was between eight and ten years old at the time of death."

"How can you be so accurate, so soon after the bones

have arrived in the lab?" Jonah was used to tests taking weeks to carry out and coming back with vague results.

"In this case it is quite simple. All through childhood, the long bones keep growing and hardening up, as do the fontanelles – the joins in the skull plates. You view the end of the femur under a microscope and compare that with the fusion of skull plates and the progress from milk teeth to adult teeth. It doesn't take long, but it is accurate.

"Boy Two was older, between twelve and fourteen. The girl is somewhere between the two of them, ten to twelve years old."

"That gives me a lot to work on for missing persons."

"That reminds me, I've also extracted one molar from each skull. The core contains good DNA material. I've entered them into evidence so they can be sent off for testing. When the profile's complete, it'll be added to the NCA Missing Person's Database."

"We'll have to get lucky though. They could be old bones, from before DNA testing. But there again, if they have been reported missing then there's always the chance that a relative has uploaded their sample, then it might flag up." Jonah paused as he made notes. "Can you tell how long they've been buried for."

"Here I'm going to defer to my archaeologist colleagues," Fiona admitted. "I've got their preliminary report here. They think the bodies were not all interred at the same time. Probably over a five to ten-year span, judging by the pattern of disturbance. Boy One was first, followed by Boy Two, then Girl One. Whoever did it worked across the hill, so standing looking up the hill they were buried from left to right."

"That's brilliant," Jonah said, making quick notes as the

pathologist spoke. "Do the archaeologists have any idea yet of how long they've been in the ground?"

"Again, their initial findings were largely right. They're sticking by at least twenty years, maybe as far back as forty years. They've taken soil samples to measure the acidity where they were buried but this is really veering more into the realms of an art than a science."

"It's okay. Did they say anything else?"

"Yes, there are techniques that they can do in their labs. They're going to coordinate with the forensics labs. Alongside the DNA tests, they'll run isotope tests on the tooth cores. These are usually done in archaeological cases with samples hundreds or thousands of years old. They should however be able to tell the rough part of the world where they grew up, maybe even narrow it down to a region. We know from their features they were probably all Caucasian but that doesn't help much."

Jonah was stunned. He hadn't even considered the possibility that they were from outside the UK, but he had to concede that he knew nothing about the bodies.

"Can I have the contact details of the lead archaeologist to phone them myself? I'd like to pin down the timeline for when they were buried a bit more closely. Even shaving a few years off each end will reduce the work needed on missing persons."

Jonah got the details, hung up from the pathologist and was soon speaking to the lead archaeologist.

"So, you said in your preliminary findings that the bodies could have been buried between twenty and forty years ago."

"Yes. But to an extent that's educated guesswork. We're not used to dating such recent events, and the presence of the paving slabs is also not something we see very often. We're not sure how they would affect the rate of decomposition. Also, there were no finds. Something like a metal stud from a pair of jeans or some jewellery or anything would have helped a lot. Aside from the remains, we got no finds at all from the site."

"Right. I've got records here of when the property changed hands. How confident would you be at dating the bones to be prior to 1995?"

"Twenty-two years ago? That's certainly possible. Have you looked at the context?"

"Context?"

"Yes. Those paving slabs are placed all the way down that slope, forming a flight of steps. They've all got a good covering of earth and grass on them. The depth of the silted-up covering is uniform, so we can assume that they all went out of use and stayed undisturbed at the same time. Who is more likely to have laid them – the current owner or the pre-1995 owner?"

Jonah thought for a moment. It was obvious – a farmer wouldn't want steps in a field for sheep. But if a few years elapsed between Tŷ Bwncath closing its doors and the field being sold, then the steps would be hidden by overgrowth. "Based on what you've said, and what I know, the slabs were almost certainly laid prior to 1995."

"There's your answer then. It fits with the evidence. The burials were aligned with the slabs as well. It doesn't look as if someone happened to place steps on top of earlier, existing burials. It's more likely that in each case, they levelled the site, buried the body, then laid a slab on top."

"So we can date them to older than twenty-two years." Jonah made notes as he spoke. "How firm is the other end of the scale, the forty years?"

There was an intake of breath at the other end. "That's

really the longest that they could have been there. But to be honest we'd have expected more degradation on the oldest skeleton if that was the case. Unless the slabs protected them more than we anticipated. It's not an exact science."

"Would you be happy if we said they were buried over a five to ten-year period, starting and finishing somewhere between 1980 and 1995?"

"As a preliminary verbal report, that would be fine. Obviously I'd like to write up my results and present them properly to the coroner at a later date. But I don't have any problem with you working to that date range."

Jonah got off the phone as quickly as he could. He leaned back in his chair and massaged his temples. The academic archaeologist had been pompous and careful with his words, but he had moved things forward.

He turned to a fresh sheet of paper and started work on a timeline stretching from birth through to burial. Boy One could have been born at any point between 1970 and 1982. Boy Two was probably born at any point in the 1970s. And Girl One's birth he placed between 1975 and 1983. He then drew ranges for their short lives, ending them all in the range for the burials he'd just discussed.

There were three big ranges, and a huge problem. But, he thought to himself, at least it now has some boundaries. All he'd have to do now is narrow things down further and further until hopefully he could attach an identity to each body.

Jonah spent the rest of the day dealing with the National Crime Agency. They had responsibility for the National Missing Persons Database. But, only being formed in 2013, they had inherited a lot of records from the Serious and Organised Crime Agency which they'd replaced.

Neither of these agencies however went back to the mid-nineties.

Soon he was immersed in the Missing Persons records. They had files on best practice and forms to fill out. He got the whole process started and sent emails to the pathologist so that dental records and DNA could be added at a later date. Despite a long afternoon's work, there was no jackpot. Three children had vanished and no one had reported them missing or mourned their passing.

CHAPTER 10

JONAH WAS glad to be finally home after the second day up at Tŷ Bwncath. Like most officers, he kept a bag in his car with spare clothes and a wash kit, but he was still glad to be in his own home.

"What called you so far away from home then?" Alex asked when they were both settled on the sofa.

"It wasn't really that far, probably less than an hour's drive." He paused to consider. "But the archaeologist and pathologist both wanted to work long days. And if I'd gone up and back the same day I'd have hit rush hour both in Cardiff and then around Merthyr."

"Was it worth it though? What did you find?"

Jonah didn't answer at first, he just rubbed his eyes. "Yes. It's tricky though. We don't know how it's going to play out."

"You can talk to me. I'm not about to phone the papers, you know that."

"Well, we found three bodies up there." He watched Alex carefully for her reaction. "They were children, most likely been up there for decades."

"Decades?" Alex was shocked. "But no missing persons or anything?"

"We don't have enough details yet. But it has been on my mind. If a child goes missing, usually it's front page news, especially if they vanish forever. I honestly can't think of three cases in this area that would match. It's baffling."

"And horrible. Three children just vanished like that?" A silence fell between them. Finally Alex said, "Any sort of commune or anything? You know where they have babies without any official paperwork?"

"But, to lose three children you'd have to have a huge community. No, I can't see it."

"Foreign then?"

"Yeah, maybe. At the moment we literally have absolutely no idea. The archaeologists are doing all sorts of tests so eventually we'll know where they grew up at least."

He got up to get himself a drink from the kitchen. Since he'd come home, he had been unable to settle down. Having spent two days in the open air his face felt hot even in the evening when he was indoors. It was a combination of sunburn and the effect of the wind.

It didn't help that a large part of the last two days had been spent hanging around, overseeing the professionals at work. He had long resigned himself to the fact that a policeman's job was mostly waiting around. The problem was that on this job, the waiting was punctuated with distressing details. He could remember both times the archaeologists had uncovered a fresh grave. He had been relaxing a bit, chatting with Dan Price, trying to get a feel for what Tŷ Bwncath was like, when the archaeologist had said, "Boss, we've got something here," and the whole mood had changed.

He realised that he'd been standing at the sink, not

doing anything. He pushed himself off and went back through to the lounge before Alex could ask what was wrong.

"Are you all right, hun? You haven't sat down for more than fifteen minutes since you got home."

"Yeah, yeah. It's just, you know, two days standing around in the fresh air, just watching someone else working. Made me kind of restless."

Alex nodded. "What was the Travelodge like?"

"Like every other Travelodge really." He thought about the weird evening mood, when they were all sombre because of what the day had revealed. But they were also near-strangers forced to share a meal. "You know what these work things are like – a bit awkward really. And we were all tired and wrung out after the day."

He wandered over to his favourite armchair and took an empty glass into the kitchen for a refill. When he finally settled down, he fished out his phone to start texting. Alex smiled across at him. "Are you really that transparent?"

"I'm just texting Emily. Checking she's okay. Nothing wrong with that."

"Why not Gareth?"

"I know he'll be at home." He paused for a moment, then said, "I might call him in a minute." His phone chirruped with an incoming text message.

Alex asked, "Is that Emily? Must be a good day."

"Yeah, she's got it charged and in credit."

"Are you all right though, hun?" Alex was genuinely concerned.

"Yeah. It's just this case. It's so bloody political. ACC Mayweather is sniffing around." He saw a frown flit across Alex's face. "Assistant chief constable. Except he isn't – he retired about three years back. Apparently retirement doesn't suit him, because he's been creeping around the office like a bloody undertaker."

"Can you figure out what he wants? Is he just bored, maybe?"

"Oh, he's not like that. I met him, and honestly, I believe that every word he says is worked out in advance to push forward some sort of agenda." He paused to gather his thoughts. "I think he's working to have the whole thing swept under the carpet. Death by misadventure. No more publicity." He took a drink and stared into his glass. Alex, wisely, let him think. "The trouble is, all this case is hung together by supposition and rumour. Now there are three bodies that might be at the same time and place as the alleged abuse at Tŷ Bwncath. And this all started because I found a photo that was close to a victim. On top of that I've got Chalky and the Riders of Annwn in the mix as well."

"How do they fit in?"

"Well, we figured that Chalky gave Green Coat Man a lift away from the station. It now turns out that Chalky grew up in Llandavy, within spitting distance of Tŷ Bwncath. There's that word again – close. He was close to where all of this took place. Not actually there with evidence to prove it, just bloody close." He sighed. "I just want a case with evidence. Actual, physical evidence. One bloody footprint or a sample I can send to the lab. Anything!"

"I've read articles in the supplements about those historical abuse investigations. They sound really slow and painstaking."

Jonah nodded sullenly. "Yeah, that sounds about right." He picked up the phone. "I'll see if Gareth is at home. You said you wanted to do something for his birthday. I'll see if he wants to come out for a meal."

"Thanks, love." She paused for a second to gauge his reaction before adding, "And you'll get to check he's okay."

Jonah ignored her and phoned Gareth to sort out the birthday meal. For all of Alex's ribbing, he did feel better to know that his children were alive, safe and cared for. When he'd hung up, he said, "All sorted. I've pencilled in a date and I can phone round and get a reservation. I'll just text Em with the date and then head off to bed. If I'm in it for the long slog, I'd better get off to my own bed for a change."

CHAPTER 11

Jonah was heartily fed up of the Brecon Beacons before he even got to Builth Wells police station. To him it all seemed to be long, sweeping A roads, one up and one down. Perfect territory for impatient drivers to risk everything in dangerous overtaking manoeuvres. Everywhere was bleak and empty, with towns nestled in the hills separated by long distances across the open moor. He longed for the close, compact streets of Cardiff where he could understand the territory.

The capital city was constantly reinventing itself and had done so throughout history. It had far more diversity than the surrounding countryside and Jonah was far happier with suburbs that had mosques or eastern European shops than he was with this open space and inward-looking towns.

After cursing his way around the Builth Wells one-way system, he finally found the place he was looking for. The historic abuse team were obviously low down in the pecking order as they were crammed into a portacabin in the car park behind the main station.

Soon he was wedged in behind a desk, facing Gareth Morgan. The officer in charge of the historic abuse enquiry was thin and seemed almost lost behind his desk. His office didn't have much spare space as filing cabinets and shelves of box files were crammed in everywhere.

"Tŷ Bwncath or Buzzard House was the file you were interested in, wasn't it?"

Jonah picked up the expression on his face – he clearly thought it was a wild goose chase. "What's wrong with the case? There's a fairly active website with accounts on there."

"Yes," Morgan sounded tired of it all already. "But that's only one part of the picture. The problem is that two factors collide. Firstly, this is a decades-old case and secondly the Internet has muddied the waters. Anyone can start a website and invite the whole world to share their stories. No end of people then create logins and blame all their problems on this or that high-profile case. What we really need is corroboration and controlled information."

"But, you must know, by the very nature of the offence, that there are hardly ever witnesses."

"I didn't say witnesses. I said corroboration. For example, one of our most common scenarios to get complaints about is private schools, either day or boarding. Now, they have so many adults on the staff and it's inconceivable that they would all be complicit in any abuse that's been going on. Our most likely chance is usually in finding teachers or assistants who were just starting their careers. This gives us two advantages – firstly they're likely to still be alive decades later. Secondly, we've found that in general they start off naive and afraid for their jobs. But once the rumours start they can look back with a new perspective."

"What do you mean?"

"Well, you might have a newly qualified teacher in their

early twenties who sees an older guy who takes a special interest in pupils. Maybe he's always organising extracurricular trips, or insists on private one-to-ones in his office. At the time it happens the teacher wouldn't have had the confidence to report it, and maybe it wouldn't have seemed too strange. However, once the stories come out, then that same teacher might be in their forties or fifties and a lot more confident. They often want to unburden themselves when the stories start flying around. Also, even if they were private, schools traditionally have very good records. If we can establish that the accused was in the right place at the right time, then that adds weight to the claim."

"Isn't it all still circumstantial though?"

"Well, yes. But this job is all about building up patterns. If an accused teacher keeps moving jobs every few years, or if all the accounts have common features, even from different parts of the country. If colleagues from different schools all report similar concerns – it creates a balance of probability." Jonah still looked sceptical. "Look at Operation Midland." Jonah frowned. "The Met ran an operation to uncover a suspected paedophile ring operating in and around Westminster, including some high-level politicians. But it all collapsed due to lack of evidence. Turns out they based it all on one informant with no corroboration. The whole thing was sponsored by the media hand in hand with the Met. A nightmare."

"So, how does this relate to Tŷ Bwncath? There were many stories on that website."

"Yes, but the website was open to the public. Anyone could read the accounts already on there and then make up their own stories to fit the pattern."

There was a silence as the two men faced off against each other. Jonah knew that PC Morgan was wrong but he couldn't see why or how. In the end, he decided to bring it back to the main topic.

"Anyway, back to the matter at hand. Surely one man, this Bryn Bancroft couldn't have run the whole place by himself? Aren't there regulations about the number of adults supervising children?"

"Have you been in there? Seen the filing?"

"I've had a brief look. It is in a bit of a mess but there seems to be a lot of material there."

"That's now. We tried to get it in order. We didn't have enough evidence to get a warrant so we had to go softly-softly with the keyholder and the owner. In the end he agreed that we could have one supervised visit and not take any papers away with us."

"Now that we have confirmed human remains we can do more."

He held up a hand. "Hold your horses, we haven't told you what we found yet. There are hardly any names mentioned in the files. There's lots of petty cash transactions, mostly for additional help. But he doesn't use names. The site seems to be most active in the school holidays, offering respite to looked after children from inner cities. As far as we can tell he was offering cash in hand payments to teachers to help out during the holidays."

"But you can't trace them?"

"No. Even if we could, I doubt they'd want to talk on the record. If they were full time teachers, then they'd be paid for the full twelve months. Over the holidays they're meant to be doing lesson prep, marking etc. So if they're working cash in hand, it's a whole world of problems with the tax man, breach of contract, all of that."

"And the councils who sent the children? They went along with this? Sloppy paperwork and poor supervision?"

"'They'd never see that side of it. And their side is well documented. You know what councils are like. Bryn was very good at raising invoices and corresponding them with purchase orders."

"But surely the council would want to know who was looking after their children for a week?"

"Nope. It all closed down in the mid-nineties. Criminal records checking was first suggested in 1997 and finally enacted in 2002. For most of this time, it wasn't even an issue. To be honest, he was pricing himself cheap so to the councils he was the golden goose. They wouldn't want to be concerned with who he was paying and what the other side was."

DC Morgan paused and glanced down at the file, as if unsure whether to continue. "I know I sounded sceptical, because that's my job. But I have been through the survivors' accounts on the website and made contact with those who are willing to talk to me and make a statement.

"Now, I'm not saying I believe all these accounts, but I've analysed them and you can see a pattern. The way the centre operated was that the children arrived at some time on a Monday, depending on how far they had to travel. It seems that either we're missing a lot of data, or it was only a few weeks every year, well spread out, that the abuse took place. On one of these weeks, on Friday night when most of them would be in bed, some children were taken out of their beds and loaded into the minibus. They were then driven a short distance to another location, where the actual abuse appears to have taken place. Most of the survivors have very poor recollection so it's likely that they were drugged before being abducted.

"As I said, that's the story that can be assembled taking the common elements from all the accounts. So, even if you did track down a moonlighting teacher, you wouldn't be any further forward. The teachers would be around during the day and go home at night. And everyone went home on Saturday morning, so the children had no contact with anyone else who worked there after the alleged abuse took place."

There was an awkward pause. Eventually Jonah broke the deadlock. "Okay. Back to basics. Now we have three sets of human remains. Surely they require investigation now?"

"It's a numbers game. Let's be really optimistic and assume that Bryn only ran ten weeks a year, and that only ten children went on each course. How are the forensics on the bones? How much do you know about them? When they were buried and how old they were?"

"We've got the ages down to a range of two years for each body. The date of burial could be at any point while it was operating."

"So, they operated over about fifteen years, so we're still looking at around fifteen hundred people to trace. I know for a fact that the numbers are higher, far higher. He was averaging fifteen children each week and working pretty much every school holiday. So, out of thousands and thousands of names, we're now looking for three children. Have you ever contacted children's services at even one council?" Jonah shook his head. "Well, you'll get an education. For starters, if you're looking back twenty to thirty years, you'll find that many councils have either merged or been split up. For example, every council in Wales changed in 1996, the year after Tŷ Bwncath closed. On top of that, the records of children get the highest level of protection. Many of the children went on from care to secure units and from there into the adult criminal justice system. You might pick them up on police systems, but you'd need a magistrate to unlock the sealed records of detention centres. Those that didn't graduate to a life of crime are often ashamed of being brought up in care and make an effort to hide their past by changing names and refusing to ask questions. You also have to remember that a lot of children who come from care try to find their birth parents and often those parents don't want to be found. You could easily spend the rest of your career filling out forms and waiting for replies and you'd still be no further forward. Listen, to pluck a number out of the air, around three thousand kids must have passed through Tŷ Bwncath on holidays. So, if you want to make a match to those bones, then you have to hit a success rate of ninety-nine point nine per cent."

"So that's it? Just shrug your shoulders and walk away?" Jonah still thought that Morgan was wrong. He was already thinking that if he could compile a list of children who'd attended a holiday there then he could use the gender and the rough age of each body to narrow it down. It would be a lot of work, but it might not be impossible.

"You've got me all wrong!" Morgan stood up and tried to pace away, but he could only take two steps. He took a deep breath, obviously trying to control himself. "I'm not callous, just practical. We have limited resources so we can't chase every rumour down to the end. I have the experience and I know this is a fight we can't win. You don't even know that the bodies are connected to Tŷ Bwncath."

"What? Of course they are! They were buried in the exact time frame that Tŷ Bwncath was operating, on their own land. Where else would they be from?"

"Open your mind a bit, please! Imagine a psychopath who likes to abduct and kill children – what better place to bury them than the grounds of an outdoor activity centre. If they're ever found, officers like you will burn themselves out investigating the history of Tŷ Bwncath without ever looking in the right direction."

Jonah felt himself getting annoyed. The true scale of the task ahead was dawning on him but he couldn't see the point of just giving up. To buy a bit of time to calm down, he went back over his notes. Something was bothering him. He found it. "If Bryn was taking them off the site for the abuse in the middle of the night, then was another adult staying there? Also, when you described the files, you said that there were hardly any names of employees. Do we know who else was working there?"

Now Morgan looked like he'd been caught out. "Well, there was a woman who worked there. She seemed to be the cook, cleaner, housemaid, you name it. And it seems that she had a room there so she could stay over."

Jonah nodded. "So? What's her name? Is she still alive?"

"Oh, she's very much alive! And abusive. We tried to interview her about five, maybe six years ago. Got nowhere."

"Well, if I could have a copy of her file, maybe I could make a fresh approach?"

"I suppose I could check."

Jonah had had enough and let his frustration show. "I'm a fellow officer, offering to work one of your closed cases!"

"It's not closed! It's pending further evidence."

And three bodies don't count as further evidence, Jonah thought bitterly. But he had the sense to bite his tongue and say nothing.

"Listen," DC Morgan carried on speaking. "I saw the look on your face the minute you walked in here. I know it's not some fancy office in Cardiff, but we work with what we are given. It may not look fancy and we don't have a lot of space but we are doing well." Jonah looked sceptical. "If you compare this unit's performance against Home Office guidelines then our conviction rate is within normal parameters. Especially considering the fact that we have several staff vacancies that we are yet to fill."

Jonah took a deep breath. All the jargon did nothing to help him calm down but he attempted to keep it businesslike. "I'd still like to have a talk with that woman who worked with Bryn." He tried to sound conciliatory. "If she tells me anything I'll make sure to pass the interview reports over to you. Save you some work."

"All right," Morgan grumbled. "She's called Gwen Davies." Jonah's shoulder's slumped. It was probably the most common name in the country, there would be one in every Welsh village. "We've been keeping tabs on her. She lived in Llandavy until recently, but now she's moved into a specialist nursing home called Golden Valleys, just on the outskirts of Merthyr. Should be quite easy to find."

"Specialist?"

"We poked around, and apparently it's got a high level of nursing care available. We think she's got breathing problems, so I'd hurry up if I were you. Might even get a deathbed confession."

DC Gareth Morgan had been given a mountainous task and hadn't applied himself to it with any commitment. Jonah need to get out – he could see that no good would come from continuing the meeting. He nodded curtly and shut his pocketbook.

"Like I said before, you've got us all wrong. We do close cases, we get convictions on what are really difficult cases. We have files full of victims who, after a lifetime of not being believed, finally get to face their abusers in court. But we don't have infinite resources. We can only do that with careful targeting of the cases that show the best chance of a result."

Jonah's desire to argue with the officer drained away from him. He knew the logic but he felt it like a body blow. No one was willing to help. Unable to stand the atmosphere, he left the claustrophobic office as soon as he could, not caring if he was polite.

His mind was spinning. Had there been three unreported child murders anywhere in the UK or abroad? He cast his mind back to the eighties and nineties. There had been high-profile child abductions, but they were just that – high profile. Surely three missing children would have made the news? Nothing had come from his work with the Missing Persons Unit either.

Sat in his car, he took a deep breath and got back to basics. Was he barking up the wrong tree? If the bodies were buried under steps that were, at the time, part of the Tŷ Bwncath grounds, then they had to be connected. From what he'd seen of Llandavy, it was a typical Welsh village. He knew the type of place – people wouldn't move out very often. However hard he tried, Jonah couldn't imagine a stranger turning up, moving paving slabs, burying bodies and then leaving again, three times over the space of ten years. Someone would notice. And even if no one in Llandavy did notice that still didn't explain the absence of any disappeared children.

Often the simplest solution was the right one. Bryn had access, both to the land and to children, so most likely he was involved, despite what DC Morgan thought. Assuming the bodies did belong to Tŷ Bwncath, and there were reports of abuse, how come there had been no police investigation while the place was open? Everything Morgan had said rang true, but Jonah couldn't bring himself to accept that the world was that cynical.

CHAPTER 12

JONAH's initial pessimism about locating a Gwen Davies within Wales was unfounded. A quick check on the Internet turned up the Golden Valleys Nursing Home. It was on the outskirts of Merthyr so Jonah could stop in on his way back to Cardiff. He decided that he'd enough of vague links and ifs and maybes. It was time to seize the initiative and gain some solid facts.

It was late afternoon by the time he parked his car in the car park of Golden Valleys and looked up at the building. It was a sprawling red brick mansion, probably Victorian and in good condition. Chimneys and roofs sprouted everywhere and the gardens around it were immaculate – manicured and well maintained.

As he approached, Jonah could see that while it looked old, it was actually very modern. The double glazing was up to date and there were new pipes and small outbuildings tucked away. Small square hazard signs on these buildings hinted that the place was closer to a hospital than a care home.

He stopped in the car park, unsure how to handle this

interview. Had Gwen Davies been a willing participant in the abuse that went on? Maybe she'd agreed to watch the children at the house while others were taken off to be abused? Or had she somehow managed to stay ignorant? If she was ignorant, was it a wilful turning a blind eye so as not to get involved? Or had she merely supported Bryn Bancroft out of some misguided love?

Jonah privately thought the last one was the most likely. With a barely suppressed shudder, he recalled Rose West. She had acted as the friendly face of the monster, luring victims to their doom. Was that Gwen's role?

He looked at the surroundings and a new thought occurred to him. The garden would take a lot of workers to keep in check. The visitors had parked expensive cars all around him. This place was not cheap. It was anything but. And yet, a retired housekeeper had chosen to end her days here? Was he looking at that fine line between blackmail and being paid for her silence?

Glass doors whispered open at his approach, and he walked into an area that reinforced his impression of a private hospital. He squared his shoulders and approached the desk, fully prepared for confrontation. "Hi, I'm here to visit Gwen Davies."

"Lovely! Does she know you're coming?" The receptionist was immaculately turned out in a white tunic that echoed a nurse's uniform.

"No, just dropping in for a chat."

"Okay. I'll get someone to find her now. Are you family?"

"No, just an old friend, Jonah Greene." With Debbie Houghton's warnings still in his mind, Jonah decided to keep this strictly unofficial.

"Fine, if you sign in there," she indicated a book, "I'll phone through for you." Jonah wrote his name and noticed that the book was turned to a nearly new page – there were only four names above his. He itched to look back and see who else had visited Gwen.

Jonah waited a couple of minutes before a nurse appeared. "Mr Greene, if you'd like to come with me." She led him through key card locked doors and into the building.

The nurse stopped briefly on the way to the day room to get Jonah a coffee and a plate of biscuits. He noted that the nurse knew what drink to get for Gwen Davies.

"Mrs Davies has a trouble with her breathing. She is on an oxygen mask and she can remove it for short periods to talk. But don't expect too much. The lack of oxygen also tires her out, so she might doze off. Come and find me if that happens and we can make sure she's comfortable."

Soon he was sat in a high-backed armchair opposite Mrs Gwen Davies in a stiflingly hot day room. His coffee and the biscuits were on a low table between them, while her tea was at her elbow. Large patio doors gave an expansive view over a lawn with the Brecon Beacons in the distance.

Gwen was dwarfed by the armchair, with a deeply lined face and black curly hair messily piled up on her head. She seemed to be sunken into herself. She had a mask on her face and the oxygen cylinder was next to her chair. No one else was within earshot.

"Well, this livens up my day, a surprise visitor!"

Jonah met her eye as he sat down. For all her age and illness, her eyes still sparkled with wit and determination.

"I'm Jonah Greene, nice to meet you." She waited to see what he wanted, one lined hand on the mask. "I wanted to talk to you about your time working at Tŷ Bwncath."

"I suppose you're police?" Jonah nodded. "Are you allowed to do that? Coming in here. Old family friend." She paused to catch her breath. "Suppose you thought you could trick the frail old lady into spilling all her secrets, did you?"

"No, it's not like that," Jonah protested. "But you did work there?"

"You know I did," she countered. "That's why you came here."

"And, what did you know of what went on there?" Jonah was feeling his way now, aware that his adversary was bright and capable of duelling with him.

"What the kayaking, long hikes, songs around the camp-fire, all of that?" There was a definite twinkle in her eyes.

She knew and Jonah knew that she knew. They looked at each other, in a brief deadlock.

"There are persistent rumours of abuse from the early eighties up to when it closed in the mid-nineties. Is there anything you'd like to say about that?"

"I've seen your eyes sliding around this place. I know what you're thinking. My heart is so black that I've sold my eternal soul for a final few months of comfort, filter coffee and cream-filled biscuits? Do I strike you as that stupid?"

Jonah ignored the question. "So you knew?"

With the mask in place, she nodded.

"You knew, and yet you kept working there?" Despite his best efforts he couldn't keep the disgust out of his voice.

"What do you think I ought to have to done?" She cocked her head to one side and looked at him with a challenge. She held her oxygen mask over her mouth while she waited for an answer.

Jonah thought for a moment. "Reported it? Resigned?"

A slow smile spread across her face and Jonah knew he'd walked into a trap.

Gwen took a deep breath before setting the mask aside. "I always remember the first time. It took me a while to put it all together. That Friday night, Bryn asked me to stay over, said he had some business in town. Wasn't that unusual, but he warned me to stay in my room. I never was good at doing what I was told, so I saw the minibus leaving with some of the kids. That just wasn't right. I don't know how far you've got, but I also cleaned at the Prince of Wales in Llandavy. Have you been there?"

"Yes," Jonah nodded, thinking of his only visit to the place and how uncomfortable he had felt.

"Well, then you've probably met the owner, one Alan Cooper." She paused to take more oxygen. "My whole life I've always managed to choose the wrong man, whether it's for a husband or a boss." She chuckled at her joke, although she was always on the edge of coughing. She took some deep breaths before she could continue. "Anyway, Alan was as thick as thieves with Bryn. The next day, I saw that all the rooms were booked out and a friend said she'd seen the minibus in the pub car park, late at night. Slowly the pieces started to fall into place. Next time it happened, I found a piece of paper while I was cleaning in the office. Alan kept a list of people. None of them trusted each other, you see, so he kept an attendance record to keep them all honest." There was another pause while she breathed more oxygen.

"So, you could have reported it then, put a stop to it?"

"Really? Is that what you think? Do you think that if one lonely nurse had reported Jimmy Savile, then it would have all come crashing down? I was just a cleaner, not even a professional like a nurse. I might not have any formal education, but I do remember a name. Once I knew the pattern I started checking for Alan's lists. Half the people who were written down were regular visitors at Tŷ Bwncath. An MP, several councillors, even a senior policeman. You know the sort of thing. Local dignitaries turning up to show they care for the little people." Again, she had to stop to breathe. Jonah surmised it was the most she'd spoken in days.

"So, what did you do then?"

"Nothing. Not at first. I was stunned, I didn't want to believe it was possible. Every quiet moment though, I saw their faces. The kids the next day. They were like empty vessels. Hollowed out, just going through the motions. I couldn't take it any more so I went to the church and I prayed. I asked Jesus to guide me." This time she stopped to stare straight at Jonah, challenging him to mock her religion. Wisely, he stayed silent. "Let me ask you something. If you had a candle, would you go to stand in the bright sunlight, or would you go into a dark cave?"

"Uh?" Jonah wanted to ask what she was on about, but he could start to see what she was driving at. This was reminding him of his conversation with Debbie. Gwen was still looking at him, eyebrows arched over her oxygen mask, expecting an answer. "Well, a candle works best in the dark, doesn't it?"

Gwen nodded. "Exactly. God put me there to shine a light. To show those poor children some love. To put the brakes on Bryn. I know you can't stop people like that." She stopped to consider her words carefully. "I know that people like me can't put a stop to people like that. If I'd have reported it, it would've gone nowhere. Have you seen how small Llandavy is? The whisper would've gone round in a couple of minutes and I'd have been out of both my jobs, no one talking to me. I'd have left the village in six months, and then guess what?" When Jonah didn't answer, she continued. "He'd have hired someone else. Someone worse. The parties would've crept up from four a year. Everything would be worse."

The stark silence between them was broken only by her

laboured breaths and the soft hiss of the oxygen bottle. Despite her story, Jonah was a policeman and still remembered the outrage he'd felt before he met her.

"You have just admitted to knowledge of a series of crimes. And that you did nothing to stop it or report it."

She lifted her head and sat forward. "Go on then. Arrest me! I'll get the doctor in here and a solicitor and we'll start talking about competency while I use my right to remain silent. If you're really lucky you might get me in court before my emphysema puts me in a coffin."

They had reached a stalemate. Jonah started working through it in his head. There had always been rumours about the very famous before the Savile story broke. But if one cleaner from South Wales spoke up, would anyone have listened? Slowly, his thoughts turned around and he started to see Gwen's point of view.

"So, you knew the whole time?" Jonah's voice was much gentler this time.

Gwen nodded. "Sometimes the Lord puts a hard road in front of you." Jonah nodded, hearing the tension in her voice. "But it's our lot to walk it as best we may. And no one can judge me now, at least not on earth. When I meet my saviour, I'll kneel before Him and make my account. I did what I could to make life easier for the children, I just hope it's enough."

"But the things you know." Jonah stopped for a second. "Surely now, in the current environment you could come forward?"

"No, I'm too old for all that. And everyone would hate me. I might even end up in court. As you said, I was there when crimes were committed. Involved even, some might say."

Jonah was stumped. He felt he should reassure her as

she was obviously upset. But he'd just suggested that she was guilty and that she should come forward.

"How far have your investigations got? Have you found out about my other indiscretions?"

"No, what else have you got in your past?"

"It's not my place to tell. I can confirm or deny your guesses but where other people are concerned I can't tell you anything."

"So, the rumours about Tŷ Bwncath? What went on there when they were taken to the inn?"

"Yes!" She would have shouted but it came out raspy with her lack of breath. "You have no idea. I spent over a decade there in a stand-off with Bryn. He didn't dare fire me because of what I knew, and I only stayed to care for the children." She paused to draw more oxygen in deep gulping breaths. "But even with my disapproval it still happened about four times a year. Four times every year that I stayed up at Tŷ Bwncath, spending half the night on my knees praying to God to do what he could to protect them. All the while, I knew precisely what was going on. Dreading the next morning, seeing those broken children getting on their buses." She burst into sobs which soon dissolved into coughs. The nurse glided over towards them. She closed her eyes and leant back.

Jonah was paralysed – he didn't know what to do. As the nurse hovered, he tentatively asked. "Should I go?"

Gwen nodded, eyes shut. She could've been asleep except for the tears flowing down her cheeks.

Jonah caught the eye of the nurse and was escorted out to the front desk. He signed himself out.

THE NEXT DAY, Jonah was in his office trying to make sense of his notes from his meeting with both DC Morgan and Gwen Davies.

He had some good information, about the pattern of the abuse and the role that Gwen had played in it. However it all relied on the assumption that the accounts were true. In fact, because of the suspected use of drugs, most of the accounts were either very vague or reconstructed from recovered memories. And Gwen Davies herself, while having very strong suspicions, was not a direct witness to any wrongdoing. He could imagine the holes a competent barrister would drive through it if it ever came to court. In fact, he could see that it would be nearly impossible to get this mess past the CPS. The combination of drugged child victims and an elderly witness who was dying was enough to scare them off.

If he could understand Gwen Davies' personality then he could decide how much weight to give to her account. He decided he needed another perspective so he arranged to meet Farida for a coffee.

At first, he filled her in on all he had learnt from the historic abuse unit.

"Then, I went straight to Golden Valleys and met with Gwen Davies."

"The housekeeper from Tŷ Bwncath? You're going to have to tread carefully there."

"Yeah, I know. I signed in as a family friend." Jonah ignored Farida's frown and continued. "I went in there wanting her to be guilty. The last surviving adult that we can trace who worked at Tŷ Bwncath. She might be our last chance to find out the truth of what went on. She was actually there when it happened."

"Sounds like you were looking for an arrest. I take it you didn't get one?"

"No, it's more complicated than that. She did admit to being the housekeeper there, and that she knew that something was wrong. Even better, she was asked to sleep over in the house when the children were taken away so she must have a good idea of what dates to investigate, where to start looking in the records."

"But?"

"But, she didn't know what to do, so she went to church and prayed. Jesus told her to stay there. To be a light in the darkness." He shook his head. "It's never straightforward is it? If she'd reported it, we could have followed that paper trail and found out who failed to act, who buried the evidence. Or if she'd been complicit, well we'd have someone guilty to arrest. But this? It's almost tempting to write it off to mental incapacity."

"You're being totally unfair!" Farida said. "If you take out the religious, talking to God aspect, what she did could be seen as a very brave and wise thing."

"Do you really think so?"

"This all started in the eighties didn't it?" Jonah nodded. "How old is she now?"

"Early sixties, I'd say."

"So at the beginning, she'd have been roughly in her late twenties. Isolated up on the Beacons with a sexual predator. I know what those villages are like. She must have felt like there was no one she could trust, nowhere to turn. And, you know what these predators are like. Now we have terms like malignant narcissist and psychological descriptions, but they haven't changed at all over time. He would have been overbearing, especially as he was an older man." She turned to look at Jonah. "I can see you're struggling to accept that she found her answer in prayer. How would you feel if she said that she went for a long walk across the moors, or sat by the sea, and after that she reached her decision?"

Jonah frowned. He tried to remember long ago school lessons about comparative religion. Did Muslim's pray in the same way as Christians? He couldn't think of a way to ask the question tactfully so he grunted noncommittally and nodded.

"Well, why don't you ask her what she did? Ask for specifics? It's all very well for her to say that she stayed there to shine a light but unless she can give you concrete examples, then it's all just hot air. Did she try to rein in Bryn's activities? Keep records? I think you should go back and interview her."

"That's all well and good," Jonah said. "But it would have helped if she'd spoken up at the time. She could've taken action there and then."

"Maybe she couldn't? She might have felt that she had no real choice."

"Do you really believe that?" Jonah asked.

"Just think back to that time. It was the eighties and we don't even know if she could drive or not. Or if she had access to a car?" Farida was starting to warm to her subject. "She would have had to have taken time off to go into a police station, be interviewed by men and she would have had very little specific evidence to give them. She didn't know in advance when the abuse was going to take place. And persuading a police force to believe her to the extent that they would mount a raid on the Prince of Wales? Even if that all worked, how long would she last under cross-examination by powerful lawyers? And when it was all over, where would she go? She wouldn't be welcome back in Llandavy. Those places can quickly close ranks and shut people out even if they live there."

"I suppose you're right." Jonah was morose at the way Farida took his case apart.

"Also, what do you remember of the eighties?"

"Well, I was there, you know."

"Think back to that time, especially how the police were viewed, especially around here. The miners' strike, followed by Lynette White. If she saw even one policeman's name on those lists of people involved in the abuse, then she would have every reason to believe that her complaint would go nowhere. In the Valleys, we were the bad guys. Still are to the old guard."

Jonah frowned at her, he had rarely seen her this passionate. She caught his look and then looked away. When she spoke, it was to the window, not his face. Her passion hadn't gone, but her voice was a bit gentler. "I know what it's like to be ignored. To not have your voice heard. Whether it's in the more conservative parts of my community or here in the police, I know. It must have been so hard for her to stand up and be counted. Maybe she did the only thing she felt she could."

"Thank you," Jonah said. "You're right. I ought to find the time to go back. Be more compassionate, listen to her, see what I can learn."

"I do wonder, we arrest so many people. How many of them felt they had no choice but to do what they did? I mean, I don't mind arresting those who choose to do wrong. But it's those who are desperate – they're a different thing." She paused, seeming to have talked herself out. "How official is this? Do you feel you can go back and question Gwen Davies again?"

"Officially, I am doing my job. We have unidentified remains and I'm making best efforts to find out whose remains they are. The most likely explanation, given the combination of the abuse rumours and the location of the bones is that the dead children were at Tŷ Bwncath, so that's where I have to focus and Mrs Davies is our best witness."

Farida laughed. "You've been rehearsing that in case you get questioned by your boss, haven't you?"

"Maybe." Jonah smiled ruefully. "Listen, do you want some fresh air? The warrant came in for Tŷ Bwncath, so I'm heading up there next week with Dan Price, the DC from Dyfed Powys, to have a poke around, see what I can find out."

"Sounds like you'll need CID support."

"Thank you." Jonah's voice was muffled as he was sitting with his head on the desk. Farida turned back to him.

"What's up?"

Jonah sat up. "I think that DC Morgan might be right. Look at this case – we've got hardly any evidence, nothing concrete anyway. Maybe it would be better to refocus our energies to winnable cases."

"I know you. It's the children, isn't it?"

"It's not just the three bodies either. I keep going back to the website. No one listened to them before, and now we've got to that stage. We're looking at events that happened twenty to thirty years ago. Every year that goes by, there's more chance that any suspects will be dead." He paused and gathered his strength. "I know you're right. I need to go back to Gwen. Chase up Green Coat Man, hassle Chalky. Shake enough trees until something drops out."

CHAPTER 13

Tŷ Bwncath hadn't changed since Jonah was last there. Together with Farida and Dan Price, he stood in the car park. It was ten in the morning and the weather was already gearing up to be hot and sticky. Jonah felt the building looming over him. He was unwilling to look at its shuttered windows, hiding its secrets. Instead, he looked around at the grounds. The undergrowth was slowly encroaching from the sides of the car park, softening the edges.

Jonah berated himself. It was just a building. One of many Victorian and Edwardian great houses in the Brecon Beacons. Was it really a house of horrors? Or just a normal building with a history?

He got out and stretched his legs. He'd parked next to the other two cars in the car park. They all grouped together in the centre of the large yard, as if afraid of the surrounding countryside.

They all greeted each other – Farida had come up on her own from Cardiff and they'd arranged to meet Dan Price here. Before they went in, Jonah wandered across to get a better look at the outbuildings. The one running away from the house up the left side of the car park was joined to the main building.

"That was a dormitory," Dan Price said walking up beside him. "One long corridor running from the main house with the rooms leading off. Then over there," he indicated the building that ran parallel to the road, on the other side of the car park from the house. "This was divided into big rooms for meetings, indoor games and the like." He turned around to the third building which had some open areas with racks as well as some doors. "And that was the equipment store. Canoes, cones, balls, all that sort of stuff."

"What was in the main house then?"

"Let's go and take a look."

With all the protests from the owner now dealt with, Dan Price had a set of keys. Soon the three of them were standing in front of the house, under a small porch roof. The metal shutter and the front door were unlocked by Dan Price and opened.

Inside was so dim that all three officers switched on torches. It didn't matter how long it had lain empty, it still had the feel of an official building open to the public. Doors were marked 'Fire Door Keep Shut'. There were emergency lights and official notices everywhere.

Dan Price led them past a staircase that rose on their right-hand side. Ahead of them was a hatch and a faded sign reading 'Reception'. "What we're after is behind reception where the office is. Do you want to see the rest of the ground floor first?"

They both nodded so Dan led them to the left where there was a large dining room and an industrial kitchen. "This is pretty much the rest of it for the ground floor." He looked around at the rooms. "I can see why it hasn't sold as it's such a big old place, I can't see what anyone would do with it."

Jonah looked around in amazement. The place had been abandoned suddenly, that much was clear. Luckily it had been cleared of food, but there were pots, pans and stacks of plates in the kitchen. Likewise, the dining room had a full complement of chairs upturned on the tables. The whole place looked and smelt like a small school that had been abandoned twenty years ago. Everything was still in place so that with a bit of cleaning and stocking, thirty people could be seated for a meal.

"It's just so weird," Jonah said. "Are there bedrooms upstairs?"

"Some, yes." Dan pointed to a door in the corner of the dining room. "If you go through there, it leads through to the corridor that runs up the side of the dormitory block. That part is ramshackle though, just prefab stuff from the fifties, not like this solid old building."

They naturally drifted back through to the hallway and Dan led them through a door marked 'Private' to the right of the hatch through into the office. There was one desk and chair under the hatch and second one under the window opposite. That one would have given a view out onto the yard if it hadn't been shuttered.

The rest of the available space was occupied by filing cabinets and shelves of folders. Rather worryingly for Jonah, there were piles of paper, filing trays and stacks of folders on both desks. He picked up a clipboard hanging from a peg by the hatch. The single sheet on it listed the fourteen children due to arrive from a children's home in Glasgow on July 24, 1995. There was a pen on a string, but the sheet was blank – they had never been ticked off as having arrived.

"Where do we start?" Farida asked, not expecting an answer.

"If we could find more of these that'd be a start," Jonah said, waving the clipboard.

The three of them started opening drawers and reaching down folders, randomly at first as they tried to find some order in the system.

After about twenty minutes of moving papers around and trying to assemble piles of similar looking forms, Jonah dropped his folder onto the desk with both a bang and a puff of dust.

"This is pointless," he said. "I've just found a stack of these sign-in sheets from 1987, in date order covering the Easter break and the first half of the summer holidays. Then suddenly, the next page is an invoice from 1991 for Hackney Council and after that it appears to be petty cash receipts from 1984." Farida and Dan stopped what they were doing and turned to him. "Let's assume, for a moment, that all the rumours are true. Let's put aside the rules of evidence and reasonable doubt. For the sake of argument, let's say that Bryn was running a paedophile ring that had regular events where children were abused. Let's go further and state that for whatever reason some of them died."

"Okay," Farida said. "I think we're all assuming something broadly like that is true. I mean that's why we're here and investigating."

"So, if that's true, and given the state of these records, I think we can assume that he would've just destroyed the records of any child who died. Probably would've binned the lot for any week where something happened."

"There might be something here though," Dan said hopefully. "Most criminals get caught because they make stupid mistakes. Yes, someone sensible would have destroyed everything. But there might be something that he missed."

"Yeah, I know what you mean." Jonah looked around. "But unless we find a file labelled 'paedophile parties' we won't know which lists are children we're interested in."

Farida looked at the papers around them. "Realistically, we'd need to get a team in here, move all this paper through to the dining room. Make organised stacks of the sign-in sheets, the invoices, petty cash, correspondence, receipts, all of it. Then each stack would need to be sorted by date."

"And when we've done all of that," Jonah picked up the thread, "we'd need to go through and look for any gaps. And cross-check it against any names that we can find on the website. That would just be a beginning."

"But you've seen the state of this place," Farida said. "Any gaps could have any number of reasons. Finding something missing isn't positive evidence of wrongdoing. And if you're looking for the dead children, well it stands to reason their names won't be on the Internet or anywhere else."

"And," Jonah continued, "we'd need a list of term dates going back over thirty years. If a week is missing from the records it might just be that the children were at school."

They all stood there, gloomily looking at the piles of paperwork, folders and files. Dan suddenly brightened up as he had a thought. "What about the abuse investigation team? They must have names that are associated with the accusations? Of the children? Surely we can look for those? Especially if they come with dates?"

"I'm not sure it'd be much help. Nothing here is in date order." Jonah shook his head. "And either they would be missing, which wouldn't prove anything, or there would be a record which would only prove that they were here on holiday."

"So you're just going to give up?" Dan Price looked incredulous.

"No! I just had this exact argument with the Historic Abuse Investigation Team. I felt that they took one look at the scale of the problem, the lack of evidence and just shrugged and walked away. I don't want to do the same thing. But, on the other hand, we could plough lots of resources into this and find nothing."

He wandered from the office and stood in the doorway to the hall. "According to my source, several times a year, children were taken from here to the Prince of Wales in Llandavy to be abused by adults. I haven't been able to corroborate it yet, but that's what I've heard. It happened on the last night here and they left the next morning. So we can say this isn't the primary site and it stands to reason that there'll be no evidence here and all this paperwork will just confirm that it was an outdoor education centre."

Jonah turned to look up the hall. "If this was happening in the last ten years, there'd be computers we could seize and give to the technical boys who'd find out how it was all organised and what pictures Bryn had been downloading." He turned to Dan. "Is it all right if I just wander around a bit? I want to get a feel for this Bryn Bancroft character. He seems to have been at the heart of it, together with Mrs Davies."

Dan nodded and Jonah started up the stairs. At the top he found several large rooms, each with three or four beds, many arranged as bunks. At the end of the corridor he found what he presumed was Bryn's room. Rather disconcertingly, a faded and dated eiderdown was still on the bed. There was a bookcase that revealed nothing except that he had a weakness for Westerns. In all it looked as if Bryn had just stepped out for a moment.

Jonah stopped and looked around, his torchlight playing over the surfaces and walls. He could imagine this place when it was all quiet. Bryn here on his own, eating his meals in that cavernous kitchen, making arrangements in the office. Mrs Davies popping in and cleaning and making all the beds and getting ready for the next influx of children.

On his way downstairs he discovered a much simpler bedroom with a single bed and a nightstand. Probably where Mrs Davies stayed over when she was required, Jonah thought. There was a Bible left next to the bed. Jonah shuddered, imagining Gwen kneeling by the bed, praying fervently while her children were away.

At the bottom of the stairs, he met with Dan and Farida who had both wandered off to explore the ground floor.

"What happened here?" Farida asked. "It's like someone shut up shop twenty years ago and never came back."

"Pretty much," Jonah said. "Bryn had a stroke in July 1995 and was rushed to hospital. He spent ten days there before he died on the first of August. It looks like Mrs Davies came in and had one last clean and removed all the food and shut it up for the next owners."

"Who never showed up?" Farida asked.

"No, it didn't sell. By the late nineties the whole land-scape of childcare was changing. There were far more regulations around running a place like this. People were starting to talk about the checks on people caring for children that we now take for granted. On top of that there were changes in the National Park Authority, and planning tightened up along with concerns about access. Too much red tape in short."

"It is spooky," Farida commented, allowing her torch beam to play across a noticeboard of leaflets that were curling at the edges. They advertised events like canoeing and orienteering, all over twenty years ago.

By common agreement, they went outside to the fresh air. The day had heated up and the inside of the house was stuffy.

"Do you need any more access to the house?" Dan asked.

When Jonah shook his head, Dan locked up, made his excuses and went back to his station, leaving Jonah and Farida alone in the car park.

"Could you show me where the bodies were found?" Farida asked.

Together, they left the car park through a gap between the buildings in one corner. After climbing a short slope, they stood on a ridge and looked down on Tŷ Bwncath and the surrounding countryside. Turning their back on the house, they carried on over a saddle in the ridge, and down to the sheep field.

"I've been walked through this by the mapping guy," Jonah explained, pointing out landmarks. "So, the way we came up, through that gap in the outbuildings, that's where the path started. There was probably a gate of some sort or even just an opening. Then the path led up to this small wood here. From here they would've gone down the steps to the firepit." He pointed to where Mr Williams had removed the slabs and found the bones. "We're lucky that it's been dry for a couple of weeks. You see those marks where the grass is fainter? How they mark out a rough circle?" Farida nodded. "That's the where the firepit would've been, with some fence posts and benches around the edge."

"Oh! That is horrible! So they would have all trooped down there for some boy scout style sing-along walking over the bodies of their friends without knowing?"

"He must have thought that putting the steps over

would stop them being found. Whereas it actually led to their discovery."

Farida looked around, as if there might be someone listening. They were alone on the hillside. "What about Leo Davidson? That photo looks like it could be from the same time as the bodies. And I know the background is just general grass and hills, but it's not impossible that it was taken around here."

"Yeah. I think it must've been a photo of one of the children from here. Like a holiday snap or something. As for Leo Davidson, I did some research there as well. Apparently there wasn't a trust or steering committee or anything like that for this place. Just Bryn Bancroft at the helm. As for outside people helping him, well you've seen the records for yourself, there are a lot of entries marked 'petty cash' and 'cash in hand wages'."

"So, we're back where we started." Farida sounded glum. "A lot of rumour, supposition and informed guesswork and no hard evidence."

"But I don't think it was a wasted day. I can picture it now. Kids from the cities, who've had a hard life in care, coming up here. Making camp fires, playing football, kayaking, all of that. And Mr Bancroft and Mrs Davies running the whole show."

"Don't go all rosy eyed though," Farida warned. "We're here because terrible things might have happened as well."

Jonah walked away from the firepit to have a proper look at the house. Boarded up and abandoned it still had a presence. The sky was clear blue, the sun was beating down and there was a gentle breeze. Up here on the Beacons it should've been a beautiful day. But Jonah's gaze was always drawn back to Tŷ Bwncath and the terrible secrets it still guarded.

JONAH STOOD in the car park, surrounded by Tŷ Bwncath and watched Farida drive away. He wanted to check the information that Gwen had given him. As the day was so nice, he decided to walk into Llandavy, to see for himself just how far it was from the house.

He checked his map and grabbed a water bottle before starting down the lane that ran in front of the house. As he walked, he struggled to do what he always did when he dealt with cases that were deeply emotive. He tried to put aside the emotional component of the case and instead focus on the logical. But every time he thought of trying to prove the links between people, other thoughts crept in. The children, possibly drugged, being taken down this exact road in the dark of night, unaware of the horrors that awaited them at the end of their journey. He pushed that thought aside and replaced it with wondering about the lists that Gwen had hinted at. If Cooper still kept records, maybe that would be a way to open up the case. But he also couldn't stop thinking of the names on that list. People who would have one evening of perverse pleasure without any shred of shame. Without any thought whatsoever about the lives that were ruined. He thought of all those people growing up with problems, drug addictions, unable to form proper relationships. He knew for a fact that many of them came to the attention of the police because they couldn't rein in their anger or control their urges.

Before he could sink too far into maudlin thinking, he came across another house, set back from the road behind a large garden. He had been walking for about twenty minutes so he stopped for a moment and looked at the building. It had a tended garden, curtains – a lived-in feeling. It was only when he saw this that he realised all the differences between this and Tŷ Bwncath which was all shut up and abandoned.

Then he continued on, discovering that the house was the first on the outskirts of Llandavy. There was a short row of cottages on the other side of the road, followed by a couple more big Victorian houses. Soon he was walking down a residential street. He turned a corner, and there was the main road to Merthyr. And over the road was the Prince of Wales Inn.

He stood stock still and stared at the big building which was framed by the last few houses that ran down to the road. The pieces fell into place. Somewhere you could get a private room, easy driving distance of Tŷ Bwncath, where people could turn up from out of town and disappear again. All it would need was a landlord who was complicit in the abuse. Whether it was for profit or personal pleasure Jonah didn't much care. He hadn't liked Mr Cooper when he met him and now liked him even less.

He now had to consider the inn as the primary crime scene. He shook his head. It had been the primary crime scene, over twenty years ago. There would obviously be no forensic evidence or anything at all useful left.

But, as his main objective was to get a feel for the place, try to get the overall context for what had happened decades ago, he decided it was time for a pint. As he walked into the pub, he stopped for a moment in the porch. The licensing plaque was there and the insurance document, both in the name of Alan Cooper. So, Jonah thought, he hadn't moved on when Bryn died.

He went through to the bar and was relieved to note that the daughter was serving. He honestly hadn't decided how he would react if he came face to face with Mr Cooper again. She drew his pint and he sat at the bar. Looking around he could tell that nothing had changed since his previous visit and, he wasn't sure, but it even looked as if the locals were the same people sat at the same tables.

"Will you be wanting food this time?"

"Just a packet of crisps, thanks." Jonah still had to walk back to his car and he knew that he had limited leeway to investigate this case.

When he had drink and snack, he got to the main purpose of his visit, trying to keep his tone light and casual. "I got the name wrong last time I was here. Have you heard of Gwen Davies?"

"Mrs Davies? Of course. She's worked here since I was tiny. Do you know..." she trailed off, unsure of how to proceed.

"Yes, I visited her at the nursing home."

"It's terrible. But she always smoked. I mean back then, everyone did. No one thought twice about it. But to be struggling to breathe like that in your early sixties." She shook her head. "Shocking!"

"What did she do here?" Jonah asked.

"Officially she was chambermaid or maybe housekeeper. But really whatever needed doing. She'd clean the bar, sweep through to the kitchen, take out the rubbish. Of course, she cleaned the rooms too, changed the beds, that kind of thing. If she wasn't here she was up the hill."

"Tŷ Bwncath?"

"Yes, that's it. She helped out there as well. Cooking and cleaning when they had kids in. She was always busy. I've no idea how she had enough hours in the day to fit it all in." She paused, looking as if Mrs Davies was already dead. "And now she's stuck in that place. Hardly able to move after a lifetime on her feet. It's terrible."

Jonah nodded his agreement. The place still felt oppressive, even without the dour figure of Mr Cooper behind the bar. With his new knowledge however the pub became even more sinister to Jonah. He took some large gulps of his pint, suddenly keen to be on his way back to his car. Ultimately, he wanted to be in the crowded streets of Cardiff, where he understood the territory. He had had enough of this inward-looking village, surrounded by hills.

He didn't go straight up the road back to Tŷ Bwncath however. Instead he wandered aimlessly up and down the main road trying to picture the scene in the eighties or nineties. Down there was where Chalky White had lived, then a scruffy schoolboy, Jonah imagined. Somewhere in Llandavy, Gwen had also been living. He imagined her puffing on a cigarette, shuttling between her house and the Prince of Wales and Tŷ Bwncath. Would she have passed Chalky in the street? Would he have met her if he tried to sneak into the pub for an underage pint?

He started up the hill and was forced to acknowledge that his fitness was not what it used to be – he was labouring and sweating. A slight twinge made itself felt in his left knee, reminding him that he'd failed to attend his last physiotherapy appointment.

The breeze had dropped and now it felt stuffy. He'd left the town behind and although he was rising onto the moor, the air was trapped between the banks of the lane. He turned and looked back at Llandavy. The ribbon of the main road cut through the village. From up here, the estate was clear to see – barely fifty houses grafted on to the edge of the village. And there, right in the centre, the building of the inn dominated the village.

Jonah toiled on up the hill. Surely at some point, Chalky White and Gwen Davies would have met. It was a small village after all. Jonah made a mental note to ask her next time he spoke to her.

Finally he saw the dirty white walls of Tŷ Bwncath and made a final effort to get back to his car. He didn't even look at the brooding house but instead got straight into his car and prepared to flee the area back to the comfort of the city.

CHAPTER 14

JONAH WAS BACK in his office in Cardiff Central, where he belonged. Before this case started, when he had returned to Cardiff from the north, once he crossed the M4 his irritation had increased with the traffic and inevitable jams.

Last night though he'd looked out of his car windows and been happy that he couldn't see farther than the houses. He'd had enough of wide-open spaces and the closed off villages even if it meant bumper to bumper traffic.

He'd arrived in the office early and settled into work determined to put the unsolvable case of Tŷ Bwncath out of his mind. His plan worked for the first two hours as he sorted through the deaths that had occurred while he'd been away. Then he got an email requesting a lunch meeting with Debbie Houghton. Why did the case refuse leave him alone, no matter how hard he ignored it? He shook his head ruefully and typed a quick reply reluctantly agreeing.

When the morning was over, he got up and went to the window to check the weather. The pub Debbie had chosen was walking distance from the station. The sky was clear, but Jonah frowned as he saw his boss, Timothy Carlton leave the station below him. He walked straight across the road to a waiting red BMW where Albert Mayweather shook his hand before they both got in and the car left.

Jonah had thought that the Davidson case was over, so he was confused as to why a retired senior officer was still involved with the coroner. As he got his jacket and walked to the pub, he turned it over in his mind. In the end he had to conclude that his boss had friends and that was all there was to it but it still sat uneasily with him.

Soon he was settled into a stylish gastropub sitting across a table from Debbie Houghton. He noticed the table was chosen so they couldn't be overheard.

"How's the cross-force investigation into the abuse at Tŷ Bwncath going?" Debbie was looking as immaculate as ever and got straight to the point.

"Why do I get the feeling you don't ask a question unless you already know the answer?" Jonah countered.

Debbie smiled warmly. "It's the first rule of public relations – you should never ask a question unless you're already certain of the answer."

"Hmm, well in case you didn't know, I've been back up to Llandavy and visited the abuse investigation team in Builth Wells."

"And what are your impressions?"

"That it's an impossible task not being made any easier by the people who are meant to be investigating it."

"Ah yes. You should talk to Amy Martin. She was on the historic abuse team before she moved to something else."

Jonah nodded. "Is she Dyfed Powys?"

"No, she was the South Wales Police representative on the team. At first I thought Mayweather had made a mistake putting her there." Jonah frowned so she continued. "ACC Mayweather put the team together just before he retired. A cynical person might say that he designed it to fail. There was a horrible clash of personalities right from the start." There was the slightest pause, perfectly calculated. "Have you met Gareth Morgan?"

"Yes, he's," Jonah looked for the words. "He's not..." He looked to Debbie for help.

"He's a competent officer, able to follow guidelines and process reports. And I'm not saying he's stupid or anything, but there's no real spark, no passion there."

"You're right, he's just plodding his way through, picking the easy cases and closing those."

They were interrupted by the waiter. Jonah chose steak and chips, together with a pint of beer.

When they were alone again, Debbie continued. "And you said you'd been back to Llandavy, is that right?"

"'That's where I was most of yesterday. Being up there, I can see how it's all connected. The house is walking distance from the village. According to Mrs Davies, Gwen, the children were possibly drugged and taken by minibus from Buzzard House down to the Prince of Wales. Which makes the pub the primary crime scene." Debbie nodded, so he continued. "And this Gwen Davies worked there as well, a bit of everything from cleaner to chambermaid. I don't like this, everywhere I turn, there she is. I know she had her reasons for keeping quiet but it still makes me uneasy. She's like the glue that holds this case together."

"Maybe you should go back and talk to her. But don't go with any preconceptions, just listen to what she has to say."

Jonah narrowed his eyes at the press officer. Why was she acting like his boss? Why was she so interested in pressing this case forward when, by her own admission, she was getting pressure from on high to drop it all together? He did know one thing, she was good enough at her job that if he challenged her directly, he wouldn't find out what her agenda was. But that wasn't enough to stop him fishing for some answers.

"I'm feeling like I'm being pulled around here. People are telling me where to go and what to do, but I'm not being given the whole picture. Do you know what I mean?"

"Sometimes, I think every day is like that in the police service," she answered. But Jonah was watching her expression rather than listening too much to her words. She was thoughtful, like she was trying to reach a decision while also staying two steps ahead of him in the conversation. "What do you think your next steps will be in the investigation?"

Jonah's first instinct was to dig in and ask why she needed to know. But she was a colleague in the police and they were nominally on the same side. "I'm going to meet with the guy who set up the survivors' website. Most of our accounts come from there. I need to find out if there's any rumours about children going missing, without tipping my hand. If I get a list of children who vanished, then it'll be a much smaller subset of all the children who went there. It could be the quickest way to get an identification on the bones."

"And you think that's the best way forward?"

"I think it's critical. The whole case we have now is based around best guesses and assumptions. There are plenty of stories but no evidence. If we can take even one set of bones, and find a name and prove that they went to Tŷ Bwncath and died there, well then we'll have achieved something."

"But will it be justice?"

"You mean, will we find someone guilty? Bryn Bancroft is dead. I doubt Mrs Davies has more than a few months to live at the very most. The stories suggest that many high-profile figures were involved, but I doubt we'll ever be able to find direct evidence linking one of them to the crimes. And if any were in their fifties or older when the abuse stopped, there's a fair chance they'll either be dead or too old to prosecute."

"I wasn't aware there was an upper limit?"

"Well, when you get someone in their nineties it doesn't take much of a lawyer to start talking dementia. The appetite for a conviction goes down when the suspect might not survive the initial hearing never mind the sentence."

"So, if there's not much chance of convicting someone, what is the point then?" Debbie's tone was kind even though her words were confrontational.

Jonah thought for a moment, back to the first conversation he'd had with Farida. "Three children died, back in the eighties or nineties, in a civilised country. Nothing I've done has uncovered their identities and they haven't been reported missing. It's like they were workhouse kids in Victorian Britain. No one cared about them. In all probability they were in care and their parents are unaware of their fate. But I just feel that someone should care. Someone should know their names.

"And hopefully, as a consequence, whoever is guilty will sleep a bit less easily, will look over their shoulder a bit more often. Because it doesn't matter how hard it is, I don't think I'll stop looking for them."

There was that awkward silence that often follows a big speech. Jonah bit down on an apology for going on a rant.

This case had got under his skin and she had asked. Finally Debbie said, "I understand what you mean."

Before the conversation could go any further, the meals arrived. Neither of them brought up the investigation as they ate. In fact, Jonah felt that he was very skilfully steered away from the topic.

CHAPTER 15

JONAH HAD ARRANGED to meet Barry Patrick, the administrator of the survivors' website that featured most of the claims about Tŷ Bwncath.

The café chosen for the meeting was underground with an entrance in the centre of the main shopping area in Cardiff. To get to the seats you had to walk through a canteen style area so Jonah already had his coffee when he started scanning the tables.

He wondered what a survivor of childhood abuse would look like. His experience told him that there wasn't an answer – it could happen to anyone in any walk of life.

He walked through into the steamy café and made it obvious that he was looking for someone. A lone man sitting at a table raised his hand when he saw Jonah approaching.

"Are you Jonah Greene? From the police?" he asked quietly.

"Yes," Jonah said sitting down at the table. He had a quick scan of the man he was here to meet. The only thing that stood out about him was his small round wire-framed glasses. Apart from that he was incredibly average. He was neither excessively fat nor thin, just a bit heavy set. He had neat short hair a dirty brown, cut neatly and side parted. He was also dressed conservatively – a polo shirt and chinos with a dark blue anorak on the seat next to him.

When they were settled, Barry started speaking.

"Another police officer then. What's your angle? Come to blow more holes through my story? Or just bury the evidence."

Jonah sat back and considered his approach. "So, you've spoken to the police before about this?"

Barry answered with a snort of laughter. "This has been kicking around for ever. Tŷ Bwncath shut its doors over twenty years ago. Of course some of us went to the police, both while it was operating and after Mr Bancroft's death. Guess what happened? Absolutely sod all." He stopped for a moment to study Jonah. "Every report that has been made has disappeared into a black hole. You make a statement, wait six months, and then chase it up. They can't find a thing. Even you," he jabbed with his finger, "working for the police don't know that there should be cases open."

"There is a unit dealing with all historic child abuse cases," Jonah said then stopped. He had been about to say that they were useless but he couldn't bring himself to criticise fellow officers. Certainly not in front of someone who was both very active on the Internet and hostile. "They are aware of the allegations surrounding Tŷ Bwncath and are looking into them. I can assure you that I've seen the files and the cases are open and being worked."

"What a load of bollocks!" Barry pushed his chair back, preparing to leave. "If you wanted to give me corporate bullshit you could've phoned. Even better, just copy and paste it into an email!"

The problem was that Jonah agreed with him, placing

him in a very difficult position. "Wait!" Barry sat down and looked even more sulky and aggressive than before. "I get that you're angry and upset."

"You don't know the half of it!"

"I need some information from you, but it has to be kept quiet. I can't have you sticking it all over the web. We don't want the press getting hold of this yet."

"Why the hell not? Isn't it about time things were dragged out into the light? This should be front page news in every bloody paper in the land!"

"Just for once," Jonah said allowing his disappearing patience to show in his voice, "I'd like to do things properly. Not go off half-cocked and allow the predators to get ahead of the information and lawyer up. We need to keep this quiet until we know more and then we can go after them."

The two men stared at each other. Neither was willing to trust the other, but could sense they needed each other.

Finally, Jonah's silence worked. "What do you need to know then?"

"Can you keep this quiet?"

"For the minute, I suppose," Barry grudgingly admitted.

"I mean it. One of the problems with the case is your website. The reports are all open to the public."

"You have to do that. It's the best way to persuade other survivors that they will be believed if they come forward."

"I understand that. But now, we need to keep some information off the web. The problem is that the defence can use it to undermine any survivor accounts. They can claim that as it's in the public domain, anyone could make it up and present it as their own experience."

"Okay then." Barry nodded grudgingly.

"We need to know of any disappearances of children at Tŷ Bwncath."

Barry blew a breath out of puffed cheeks. "That's very tricky stuff. How much do you know about how they operated?"

"Not a huge amount. I'm here to learn."

"Well, drugs were involved. We think they drugged the hot chocolate on a Friday evening. That's very clever you see because clear memories don't exist for a lot of them. But disappearances? You're going to have your work cut out on that one." When Jonah looked confused, he continued. "You see this was back when there were still children's' homes. But, after one of those nights, the groups were all split up."

"What do you mean?"

"Well, the place was block-booked, you know that. So the kids who came for a week's holiday would all know each other. Either they'd be from a single children's home or one local authority's care system. But I can guarantee that six months down the line, after one of those weeks, none of them would be together. When you're in care they can just shuffle you around and the children get no say in it whatsoever. This was before mobiles and email and stuff like that drifted down to kids in care. So they all lost touch. Some of the homes were shut, in other cases they just increased the turnover whichever way they could – out of area transfers, fosters, adoptions." He paused for a second. "Makes it much harder for them to form support networks and difficult to corroborate the stories, when the memories finally started coming back." He paused and shook his head. "I dunno, man, that was like the final cruelty, you know. I'll never understand why the abusers do what they do, but you accept it as a fact of life. It just is what it is and they are what they are. And I can see from a logical standpoint it works in their favour. It destroys evidence, it stops survivors banding together. That's really why I started the website. When the Internet came along I saw a chance to break the silence. It doesn't matter now, where the children are moved, we can reconnect them. We've all got a chance to support each other wherever we come from, whatever has happened in our pasts. But it's a long-term project. Some of us take fifteen to twenty years to find each other and start to come to terms with the memories."

An awkward silence fell across the table. Jonah couldn't imagine what Barry had been through and how he had turned it around. He started to see the reasons for Barry's belligerence and he certainly couldn't fault his logic in starting the website.

Barry kept his silence. Jonah felt that the other man had said his piece and was now waiting for a response.

"Thank you. So it would be really hard to track if anyone disappeared after visiting Tŷ Bwncath?"

"Like I said, it was almost impossible for the returning children to keep in touch. And often experiences like that drive groups apart." He paused and studied Jonah. "But that was news to you, so what were you on about? Disappearances? Are there bodies? There were always rumours, but you know that was completely out there."

Jonah was stunned. With no next of kin and only the coroner, pathologist and a handful of police and archaeologists aware of the discovery, they had been able to keep the discovery of the bones quiet for the minute. There certainly had been no need for a press release.

"Oh. Now you've gone quiet. I've stumbled onto it, haven't I?" Barry looked intrigued. "There were always people who said that some of them didn't come back from Tŷ Bwncath. I mean some of it must've been bullshit, but when you start to get six or seven different accounts..." His voice trailed off as he considered the implications of what he said.

"You can make whatever assumptions you want," Jonah said, recovering his composure. "But remember what I said earlier, I want this to be done properly. Don't go encouraging people on the forum."

"Yeah, but those children. The ones who swore that sixteen went on a weekend away and only fifteen came home. They were never believed, ridiculed, most of them even started to doubt themselves."

"So do the right thing. Give us a chance to do our job and give them the justice they deserve." He paused wondering how far he could push Barry. "Could you give me a list of the user names of people who've made claims like that on the forum?"

"You're lucky, I went through the Tŷ Bwncath section before this meeting." He produced a bit of paper and started scribbling names on it. They were odd combinations of numbers and letters, like wɪdeBoi, looking more like passwords than names. "Here are a few to get started with. Once you engage them, they might lead you on to others. You have to understand, none of them are quick to trust. Don't push them, go slowly. And, whatever else you do, only ever promise what you can deliver. These guys will be really suspicious of you and if they catch you in a single lie, then you'll be dead to them."

There was another awkward silence as the two men surveyed each other across the table. Finally, Barry broke the silence. "Can you at least confirm that you've found bodies? That it really is true?"

Jonah took a deep breath. He pocketed the list of user names. He could see the desperation in Barry's face, the need, hunger for validation. But on the other hand, he had his job and his career to consider. And he had his professional duty and his duty to those children who were buried on a lonely Welsh hillside. If this news got out now, then their killers might never be found.

He was sat opposite someone who was hostile to the police. Someone who had access to a website which was in contact with thousands of abuse survivors. If information was a plague, then he was the perfect patient zero. Once he got hold of the facts, the genie would be out of the bottle.

"I can neither confirm nor deny anything at this moment," he said wearily. He wished he could say more but he truly felt his hands were tied.

"Bollocks! You had me going for a minute. I thought you'd be different to all the other bastards. But you don't care who you throw to the wolves, as long as you protect your bloody careers and your bosses. You know, those people who give you orders, sit in their fancy offices with stars on their shoulders and tell you what to do? Senior police officers? Next time you're in the same room as one, just think this. They might get their rocks off hurting children. I couldn't stand to be in the same room as one, never mind take orders from them!"

He turned and stormed off and this time Jonah had no desire to call him back. Had he made the right decision? It was impossible to tell.

CHAPTER 16

Jonah was back in the car park of Golden Valleys. When he'd got back from his strained meeting with Barry from the website, a message had been left on his desk. It was from the receptionist at the nursing home – Mrs Gwen Davies would like another visit. He didn't like this case. It would take time to follow-up on the usernames from the website and now he was called back to talk to the housekeeper. He could ask her about details and dates but he had a fairly shrewd idea as to how forthcoming she would be. And he wouldn't have any new information so he had no new questions to ask.

He knew he was getting obsessive so he had decided to wait until the forensic results came in on the bones before doing anything else. In his weaker moments he had been back to the website to read more accounts of what had happened at Tŷ Bwncath. Allegedly happened. They were always distressing and he didn't know why he did it. But no matter how hard he tried, he could neither walk away completely nor throw himself into the investigation headlong.

But now he was waiting to see Gwen again. With the state of her health, he knew that any delay might mean he never got to see her again. He took a deep breath before leaving his car. He made the usual efficient, expensive progress through the corridors and was soon seated opposite Mrs Gwen Davies with the same coffee and biscuit selection.

"Thank you so much for coming. I know we didn't see eye to eye before but I've asked around and it seems you are a good one." Jonah nodded, privately thinking that she looked awful. Her skin was dry and waxy, her lips almost blue. "I can see that look in your eyes. I've asked the doctor and it won't be long now. Oh, don't look so shocked. I'm dying and I've known it for a while. I'm just coming onto the final lap. But I do need to make a confession."

"But why me? Surely a priest would be more suitable?"

"Ha! The church hasn't done me any favours." Although she looked more ill than ever, her eyes still burned bright. "I know the message of love and forgiveness is good. But until they get tough on the paedophiles instead of hiding them, I just can't be doing with them." She paused again to breathe oxygen. "You're police and a good man. I think you'll do to hear my confession."

"You are aware that as a policeman, if you tell me about any crimes you have committed, I'll have to investigate them?"

She nodded. "Yes. I'm not doing you any favours. I won't even tell you which year it was or which city. I suppose if you worked hard, you might get there. But I'll be gone by then, and facing a sterner judge than any here on earth."

"Okay then," Jonah said. He was unsure of how to proceed. "What's on your mind?"

"I used to be married. Before I moved to Llandavy, in what feels like another lifetime. And he was a useless bastard. Charming enough when he was sober, a monster when he was drunk. Unfortunately once he had access to me and my wages he was drunk most of the time." She paused and used the oxygen mask to hide behind and gain time to order her thoughts.

"One night, and I remember it now like it was yesterday, he'd had a skinful and started in on me. He'd just dragged me out of the bedroom by my hair. I was on all fours, blood running down my face. He was so drunk he'd forgotten for a moment what I was supposed to have done wrong. I curled up on my side in case he started kicking me. Lying there on the carpet, I looked up at him swaying at the top of the stairs. I thought, what if he just fell down?

"I didn't even consider the question. I kicked out with both feet and caught him behind the knees. He went straight down the stairs."

"What did you do? Did you call the police?"

Gwen gave a laugh that came out as a weak bark. She struggled to get her breathing back under control. "No, it was before all the domestic violence awareness nonsense. I didn't call the police. I staggered down the stairs and climbed over his body. He was lying there with his neck at a funny angle. Like a puppet whose strings had been cut. This wasn't the first time he'd been free with his fists, so I had a system in place.

"I put my shoes on and my coat over my nightie and went round to a neighbour who I knew and who had a car. She never commented or judged, she just took me straight round to my sister who lived in the next town over. It was just one of those things. None of the women ever said anything about it. It was just what we did."

"But surely..." Jonah was at a loss for words.

"Surely nothing." She waved away his doubts with a bony hand. "Everyone knew the old bastard liked his drink and was loose with his fists. The next day, the police called at my sister's house with the bad news. I told them he'd knocked me around and when I walked out he was still alive and very drunk."

"And you got away with it?"

She simply nodded. "They decided that we'd had a row, he'd passed out from the drinking. When I slammed the door, he woke up and ran after me. Stumbled at the top of the stairs and fell. The neighbour and my sister confirmed my story, without ever knowing the truth. I was covered in bruises."

"All this time, you've carried this secret?"

"Yes. It's what's driven me. I've been through hell and come out the other side. Since then I've given my life to making things better for others. Only small things sometimes, other times I've given some poor wretches the only home they've ever known. The only love they've ever had."

"And you've never wanted..." Jonah tried to find a tactful way to ask a personal question.

"Children of my own? Oh yes, I'd have loved some of my own. But, you know, God moves in mysterious ways. Any children I'd have had would've had a bastard for a father, and eventually a dead one. No, I've done my good in this world without having any of my own."

The silence stretched out between them, broken by the hiss of the oxygen tank and her laboured breathing. Finally Jonah spoke.

"Do you feel better now?"

"Yes, I do. I feel a bit lighter. I know it's a mortal sin to take a life. But I can't feel sorry about it. The world is a better place without him in it. That's another strike against the church. For them everything is black and white. They would have had me stay in that prison of a marriage until he killed me. That can't be right, can it?"

Jonah shook his head. He couldn't bring himself to say anything to condone a murder. But he could also see her point of view. Unable to reconcile these two points of view, he chose to remain silent instead.

"How are you getting on with Tŷ Bwncath?"

Jonah looked up and changed gears. "It's slow going. It was a long time ago and there aren't many records left." He hated himself for sounding like the historic abuse investigation team.

"I thought that might be the case." She nodded to herself and closed her eyes. Just as Jonah was wondering if she was asleep, she spoke again without opening her eyes. "I left you a present. It might make a difference."

When the silence stretched out again, Jonah asked, "Where is it?" He looked around but there was only her coffee cup on the table next to her.

"Oh." She opened her eyes suddenly. "The present? I've told my solicitor to tell you where to get it once I'm gone. Much better that way." She reached for the oxygen mask. "I think I need a nap. Thank you for coming, but you'd better go now."

"Okay." Jonah paused, he couldn't exactly wish her well or tell her to take care. "Goodbye." He knew it was the last time he would see her.

He signed himself out and turned to go. As the doors opened onto the car park, he heard the familiar crackling bark of a motorbike. Not a refined purr like his wife's machine, but the harsh note of another engine, just as familiar. Jonah looked across the car park to the road. In the entrance to the car park, Chalky White stopped, with the man in the green coat on the back of his bike. Jonah couldn't believe his eyes. All these weeks of searching and suddenly his quarry was right in front of him.

The two men on the bike leaned together, helmets touching and had a quick conversation. The man on the back looked straight at Jonah. Then the bike accelerated rapidly, the exhaust note bouncing off the walls and hills.

Jonah sprang to life and ran to his car. Then he realised that the noise of the bike was already fading. He had absolutely no chance of following them. But, Chalky had been bringing Green Coat Man here, so one of them must know Gwen Davies. Slowly, he walked back to the reception.

He showed his warrant card. "I just need to go back a couple of pages through the sign-in book," he explained.

"I'm not sure," the receptionist said, her hand hovering over the telephone receiver. "Maybe I should check. You know, patient confidentiality."

"There's no need," Jonah exuded reassurance. "This is in plain sight, open to the public. I just need a minute." He started leafing backwards as if he had every right. To his relief in his peripheral vision he saw her hand withdraw from the phone.

There it was. Right below Jeremy White. The name that had eluded him for weeks. His brain made the connections – the coat, the walk, that rabbit in the headlights look – it all fit together.

AFTER THE MEETING with Gwen Davies, Jonah felt the need to stay out of the office and get his thoughts together.

As he was already in the area of Merthyr, he decided to head back into the hills to have another look at Llandavy.

At first he stopped for a quick pint in the Prince of Wales, but he couldn't really settle. Now he knew they had rooms, he could see that one end of the bar was marked reception and there was a door marked 'Residents Only'. Everywhere he went, he was following in Gwen Davies' footsteps. She had cleaned in here, bustled through to sweep the kitchen, snooped around in the office.

With a shudder he realised that as well as Mrs Davies working here, children would've been brought here in the dead of night. Right under the noses of the Llandavy community they were shipped in and out of this building in the darkness. He supposed there must be a rear entrance, straight from the car park into the residential part of the hotel. He no longer thought the events were alleged. The more he read, the more people he spoke to, the clearer the picture became to him.

He looked around the bar at the few regulars and the dust motes dancing in the sunshine. It looked like any bar in any small Welsh town or village. But his eye kept being drawn to that door marked 'Residents Only'. Even though it was a warm day, for him the atmosphere was chilly. He drained his glass quickly so he could leave.

Instead of going back to the office, he turned away from the road back south and headed up into the hills. Something Mrs Davies had said was bothering him but he couldn't put his finger on it. He hoped that a bit of solitude might clear his mind.

He found a spot to park in a field entrance where he wasn't blocking the narrow lane then stood leaning on the car roof and looked at all of Llandavy spread out below him. From up here he could see how the village was enclosed in folds in the landscape with the road slicing right through the middle.

The large Victorian building of the Prince of Wales sprawled along the side of the main road. Off the other side was the modern estate. Further down in the valley to the right, there were faint glimmers where the light caught from a lake hidden behind some trees.

He tried to picture everyone involved moving around down there. Mrs Davies and Chalky. It looked more likely now that they knew each other. And what about Bryn Bancroft? Did he come down into town of an evening and drink at the inn? Or did he stay up in Tŷ Bwncath, isolated from the village? Gwen had said that someone told her about the minibus so the village might have been aware of what was going on. So Bryn was probably welcome at the pub. He made a mental note to look further into Alan Cooper's past, see if there was any earlier link between him and Bancroft.

It was too convenient that a serial sexual predator like Bryn Bancroft happened to set up a business involving children in a small Welsh village only to find a willing accomplice who owned the local hotel.

Jonah craned his neck around, searching the hillside behind him, but he couldn't see any sign of Ty Bwncath. He knew it was further up the road to the left, even if he couldn't see it from here.

He sighed and realised he'd spent too long away from the office. He hadn't gained much insight, except that it was impossible that Bryn worked alone. From the active involvement of the Prince of Wales with the quiet complicity in the village to wilful ignorance from the councils sending the children; in fact a whole a system had enabled his behaviour.

He checked his phone and found no signal bars at all. Not that surprising really, he thought. He returned to his car and headed back to Cardiff.

He skirted Merthyr Tydfil but wasn't far down the A470 when his phone started buzzing. And then he ground to a halt as all the traffic around him stopped. He tried to make out what was going on but couldn't see anything, just an endless line of brake lights.

He risked a glance at his phone and found that he had multiple messages from work. With a sigh, he decided to take the risk and unlocked his phone to pick up the messages. If he got pulled up for using his phone while driving, he would flash his warrant card and argue that it was for work and the traffic was stationary.

Most of the messages were his boss, Timothy Carlton, asking him to call in as soon as possible. When he got through he received bad news.

"There's been an accident on the M4. Between junctions thirty-three and thirty-two. The road is closed and they're talking about the air ambulance. As you can imagine it's backed up all the surrounding roads to gridlock." Jonah gave up on trying to drive and opened the map onto the passenger seat. As he'd thought, we has heading straight for junction 32. He glanced at the map again. The main route into the city was already blocked. People with satnavs and commuters would already be trying to drive around the blockage, spreading the chaos outwards.

"Are you driving? I asked where you are now?"

"Well," Jonah said, inwardly cringing, "I was heading south down the A470 back into town. But I just got past Pontypridd and the traffic is solid. Haven't moved at all in the last five minutes."

"Damn! It's looking likely that we have fatalities. And

it's all hands to the pump. It's a multi-vehicle RTA. And you're stuck in it." There was a pause. "Maybe we have to rethink the balance of your work. I know we said that you should cooperate with Dyfed Powys but this is not good. I need you in Cardiff. Could you step back to a more consulting type of a role with this? Spend less time on the ground?"

"Facilitate between the different bodies, you mean?"

"Yes, that sort of thing."

"I could try. But this is three fatalities of children that were never reported. I feel that it should have priority. This is a key part of my role – to identify remains and the facts of their death. It's information that you need for an inquest."

"Well yes, that much is true. But you have to bear in mind the historic element of the case. It cannot be allowed to interfere with current cases like the one unfolding on the M4 right now."

"What exactly were you doing in Merthyr Tydfil anyway?" Carlton's voice was dangerously quiet.

"Well, I was interviewing Mrs Davies. She worked at Tŷ Bwncath. Her time there completely overlaps with the range that we were given for when the bodies were buried."

"And has she told you anything concrete? Anything that would lead to us establishing an identity for any of these remains?"

"Well, no. Not concrete. But she is very useful in establishing the whole background to..."

"No! This isn't the kind of job where you can do deep background! We're not writing a book, we're trying to solve crimes."

"Well there are three bodies. People don't just bury dead children when they've done nothing wrong! How can three children just disappear completely and no one cares?"

"If you find evidence of a crime, report it up to CID. If you find out who the children are then we can process the forms and inform the next of kin. Aside from that we have current cases here in Cardiff." There was a pause as they both considered their options. Carlton broke the silence first. "Listen. Resources are tight at the moment. I know I emphasised the cross-force communication at the outset of this case. But now we have three sets of unidentified remains and what could be a protracted cold case. Any further expenditure on this will have to be run past me first."

"Okay. I'll do that. And, when I get out of this traffic, I'll go straight over to the scene of the accident. See if I can get a head start on the paperwork."

They made their goodbyes and Jonah resisted the urge to throw his mobile across the car. He was not a naughty schoolboy and hated being treated like one. On the other hand a small voice at the back of his head said that he had been keeping the coroner out of the loop while he went up to Llandavy. He was torn between wanting to walk away from the whole mess and knowing that if he did no one else would try to get just for all the victims, both living and dead.

Seeing that the traffic was stationary, he opened his door and tried to see what was going on. Unable to see anything he got out and stood on the sill of the car to get a better look. Car roofs as far as the eye could see. He fingered his warrant card in his pocket, but the truth was that there wasn't a gap wide enough for his car even if he'd been a chief constable late for a meeting.

He sat back down and crawled painfully along together with all the other traffic. Eventually, nearly an hour later, he got to the motorway. Ignoring all the other vehicles, he weaved his way through the cones and finally got flagged down by a uniformed traffic officer. He presented his warrant card and went to where the last few cars were parked up, right over on the hard shoulder.

Soon he was talking to a traffic officer.

"You're a bit late to the party."

"Yeah," Jonah said sarcastically. "I got held up in the traffic!"

"So, what are you doing here?"

"I was off my patch and got chewed out by my boss. I'm the coroner's officer."

"Shouldn't you be working in the office?" Jonah raised his eyebrows. "Okay. Looks like you'll have two to deal with. That car over there," he pointed to a mangled block of metal, "the driver didn't make it. He was gone by the time the firemen cut him out. He's already on his way to the morgue in the Heath. There was another one went in the ambulance but she had severe internal bleeding. Without X-ray vision, there's no telling how that will work out. But there are a lot of casualties heading to hospital so she'll have a bit of a wait. Don't want to be morbid, but it might be worth getting paperwork started on her as well."

"I'd better get back to the office, start making calls and filling out forms then."

Jonah got back in his car, unsure of what he had achieved either with Mrs Davies or the traffic officer.

JONAH LEFT THE M4, wove through the cones and waved to the officers who were still controlling the scene. The traffic was still awful – not the complete gridlock of the accident, but the heavy, bad-tempered traffic that follows once the cause of the congestion has been passed.

It was already late and he briefly considered stopping in at the station to start on the paperwork. But he knew that Timothy Carlton wouldn't be there so he saved his efforts for when the coroner would be in to see him working on the case he was supposed to be.

When he got home he was still tense from everything that had happened in the day. Meeting Gwen and having a difficult drive home punctuated by an argument with his boss. Even after a stiff drink and a longer than usual walk with Pickford the dog, he still felt he hadn't settled down.

"Tough day at work?" Alex asked.

As usual Jonah quietly cursed his wife's perception. "Yeah. I got into a row with my boss."

"The coroner? He's usually so laid back. What did you do?"

Jonah considered arguing the point. There was no way that Alex knew what had happened today. But in the end, he decided to cut to the chase. He quickly recapped all the events of the day, trying to downplay his wrongdoing.

"So, you didn't tell your boss when you went off your patch, tilting at more windmills to do with the Tŷ Bwncath case."

"It wasn't tilting at windmills! There were only three people we've definitely identified as being involved. Bryn Bancroft is dead, we don't have enough evidence to put pressure on Alan Cooper and that leaves Gwen Davies. She's a first-hand witness to what went on and she requested to see me."

"Why didn't you run it past the coroner then?"

"This whole case is tied up in politics. He would've said

no. The thing is she's dying of emphysema. This could have been my last chance to learn the truth."

"Couldn't you have sent someone else?"

"No, she's already sent other officers away with a flea in their ear. But she would talk with me."

"So, you burned bridges with your boss. Was it worth it? What did you learn?"

"Nothing. That's what makes it so frustrating. She wanted to confess to something that happened years ago when she was young. It all went nowhere in the end." He paused to consider the day. "Well, not wasted. She probably felt better for confessing."

"So, it was a wasted day?"

"Yeah. Very stressful and achieving nothing. Except to poison my relationship with the coroner." He saw Alex getting ready to give him a hard time about the way he carried out his work. "Oh, you don't need to bother. With the lecture, I mean. I know I stuffed this up. That's the problem with this case. It promises so much but delivers nothing. I've decided to drop it. The archaeologists have ordered up a whole load of tests and when the results come in I'll write those up. But that's it. I'm done with this. I'll start to be good."

Alex came over and gave him a hug, glad that she didn't have to tell him off. It did mean that the rest of the evening passed in better humour. With his late arrival, they decided to get a Chinese takeaway.

However, when he got to bed, he still couldn't settle. He half-slept for a few hours before giving up and went back downstairs. He sat on his sofa at two thirty nursing a drink and trying to remember his nightmares. As always they eluded him. He had incorporated today into his dreams but now it had evaporated to vague impressions of being pushed downstairs that somehow combined with his usual fears of being constrained and swords. In the end he dozed for a bit before it was fully light.

Today was the beginning of a new day, he thought. He would start to repair the bridges with Timothy Carlton by having a shower and a shave and getting in to work early. And then start by processing the RTA.

CHAPTER 17

Fortified by strong coffee, willpower, a shower and some clean clothes, Jonah determined to tackle his stack of work in a professional manner even though the work was going sluggishly. The woman with the internal injuries hadn't made it so he had two sets of paperwork to process.

Once he'd dealt with her file, he moved on to the stack of other cases that were waiting for him. He interspersed his work with coffee and when he fetched his fourth cup, Jonah felt he deserved a break. He knew exactly what he wanted to do, what he had been thinking of since he sat down that morning.

He pushed the door shut and made sure the piles of paperwork were all in order. All he had left to do now was wait for replies to complete the cases. Remembering his row with the coroner yesterday, he felt as safe as he could from repercussions.

He pulled the keyboard nearer and typed in the two words he'd learnt in Golden Valleys visitors' book. Sean Barnes.

He'd first run into Sean a few months ago through

Emily. He was a friend or admirer or stalker of hers –
someone that she knew anyway. At the time he had checked
him out and all he'd found was a predicable list of minor
offences. He squinted through the records again. It was
mostly cautions. He had never served prison time but was
known to the system.

Unfortunately no phone number was listed and the last
address was marked as no longer valid. With a sigh and a
nervous look at the door he picked up the phone and soon
got through to the local neighbourhood team. It wasn't long
before he was speaking to the right person.

"We do know Sean Barnes. Not a lot to report really.
He's fairly low level in whatever he does, not affiliated to
any gangs or organised groups. He doesn't mind buying and
selling stolen goods, a small amount of drugs now and then,
but nothing to really bring him to the notice of any of the
task forces."

"I've got his record up here, he does seem to have the
luck of the devil."

"Ah well. He was a looked after child. Now, most of
them just drop through the cracks on the day after their
eighteenth birthday. But our boy Sean, he seems to be on
the books of half a dozen agencies. We try to nick him for
breach of the peace or handling stolen goods and it's
suddenly all managed and explained and he gets bound
over or cautioned til the next time." Jonah could hear the
exasperation in the other man's voice. "Doesn't matter
though. Sooner or later he'll run out of do-gooders to bail
him out."

"Suppose I wanted to have a chat with him? There's
nothing much on the system."

"Is this a formal request? If we have the paperwork we
can probably round him up in a couple of days."

Jonah thought quickly. The photo had been assigned over to the case of the three bodies found in the grounds of Buzzard House. But on the other hand he was under strict instructions to clear everything past the coroner and this was a very tenuous link.

"No." Jonah sighed. "He's peripheral to a case. If I could just have a quiet chat."

"To do that, you'd have to spend time in the area. There are certain pubs, cafés, where he might hang out. Trouble is, once word got out you were looking for him, he'd probably hole up." There was a noticeable pause. "Do you want me to put the word out? Quietly like? We'll probably run into him sooner or later."

"Yeah, that would be great. Thanks."

"Okay, I'll let you know if I hear anything. Was there anything else?"

"Yeah, there was one other thing. I've been through the records and there's nothing, but do you know of any links between Barnes and the local chapter of the Riders of Annwn?"

"The Hell Hounds?" There was a pause. "No, nothing at all that I can think of. Mind you, he's a low-level dealer so there's always a chance he either buys from or sells to one of them, isn't there? They're not so insular when there's a drug deal to be made."

"That's true." Jonah made a mental note to check that avenue if he ever got to talk to Chalky or Sean in person. He said thanks and hung up.

Jonah sat back away from his desk. He'd run into another dead end. Or had he? A thought occurred to him and he fished out his mobile and arranged a meeting before heading out for his lunch break.

Jonah entered the café, scanned the tables for the

person he was meeting and eased himself into the cheap plastic chair. When he was seated, he said hi to Emily. She had been sitting on her own at the table, not ordering anything and ignoring the glares from the owner behind his counter. They ordered large lunches and a silence fell between them.

"So, Daddy, why did you want to meet for lunch?"

"What do you mean? You're my daughter, can't I take you out for lunch?"

"Yes, but it's the middle of a workday and you've come up here on your lunch break. Something's up. I'd have been around at the weekend most likely." She paused and her face lit up. "Unless it's a secret, something you don't want Mum to know?"

"No, nothing like that!" Jonah was silently proud that his daughter was so perceptive. "No, it's just, you remember a while back, we met in the launderette?" Emily nodded. "And you had that older guy who was interested in you? Well, it turns out I need his phone number."

"Sean? Why, is he in trouble?"

"Not trouble, no. We've picked him up on CCTV in the vicinity of an incident. We just need to ask if he saw anything."

"Dad! You sound like you're giving a press conference on TV. You can tell me, you know."

"Okay, okay. Well it's not that exciting. He's not a suspect or anything like that. He just happens to be useful for a bit of background."

"I haven't seen him in months. He kind of comes and goes."

"Do you have his phone number? Address?"

Emily laughed then, shaking her head. "Dad! You're so old-fashioned!"

"So, bring me up to date then."

"He's one of those people who doesn't have one address. Like I said, he's here and there."

"So, he's homeless?"

"No. He doesn't sleep on the streets drinking Special Brew at nine in the morning. He just sofa surfs. Sometimes he'll pick up a spare room, somewhere off the record. You know, like spare room dot com or one of those sites."

"Why? Is he hiding from someone?"

"You really have no idea how things are now." She shook her head. "Listen, around here, you can't get anywhere official to live for under five hundred a month. If you go through an estate agent, then it's at least a month in advance, plus the same for a deposit, if it's not six weeks. And they want to see bank accounts and payslips and all that. So, before you pay anything else, like arrangement fees, moving, paying off bills, anything at all, you've paid out at least a grand and probably more. And there's no guarantee you'll get your previous deposit back at all, never mind before you have to pay to move in to your new place. There's no one that I know who can just find fifteen hundred pounds to move house."

"So, what do they do then?"

"Well, a kind of grey market. Sublets. People with spare rooms, sheds, converted garages. Short term, cash in hand."

"And no guarantees I suppose." Jonah stopped and thought. "And no landline or address?"

Emily laughed again. "No, people don't have landlines. Even settled people with proper flats and everything they have their Wi-Fi and their mobile and that's their life."

Jonah realised his view of home was stuck firmly in the 1970s. He imagined people coming home from a job, sitting on the sofa watching whatever program came on next on the

TV. Emily's generation were doing cash in hand jobs, zero hours contracts, whatever they could find. Sleeping where they could as well, binge watching entire series of shows on their phones. No roots, no sense of belonging anywhere.

"That's why you get people ghosting," Emily explained.

"What the hell is ghosting?" Jonah was irritated by how old and out of touch he felt.

"You know, if you want to break up with someone and not actually talk to them. You just block them on all your accounts and move on."

"So one day you'd have a boyfriend, then the next he's just disappeared?" Jonah could hardly believe what he was hearing.

"Well yes. It cuts both ways, women do it too. And it's not really serious relationships, it's more, you know, hook-ups over Tinder and things like that." Emily blushed and looked at the table.

After a pause, Jonah picked up the thread again. "So, this Sean Barnes, he's a ghost? He might be living in someone's garage with a pay-as-you-go phone?"

"Maybe. I know people who know him. When he was interested in me he was always wanting to swap mobile numbers for you know, Snapchat or WhatsApp. I didn't want to encourage him, otherwise I'd have his number and I could give it to you and you could see if he was still using it."

"I thought people lived on their mobiles now? You mean he might have changed his number as well?"

"I does happen. You know, you drop your phone and can't afford to have it fixed. Or someone's stalking you. Or you just want a new start.

"Don't look so downcast. It's easy enough to ask around. He's bound to have friends somewhere. Someone will know his number. That'd be a start for you, wouldn't it?"

"Yes, but don't you go encouraging him."

"And you don't need to do the whole overprotective father thing. He's harmless and I'm sure he's moved on."

"Okay. Well as soon as you have his number, pass it on to me and I'll do the rest." There was a movement behind Emily and Jonah looked up to see the waitress come out from behind her counter. If he hadn't been distracted he'd have seen the gleam in Emily's eye, eager to help her father track down a suspect.

As it was, he moved aside to let the waitress set the plates down. The rest of the meal passed in general conversation about his work, mostly the big accident on the motorway and the ever-changing cast of people who moved in and out of Emily's orbit.

CHAPTER 18

JONAH WALKED to the coffee shop for lunch with a heavy heart. Debbie Houghton had asked for another meeting. He had spent the last couple of days burying himself in the routine work of helping the coroner. He was aware that he had avoided another row with his boss and the working relationship was slowly getting back to normal. Jonah was waiting for the results to come back from the forensic tests on the bones before he made any more official moves on the case.

Timothy Carlton surely couldn't argue with moving the case forward once scientific results came in. Until then he would, at least in appearance, not work on it. The other avenue – the death of Leo Davidson had also reached its natural conclusion. In his own time though, he'd checked the website information he'd been given. Painstakingly he had pieced together the accounts from different members, and cross-referenced them on his own chart. He had hit a big problem. The entire field had been searched and only three bodies had been found. But he had at least ten independent reports of different children vanishing after a visit to Tŷ Bwncath.

Were the independent reports wrong or were there more undiscovered bodies? And if so, where? Jonah was painfully aware that the field they had analysed with the archaeologists' technology represented only one quarter of the land that had been sold off from Tŷ Bwncath to the farmers. He also knew that he was doing this under the radar so there would be no budget for a further investigation.

He wondered what the mindset of Bancroft would have been. Once he'd buried three children under a paving slab, would he suddenly move on to another site? Or did the burials he had found represent an overflow from a main site? Would they have to take the house apart like they did with Fred and Rosemary West's?

He shook his head. There was no point in following those thoughts through. There was no way he'd ever be able to follow up. This sense of frustration, combined with the continued workload of the official cases meant that he'd pretty much given up on the whole business.

Then Debbie Houghton had asked him to meet for coffee again. He couldn't deny that she had helped him in the past, but he was happy that he had put it behind him. He spent two days trying to duck out of the meeting but in the end she refused to take no for an answer so he decided to go along so he could tell her in person that the case was over.

When he went into the coffee shop, he couldn't see her immediately so he bought himself a coffee before heading upstairs. As he cleared the top of the stairs a woman half stood and waved him over. She was at the end by the windows overlooking the high street so he had time to look her over. She had iron grey hair and Jonah guessed her age as anywhere from forty-five to maybe sixty. She had earth-toned clothes, a full skirt and ethnic top. As he got closer, Jonah saw that she wasn't alone. Debbie Houghton was also there together with an older man. He looked retired, nearly bald wearing glasses.

"Jonah Greene, I'm Jo Murchie." They shook hands. "I believe you've met Debbie before." Jonah nodded suspiciously at her. "And this is Carl Hyde." Jonah nodded at him too.

He felt off balance – he'd been invited for a coffee with one person and now felt like he was being interviewed for a job. He sat down and looked at all three of them. He wasn't going to be the one to start speaking until he knew what exactly was going on.

"I expect you're wondering why we've agreed to meet with you?"

"That makes it sound like I've requested and been granted an audience. I thought I was here to have coffee and a quiet chat with Debbie. We have met before but she didn't tell me that you'd be here. I didn't expect to be faced with a panel. What's going on?"

"Could you give us five minutes to explain what we do and then you could see what you think?" Jonah nodded warily. "It's a bit delicate really. First of all, you're investigating everything that went on up at Tŷ Bwncath?"

"Yeah. It's looking more and more likely that the rumours are true but I'm not sure we'll ever be able to prove anything. The verdict is in on Davidson and the remains we found look like they'll never be identified. The budget's evaporated and I've run out of leeway with the coroner."

Mr Hyde leaned forward and said, "We've had Tŷ Bwncath on our radar for years, well decades now. As you say, proof is always difficult. Somehow the owner operated almost alone when it came to organising the abuse and as far as we can tell the victims were drugged. So unless one of his group has a last-minute attack of conscience, there's no official way to prosecute."

"Sorry, but who are you?" Jonah asked.

"I worked in various roles for the council before I retired. Mostly social services. I offer an oversight to everything." He fixed Jonah with a hard stare. "Before we go any further, we need to establish something." He turned to look at Debbie who nodded to indicate that he should continue. "What rank are you? Sergeant now? So, if an inspector or chief inspector say, asked you for a favour would you do it?"

"That depends on what kind of favour."

"Well, you know the kind of thing. Look the other way when something happens. Or lose some evidence. Or choose to be less diligent on one case rather than another. That kind of thing? Usually with a hint that it'd help your career to be seen to be helping a senior officer."

Jonah took a deep breath. "I'm not saying that I either would or that I wouldn't. I guess that my answer is still that it depends." He thought back to the case of Patrick Kinsale where he'd actually swung the other way and gone against his superiors in order to find the truth. He decided not to mention it now though. "Is this about the Tŷ Bwncath case? Because if it is, there's no way I'd help a paedophile get out from under a case."

Debbie nodded. "I knew you were sharp. But you have to bear in mind that often these people know how to manipulate. They break the case up into small parts and collect on favours. They can undermine a case without the person who's helping them having any clue what the bigger picture is."

Jonah saw the glances between the three of them, feeling annoyed that he'd been called here under false pretences and then grilled. "Did I pass the test then?"

"Yes. Although after that business with the homeless man a few months back we thought you'd be the right kind of person. Not willing to play the political game but more interested in doing the right thing."

"Right kind of person for what?" Jonah narrowed his eyes.

Instead of answering, Debbie Houghton nodded at Carl Hyde who picked up the baton again.

"Can I ask, are you happy with the way things are going?"

"What do you mean happy?" Jonah was getting irritated with the way they passed the conversation around to avoid answering any questions.

"Well, that you can't get any traction on this Tŷ Bwncath case? That the people who abused these children are most likely going to walk free."

"Of course I'm not. But I'm a policeman. Sometimes it's part of the job. You know where the guilty are and for whatever reason you can't prosecute them." He shrugged. "It is what it is."

"It doesn't have to be." Debbie Houghton interrupted. Jonah turned to her, ready to give her his attention. She worked with the police so he thought she'd have more of an idea what the reality was.

"What exactly are you suggesting?"

"It's not a suggestion," Mr Hyde said. "It's the way things have been working for years. We just wanted to explain it to you and see if you wanted to fit in with us."

"And if I don't?"

"Well, we'd rely on you to be discreet. We are on the

side of good." Jo Murchie spread her hands to show there was nothing to hide.

"All this is very well and good," Mr Hyde picked up the thread. Jonah had a sense that they all knew each other well and the conversation flowed from one to the other seamlessly. "But we should all be on the same side. We can argue back and forth all day about what's right and what's wrong. But let me tell you how our little conspiracy got started and maybe you can decide from there." There were nervous glances from the two women but he continued anyway. "It was all a long time ago now and I'm sure DS Greene has better things to worry about. At the time I was in education for what was then Gwent County Council. I heard rumours and whispers about a senior teacher. That he was interfering with young boys in his charge. So, I had a series of quiet meetings, much like this one." He paused and looked around. "Of course, those were different days. No Starbucks so we met in pubs here and there, up and down the county. What I found did indeed trouble me. I'm sure you know the pattern. This teacher, and no I won't name him as he's dead now, kept on moving from one school to the next. Never stayed anywhere more than five years.

"I spoke to his colleagues. I kept hearing the same thing with different words. No one would go on the record and it was all hints and suspicions. But when I started to put it all together it was damning."

"So, you put a case together?"

"Impossible." He shook his head. "It was all circumstantial and half the people we spoke to were scared. This teacher was really good at networking and was in with governors and head teachers, so if anyone was going to start badmouthing him they would fear for their career."

"What about the children? His victims, surely they would grow up and come forward?"

"He picked them from mostly troubled families, lower socio-economic groups. And this was a high-status individual. Even when the rumours started to circulate, he'd move on to a different town, a different council so it was hard to pin him down. He even did some time in private schools to get away from the LEA. Also, to accuse someone of something so serious, you need corroboration. The very nature of these offences means that outside confirmation is nearly impossible to find."

Jonah nodded, this was exactly what he had seen throughout his career. Some days it seemed that the system was stacked against the victim. "So, what was the answer? I'm guessing we haven't all met here to say how rubbish the whole system is."

"Well, we marked his card." Jonah frowned, so Carl Hyde continued. "We used the very things that protected him against him. We carefully vetted the people around him and found those who thought like we did. Governors and people in the LEAs around the area. He was good at hopping between councils so we had to keep the pressure on."

"What happened to him?" Jonah was horrified at what could happen behind the scenes, but also fascinated.

"It took him a year or two but he seemed to catch on. School policies would change and he wouldn't get unfettered access to children. Extracurricular events like school trips, plays and the like were a favourite of his until other teachers started volunteering to help out. He got refused for a couple of promotions as well. Once he worked out that his opportunities were being restricted, he took early retirement."

"If there was a whispering campaign, why didn't he complain? Kick up a fuss about being unjustly accused?"

"Because it wasn't unjust. Think for a moment what would happen if that story was published in the local press?"

"Then his victims would read it." Jonah spoke slowly as he worked through the likely scenario. "It would encourage them to come forward. It would finish him off, ruin his reputation."

Carl Hyde sat back with a slow smile. His entire body language was that of a teacher whose pupil has just learned an important point. The same truth was dawning on Jonah, but he was less impressed.

"But you can't just spread misinformation about an innocent man! Hound him out of his job!"

"He was hardly innocent!" This was Jo Murchie.

"He was never proven guilty," Jonah argued back.

"The whole system is stacked against the victims." She was starting to let her passion show. "We don't take these kind of decisions lightly. And can you tell us what else we could do?"

Jonah was stumped and fell silent. There was no right answer.

"We are an informal group of like-minded individuals. We all have one overriding concern – the welfare of children. We know the predators form networks, that they help each other out, so we thought the best thing to do was to form our own alliance for good. Use their own tools against them."

"So, you all just meet together and work against someone who you've taken against?"

"No!" Now Jo Murchie was starting to get annoyed with Jonah's devil's advocate argument. "We don't just take against people. We collect independent evidence. About people who exhibit certain signs. Like arranging their lives to have uninterrupted, private time with children. Like being a bit rootless and moving around to avoid suspicion. Recently we've been able to track them online as well. We put everything together to form a picture. We don't do this lightly."

"And what exactly do you do?"

"Whatever we can. We have influence over some school governors, senior teachers and other professionals who are willing to have names passed to them. We have contacts in the LEA. We are also building up contacts in the police."

"I thought you just said that the police were useless?"

"Not precisely. You do the best you can in a system that is totally stacked against you. Back to what we were saying about how one senior officer could ask for favours or suggest that you look the other way? We found a way to turn it to our advantage. A minor offence could result in a caution. Or, with a nod from us, it could trigger a formal arrest. Which in turn could lead to their house being searched. You must have seen on the news how unfortunate people get arrested for something minor only for the police to then find child pornography on their computer. It also acts as checks and balances. If someone gets that far and the police find nothing, well, we'll back off." She paused for effect. "Like I say, we only have one concern. One question that we ask ourselves every time, in every case. What is best for the children?"

"So you don't protect the rights of the teachers, the people who volunteer at scout groups and sports teams? You don't care about them?"

"No!" Carl Hyde leant forward and slapped his hand on the table. "The world was built by them. The old white men like me make the laws, they enforce the laws, they sit on committees and make judgements. Who else is going to think of the children? The people we're after are the system. They have everything in their favour already."

There was a pause as all of them considered what had been said.

"Seriously? Do you think this is real? A massive conspiracy of paedophiles controlling everything in their favour? I know you get isolated pockets, like children's homes in North Wales."

"I don't think there's a huge club with monthly fees and membership cards, no," Jo said. "But they do tend to group together. And it's not that isolated. There were the cases in North Wales, plus Rotherham, Bradford, Jersey. They're just the ones that we know about." She stopped to compose herself. Jonah could see her slipping into seminar mode and wondered if she'd been a teacher or professor. "I think there are many factors here. You remember all that fuss about David Cameron and the pig's head?" Jonah nodded. "That was part of a system that operates by fear. Cameron was expected to pay and when he didn't they dropped the bomb. Whether it's having affairs or being gay or joining a dining club that trashes restaurants and burns fifty-pound notes in front of homeless people, it binds them together. They've all done shady stuff and are all afraid of being found out.

"It also creates the perfect environment for paedophiles to operate in. There is no incentive for people to persecute them as to do that would take away their power over them. In my experience, predators of all types tend to cynically climb to positions of power and they have little fear of detection."

"Are you saying there are enough of them to infiltrate every council. Surely that can't be true?"

"But you see, you only need one person at the top to make a big change all the way down. No one has to know why but the whole thing operates by a mixture of incompetence, apathy and underfunding. Just by promoting and supporting the worst candidates the whole thing goes badly wrong. You only have to look at the mountains the social services departments in Bradford had to climb just to get people to listen to their concerns. Not everyone who stood in their way was a paedophile, but they would have been incompetent or lazy or prejudiced. Or they would have acted because they owed favours, or had political reasons. To tackle these people you need not just brains, but passion, a desire to see the right thing done, no matter what the cost. Never underestimate the damage that can be done by someone who doesn't want to rock the boat."

"All of this is very interesting, and very academic." Carl Hyde leaned forward as he interrupted. "But either Mr Greene here will believe us or he won't. Either he will help us or he won't. Debbie, I believe that you have a way that we can move this all back into the realm of practical help."

Jonah looked over at Debbie, who nodded solemnly. "The Tŷ Bwncath case could be one of the most important we've ever seen. That's because you have physical evidence. We know that children disappear all the time, but it appears that Bryn made a serious mistake this time. We have the bones. They can tell us a lot. If we get even one solid identification, then we can start to unravel the paper trail back to those organisations and individuals who had a duty of care." She stopped to look at Jonah. "Can you see the one weak spot yet?" Jonah shook his head. "Well, the evidence. If they, whoever they are, can get to that evidence, lose it, or break the chain of custody, then the case will collapse."

Jonah protested. "There are whole units, probably

whole courses that I've sat through on proper procedure for evidence collection. Everything is signed for, duplicated, copied, and logged. It can't just go missing."

Jo Murchie raised her eyebrows at Jonah. "You've never heard of a case where evidence was lost? Or fabricated? The Stephen Lawrence enquiry found that entire lorry loads of paperwork vanished. But there's an even more relevant example. Right here in Cardiff, there was the Lynette White murder trial." Jonah winced at the mention of the name. "It started with the murder in 1988 but it only finished a few years ago. Despite the fact that the original convictions were overturned as being unsafe, and the fact that members of the public were convicted of perjury, no police officers were ever convicted of any offence. And you know why? Because when the trial date came around in 2011, the prosecution was unable to produce the evidence. It had disappeared. Of course, it turned up again, sitting in the corner of an office, in the same box that the IPCC had sent it in." She paused to draw breath. "So, all the courses you went on are useless. We can only conclude that evidence can, and will, be compromised when the pressure is there from the very highest levels to do so."

Jonah opened his mouth to argue, before realising how true it was. Even in these days of computers, all the data was input by humans. All it took was some bad data and missing evidence and cases could collapse like a house of cards. The whole weight of what they were saying came crashing down on him. Could he operate in a twilight world where computers were hacked and interviews conducted without oversight? Working in the shadows to do right, instead of under the spotlight of all the police rules and regulations?

He realised all three of them were looking at him expectantly. "What would I be expected to do?"

"The first thing would be to confirm our suspicions, and to confirm to you that we're telling the truth. What efforts have you made to identify the three sets of remains found at Tŷ Bwncath?"

"The pathologist has taken samples from a tooth from each body. Those have been logged into the system and sent off to a specialist lab for DNA testing as well as isotope analysis to give us a broad idea of where they grew up. We don't even know if they are UK citizens yet."

"Right." Debbie nodded. "Could you chase that up then? You're the coroner's officer, identification is your job. You simply need to establish that it's all proceeding well."

"Is that it?"

"We've had reason to suspect the evidence system has been compromised for a while." Carl Hyde rejoined the conversation. "This will both provide a test of our knowledge and also might prove to be an opening skirmish in our battles over Tŷ Bwncath."

"And if I do find anything?"

"I think that it would be prudent, until we know more, to go straight to Ms Houghton here in the first instance. Until we can be certain of where on the field of battle your superior officers are placed."

Debbie leaned across and placed a folded-up sheet of paper on the table. It was a lined sheet of A4, folded into quarters. "This is a list of South Wales Police officers that we trust. We've looked into it and there's nothing to suggest that they'd be a problem."

"You are joking!" Jonah was outraged. "You're saying out of all the thousands of officers, the only good ones can be listed on a single sheet of A4?"

"No! It's just that we've had personal contact with these people. They've always done their job, regardless of the politics or cost. There must be others out there but we can't be as certain as we are for these ones."

Reluctantly he pocketed the piece of paper. Jonah nodded, his irritation with the older man's pompousness building. He had a family meal that evening to celebrate Gareth's twentieth birthday and wanted to get back in time to clear his desk so he could leave early.

"Anyway, it sounds like we're all done here." Jonah was deliberately brisk. "I'll chase up that evidence and get back to you." He was relieved that he wasn't being asked to do anything illegal. He didn't believe their theories – he didn't want to believe them. It was the stuff of superheroes and films – not the reality of police life in South Wales. But all he'd been asked to do was his job, so that wouldn't present a problem.

CHAPTER 19

JONAH GOT BACK from lunch with his head spinning. He found the tale he'd been told pretty hard to take. Was he supposed to believe that there was a nationwide conspiracy protecting and organising all the paedophiles? And that the force's PR officer together with a retired civil servant and senior social worker could oppose it. He shook his head as he sat down at his desk.

On the other hand, he thought, Albert Mayweather hadn't stopped interfering even though the verdict and the funeral had taken place. He had never been able to figure out why he'd taken such an interest in the case.

He didn't have time to think about it and resolved to put it from his mind and concentrate on the routine paperwork. However, before he'd even opened the first folder, Denise buzzed through to tell him that the coroner wanted to see him as soon as possible.

He sighed, feeling that the world was conspiring to keep him from his work. As he walked between the offices he thought over the last few days since he'd been told off in the traffic jam. He'd been keeping his head down well and not spending time or budget on anything he shouldn't. He wasn't even working on the Tŷ Bwncath case in his spare time.

Even though he knew he'd done nothing wrong, he was still nervous going into the meeting and decided to let the coroner talk first.

"So, this big RTA on the M4, how are we progressing with that?"

Jonah frowned. Road traffic accidents were usually straightforward. As the coroner's officer he needed to be alert to make sure it was what it appeared, but this had all the hallmarks of a simple accident. It had happened at rush hour, and there had been a sudden downpour during the day which was the first for several days. When the rain hit the dusty roads it made them treacherously slippery for the evening commute.

"It's pretty much complete. There were two fatalities. I've spoken to the first responders and double-checked with the pathologist. It all looks above board." He thought for a moment. "I think one was certified at the scene, the other died in the ambulance before they got to hospital. It's been confirmed that they both died of injuries sustained in the accident." Occasionally a driver would have a stroke or heart attack and trigger an accident, making the paperwork far more complex.

Carlton nodded slowly, steepling his fingers and gathering his thoughts. "It's that second death that needs looking at a bit more closely. I need a minute by minute breakdown from the paramedics as to what exactly happened from the moment the collision occurred. Where everyone was, what time they arrived on scene, and the precise time of death. A complete timeline."

"Pardon me asking, sir, but why? You already have identity established, place, cause and time of death. That's enough to issue a verdict. The inquest should be a formality."

"It's very tricky. The parents of the woman who died, well her father is a surgeon at the Royal Gwent. They are quite political and their main area of concern is, understandably, the state of the NHS. Now, their daughter died while the ambulance was waiting in the car park so there has been a suggestion that I could record a narrative verdict. Apparently it's fairly routine to treat patients in the hospital car park when there aren't enough beds. So, we need to look into the availability of ambulances and wait times and whether they were a contributing factor."

"I thought you were independent, answering only to the Home Secretary?"

"That's the theory, yes. In practice everything has shifted in terms of the regulations. But the father is an old friend and in part I do sympathise. That's why the pressure is there. If I speak out, it'll give more weight to the complaints. And obviously Jim, the father, is upset and he wants a focus for his grief. It's an impossible situation." He saw Jonah's confused expression and continued. "I still have links, connections I suppose, with the medical community. I worked there for many years and only took this job because it became too much. It was too hard to work in an organisation that was being underfunded and dismantled in the name of austerity. I hate what the Conservative government are doing to the NHS. So I totally understand the groundswell of anger from people working in the health service. But here in Wales we're caught between a rock and a hard place. To criticise the NHS is one way to have a go at the UK government, but on the other hand health is devolved and we have a Labour run assembly. So anyone of any political persuasion could criticise my actions." He stopped to run a hand through his thin hair. "I wish I knew a way through this mess. I wasn't cut out for all the politics." There was a short pause which Jonah didn't know how to fill. "Well, first things first, I need you to gather all the evidence for me. Let's see what we've actually got. Whether the victim actually had a chance of surviving if they were promptly conveyed to a hospital bed instead of being treated in the back of an ambulance in a car park."

Jonah was aware that this was a major olive branch from the coroner after their recent argument.

"Right. Of course. I can access all the files and find the paramedics and people who were attending. It's going to be harder to pin them down to what effect the delay would have had on the patient."

"Yes. I know that all too well. When I worked in the NHS, no one would give a straight answer to a question like that if they could avoid it. But interview everyone, build a comprehensive timeline and submit it to me. I'll make the final decision."

Jonah groaned inwardly. It sounded like more work with very little outcome. There was a procedure that was always followed in road traffic accidents. If one driver was liable to be charged with death by dangerous driving, then maybe unlawful killing would be the verdict. Otherwise it would be accidental death. There would have to be an inquest but it should be a fairly perfunctory affair.

Unless Timothy Carlton decided to get into politics, in which case he might record a narrative verdict and mention the state of NHS funding. Jonah had a lot of sympathy with this – the police were suffering along with everyone else.

But for the moment it just meant more work and less time to get ready for his evening out.

"Listen, sir." Jonah knew he had to tread carefully. "I've got a stack of paperwork on my desk. I was planning to clear it all down and then head home on time. I've got a family event this evening and my wife will kill me if I'm late. Could this wait..."

"Til tomorrow? Of course. I know it's going to take you a few days to find everyone as they are all shift workers."

"Thank you, sir." Jonah nodded, relieved that he finally had an opportunity to get his day back on track. He settled down at his desk and cleared a few more files into the right piles. Then the phone rang.

"DS Greene, coroner's officer."

"DS? Is that Detective Greene?" The voice was professional and female.

"Yes."

"It's Ms Donelly. I'm the administrator at Golden Valleys Nursing Home. I've got some bad news for you."

Jonah quickly made the connection. "Is it Gwen Davies?"

"Yes, I'm afraid to say she passed away quietly in her sleep last night. She left us a list of people to contact including you. I'm sorry for your loss."

"Thank you for letting me know. Do you know who's arranging the funeral?"

"Yes. We can pass your name across to be added the invite list."

There was nothing more to be said, so Jonah thanked her again and said goodbye. He got up from his desk and went to stare out of the window.

He had realised that Gwen was very ill, so he had known at the back of his mind that she didn't have long. But he had always hoped that he would have more time to talk to her. He kept thinking of questions that he wished he'd asked her. He bowed his head and said a quiet prayer for her. He still wasn't sure if she was a good person or not, but she had done her best in a difficult situation. He hoped when his time came someone would think the same of him.

CHAPTER 20

DESPITE THE INTERRUPTIONS, Jonah managed to succeed in his main aim. He signed out of work at five pm, having cleared his desk, then went home, had a shower and a shave and was ready on time for the family meal. It was Gareth's twentieth birthday and they'd agreed to meet at a fancy gastropub. Jonah was sure that over the weekend Gareth would meet his own friends down the pub to celebrate but was grateful that he'd chosen to spend time with his family as well. It had been an intense few days and quality time with his wife and kids was just what Jonah needed. He did his level best to push any thought of Gwen Davies, Llandavy and Tŷ Bwncath from his mind. He was sad that she'd died, but he was equally determined to have an enjoyable family dinner.

Alex and Jonah arrived at the pub on time and found Gareth in the bar. When they were shown to the table, they asked where Emily was.

"No idea," Gareth shrugged. "I half expected her to ask for a lift or something. You know, like half an hour before she was meant to be here." There was a rueful chuckle.

Emily was not the most reliable family member. All three of them checked their phones.

"She's probably just forgotten," Alex said gently. It was familiar territory, trying to support her stable son while not openly criticising her flaky daughter at the same time. "You know what she's like. She'll be back tomorrow, all sorry and contrite. Let's just have a good night!"

But their determination to have a good time seemed to be tempting fate. The evening didn't flow at all, and each of them kept subtly checking their phone. Emily's empty seat dominated the table where the three of them sat. As if they were grieving, they couldn't stop staring at it.

Whenever the conversation lulled, Jonah found his mind drifting towards Gwen Davies again. She had implied that she knew everything but now he would never know what she did or didn't know.

Finally the meal struggled its way to coffee. Jonah asked, "Shall I phone her or send her a text?"

"I sent her a text when I got here." Gareth checked his phone. "No reply. Leave her. As you said earlier, we all know what she's like. I had a great time, thank you!"

There were mutters of you're welcome from Jonah and Alex. She seemed to have picked up on Jonah's mood and was subdued as well. No matter how Jonah tried, he couldn't drive the case from his mind. Despite his earlier resolve, his low mood after learning of Gwen's death had bled over into the evening and that coloured the normal occurrence of Emily missing a date.

BY LUNCHTIME THE NEXT DAY, Jonah had a small niggle of fear. He knew it was part and parcel of his job –

having seen the worst meant he couldn't help but worry. In the end he took the easiest option and phoned Gareth.

When the pleasantries were out of the way, he dived straight into his question. "Have you heard from Emily today?"

"No, why?"

"I know she's unreliable but either me or your mother would usually have had an apology by now. I just wondered if she's sulking or avoiding us because she missed the meal?"

"No." There was a pause as Gareth thought. "No, I didn't hear from her at all yesterday. Maybe the night before? We do keep in touch but not all the time you know. I could see when she last checked WhatsApp if you want?"

"Yeah. Do you know any of her friends? Could you ask around?"

"If you're worried, I could swing by her place this evening if you want."

"Yeah, please. Don't make a big deal of it, just you know, I'd like to know she's okay. Let her know that we're not mad with her at all."

"No problem."

THAT EVENING the three of them, Alex, Jonah and Gareth were sat around the kitchen table.

"Have we got enough for a missing persons?" Alex asked. She had the knack of going straight for the jugular, asking the question that the other two were thinking and not daring to voice.

"Not really," Jonah said. "She's not vulnerable at all and we have had recent contact. Although it has been forty-eight hours since anyone we know has seen her."

"Her phone goes straight to voicemail, and she hasn't

replied to any of our messages." Gareth looked at his own phone as if it contained secrets. "That means either she's gone out of signal or it's switched off for some reason."

Both his wife and son looked to Jonah for advice. This was his job after all. He chewed his lip as he thought out loud. "She knows I worry because of my job, but she is also really flaky. She could've dropped her phone in the bath or run out of credit or anything." He looked at both of them. "Why don't we get the message out. All her friends. All her accounts – send her texts, voicemails, you name it and tell her to get in touch as we're worried. It's the first thing that we'd be expected to have done if we did want to make an official report. We should leave it at least til tomorrow morning, maybe even lunchtime. If nothing at all comes back by then, we'll have another think about how to move forward."

"You're the boss in this area." Alex tried to sound supportive but couldn't hide the worry in her voice. "We'll look back on this in the future and laugh about it. Us three sitting around a table worrying while she's out having a good time somewhere."

"If that's what she is doing," Gareth said bleakly.

"We can't be thinking like that," Jonah said. "We've got to keep positive. It's not the first time she's dropped off the radar. I'm sure she'll turn up sooner or later."

The other two nodded. Gareth made his excuses and left, and Alex and Jonah started clearing and doing the washing up. They were both restless but neither wanted to acknowledge what the worst case could be.

JONAH WENT into work the next morning after a restless night, still wondering about Emily, but knew he had to make good on his promise to the coroner as well.

The woman who'd died was Jocelyn Fletcher. He made up a list of all the people who interacted with her from the moment the accident had been seen on CCTV and other drivers had phoned it in. The list was long, even before her ambulance had left the motorway. Firefighters, paramedics and traffic officers had worked together to stabilise her and free her from the wreckage of her car.

He went back over his notes and his pocketbook and constructed a rudimentary timeline. From what he could surmise, Ms Fletcher had arrived at hospital just under an hour before she died.

Jonah frowned and went back over his notes but that seemed to be correct, even though she was listed as having died in the ambulance. Reaching for his contact book, he called through to the shift manager of A&E and outlined his concerns.

"That sounds about right. If it was a busy period, she could have spent at least an hour waiting in the ambulance."

"But what about treatment? Surely a delay like that could be dangerous?"

"Well, yes, but we use our triage nurses to go round the queue of ambulances and then they can tend to the patients in each one as they require." Jonah tried to form another question but couldn't find the words to be tactful. "Listen, it's not perfect but we're the sharp end of the whole system. When you get cuts in social care, in mental health, in hospital bed numbers then it all focuses down to here. We don't have enough space for our intake and without enough beds we can't move people out of A&E onto a ward as fast as we'd like, so we have to hold them either in a cubicle or in the corridor until a space frees up. Honestly, if someone's seriously injured, it's best if they are treated in the ambulance because that's a better environment with better equipment than a corridor."

Jonah took a deep breath and suppressed the frustration he was feeling. He asked for the nurse on duty who had tended to Ms Fletcher in her last hour to give him a quick ring back when she came on shift. That would be later in the afternoon, but he only really needed to confirm the time and ask if any intervention like surgery would have saved her.

When the call was over, he understood the coroner's frustration. It couldn't be right that nurses were being assigned to work in ambulances that were queueing to get into A&E. He looked at the rest of his timeline and put in requests for calls back from the traffic officers and firefighters.

Focusing on the delay in treatment, he broke down how long it had taken to get Ms Fletcher treated. First the scene would have to be made safe, both from other traffic on the motorway and from leaking petrol and other hazards. Once that was done, the firefighters would have started cutting her free. He'd watched firefighters extracting people before and while it looked brutal as they cut their way through a car, in reality it was a cautious, almost delicate process. The paramedics would have worked alongside the firemen to assess and stabilise the patient. And with all of this, the paramedics would be triaging the other patients on the road. Finally, the ambulance would leave the scene.

Jonah decided that he'd done enough to satisfy Carlton, so he left early intending to take a long lunch. First, he drove around the suburbs of Canton and Splott together with the shabbier ends of Roath and Cathays – an area that he thought of as bedsit land. Here were the students who weren't living in the fancy new blocks springing up in the centre. Sprinkled among them were post-grads who had completed their course but hadn't yet left either the city or the student lifestyle.

Jonah began the boring legwork part of a job that would usually be handed out to uniform, banging on doors and in some cases waking people up. Everyone knew who he was talking about and underneath his worry, he had a momentary surge of mixed feelings – fatherly pride along with his concern. Emily seemed to be well known and well liked, but he was also aware that his little girl was growing away from him. He hardly recognised any of the people – he was working from a list of contacts known to Gareth to which Jonah had added suggestions from the people he'd asked. All too soon though, he ran out of contacts. He'd managed to stay calm each time someone suggested that he try her phone. Now he had to admit that she had vanished.

Despondently he returned to the station, went upstairs, and slouched down at Farida's desk in CID.

"What's up?" she asked, seeing the look in his face.

"Can't get in touch with Emily," Jonah said. "And I have no idea if or when I should be making it official."

Farida frowned. "When did you last see her?"

"We had a family meal the night before last that she didn't show up to. I had a message from her the day before that."

"So, we can reasonably say that three days have passed without contact?" Farida was making notes.

"I haven't decided whether or not to make it formal yet." Jonah waved at her notepad.

"Neither have I," Farida countered. "But without the

facts we'll have no idea, will we? Could she be classed as vulnerable in any way?"

"No," Jonah shook his head. "No, she's not. A bit unreliable sometimes but nothing we could swing as vulnerable."

"Okay, and what efforts have you made to find her?"

Although he appreciated Farida taking the time to help, he found it rather disconcerting to be on the receiving end of the questions. As efficiently as he could, he outlined the steps they'd taken so far.

Before she spoke, Jonah could read the concern in her face. "It does sound like you have reason to be worried. Has she ever done anything like this before?"

"No, she knows that because of my job I'm more likely to worry, so she makes a point of keeping in touch. Even if she doesn't want to talk, she'll reply to let me know rather than just going silent."

"We could definitely put it all through as something official. Obviously there'd be a bit of leeway given that you know the system and know whether or not you'd be wasting our time. But if you did that, once you've put your initial investigations into the system, you'd be taken right off the case and kept away from it. Suspicion might even fall on you. It's a lot to think about." She paused for a second. "What does Alex think?"

"On the one hand she is worried sick, as any mother would be. But she also knows that this is my job, so at the moment she's deferring to my experience."

"Do you think that might change? She might want to raise a missing persons on her own?"

"I don't think so. We're talking to each other and making joint decisions." He stopped and stared across the sea of desks to the window, through which he could see the trees glowing green in the sunlight. It seemed impossible that the bright sunny world could exist out there and CID be dealing with the darkness in here with only a pane of glass to keep them apart.

Was his daughter out there somewhere? He knew that she was, but he was grappling with the sense of the unknown. Where was she? Why wasn't she in touch? Surely by now she would have received at least one of the messages? He found himself hoping that the whole affair would end in embarrassment all round. She would be found and the whole thing would be a misunderstanding. But he knew in his experience that wasn't the only possible outcome.

"I think I'm going to have to open a missing person's report," he said finally. "Can you start the paperwork?"

"You need to phone Alex," Farida said kindly. "Ask her to bring a photo when she comes. Then we'll need to sit you down and get the details from you. Who you've already spoken to and as much information as you've got about her life. We can keep it all under the radar for a bit, but we can check her mobile, see if she's using her bank accounts." Farida paused and studied Jonah. "I'm sure you know this but it has to be said. She's over eighteen. We might find her and she might not want any further contact with you or Alex."

Jonah shook his head. He had his gut feeling as a policeman – something was wrong and she needed help.

"One thing, though," he said. "Can I be the one to talk to Alex? Let her know that we're making it an official case."

"Of course. In all of this you are the central stakeholder. You're in charge – however you want to do it."

Jonah chuckled to himself, the first moment of lightness he'd felt since Emily had missed the meal. "That reminds me, I didn't ask how your family liaison officer training went?"

"It was really good. Very interesting. When you get assigned to a case you can end up almost living in someone's home. Being there all the time, making coffee, chatting and listening. And that is at a time when the family is going through the worst time of their life." She stopped for a second to study Jonah, see how he was bearing up. "Of course, there's another side to it. So many of these cases, it'll end up being someone in the family who's guilty. So you have to keep your eyes and ears open, all the while being the friendly face of the police. It's not going to be easy." Jonah raised his eyebrows. "But in your case I trust your instincts and I know you – it's not your family that'll be under the microscope, we'll just focus on finding Emily."

There was an awkward pause. Finally Farida broke it. "So, you need to get in touch with Alex. Once she knows then we can get going with the formal stuff."

"Right. She's at home at the moment. I'll go and bring her in. We can get photos, phone numbers, all that kind of stuff at the same time."

AS SOON AS Jonah opened the front door, he heard the question. "Have you found her yet?"

"No, love." He wrapped her in a hug. "I've been speaking to Farida at work. She thinks we can get the police involved in looking for her."

Alex burst into tears, but not for long . She fought for control until she could speak. "That means you think something awful has happened, doesn't it?"

"No." He was gentle with her. "It means that I've spent

quite a bit of time today pounding the streets, looking for her and worrying about her. It's time to get a bit of help, get things on the record so that we can find her. These people know what they're doing. They will find her."

Alex took a deep breath and composed herself. "Right. What do we need to do?"

"We need recent photos, on our phones or real photos, doesn't matter. And all her phone numbers, contact details, all that stuff. Can you come in with me now, to make a formal missing person's report?"

"Yeah, of course. We'll do it together."

Soon Alex and Jonah were in his car and driving towards the office. For the whole journey, she sat in stunned silence.

"So, you really think Emily could be in trouble?" She looked across at Jonah for some reassurance or support as he parked the car.

"I don't know. She has gone quiet. I've talked over it with Farida and we've decided that it does meet the burden for opening a formal case. That's all. It doesn't mean she's been hurt or anything worse."

"So, what happens now? Will we see her face on posters and on the TV news? I'm not sure I could cope with that right now."

"No," Jonah shook his head. "We're going to start very low-key. Get the beat officers where she lives out on it. They can put a search on her phone and her bank accounts. Get some of the technical boys to look over her social media. Nothing will be made public at this stage."

"What happens then?"

"Well, it depends. If we turn up anything at all then we'll follow all the leads down. And of course, she might still turn up while we're doing all of this."

"And if she doesn't? What do we do then?"

"Then, there'll be a case review. That's when we'll decide whether or not to go public, or broaden it out to other forces. That kind of thing."

"Other forces?"

"Yes, they'll want to know if there is anyone else around the country that she could've gone to?"

"Like who?"

"Family friends, cousins, uncles, that kind of thing."

"Well, we don't really have anyone. I don't think she'd have gone to the New Forest or anything?" This had been the site of many family holidays when the children were small. "I'll have a think and try to find a way to get in touch with our distant relatives and see if she's there. But I don't want this getting out and starting a panic. I'll have to choose my words carefully." There was another pause. "At least I've got you," Alex said.

"What do you mean?"

"Well, you work for the police. You'll be able to keep an eye on things, let me know how it's going."

Jonah shook his head. "Probably not. The first place any enquiry will look will be at the parents." He held up his hand at the shocked expression on Alex's face. "Obviously, as I am police, they won't come down all heavy handed and interrogate us to see what we've done. But on the other hand, if they didn't at least check us out, quietly and subtly, then they wouldn't be doing their job properly." He stopped for a second. "It's an impossible situation for them. No one wants to accuse a colleague but then no one wants to be the one who let a killer go because he was working with them."

"The whole thing is a nightmare." Alex nodded. "I just want Emily home. The more we talk about it the more worried I get. Where do you think she is?"

Jonah went silent for a moment. "I really don't know. I don't have a sense of anything bad and I'm not just saying that to calm you down. You get a gut feeling in this job and mine is saying that we will find her."

"And as a mother, I don't feel that gut-punch that I'm sure I would if she was gone."

"Well, let's just hope our instincts are right on this one," Jonah said before lapsing into silence as he got out of the car and led her into the building.

CHAPTER 21

Jonah was frustrated with not being able to get involved with the search for Emily. He knew all the reasons but he was still champing at the bit. In the end he persuaded Farida to join him for lunch in the canteen.

"I hope you're not going to ask me about Emily," she said as she sat down.

"I would love to, but I know what you're going to say."

"Well, I can tell you that there's no news so far," Farida said with a quick look around to see if she could be overheard.

"Nothing? No bank or phone activity?" Jonah was clearly worried. Farida chose to answer by shaking her head. When the silence had stretched somewhat uncomfortably, he decided to change the subject. "Has there been any progress on Sean Barnes? I know you can talk about that."

As Sean and Emily lived in the same area, Jonah had explained to Farida that he had asked for any reports about Sean's location to be passed to him. Since Emily had been made a formal missing person, he'd asked Farida to be the main point of contact. He couldn't risk the beat officer getting in touch with him and having anything passed on about Emily. If anything had happened to Emily, he wanted to be sure that whoever was responsible was not only caught, but successfully prosecuted.

"Yeah, I could talk about it if there was anything to say. Have you made no progress in linking him in to either your Tŷ Bwncath bodies or the Davidson case?"

Jonah shook his head sadly. "It seems whichever way I turn, I get blocked. The Davidson case is dead now because they've got a verdict."

"What about three bodies up on the Beacons? Surely that can't be shut down without any investigation?"

"It's not shut down, but no one's helping either. I've got to get clearance from the coroner before spending time or money on it. It's nothing overt but it's not a popular case." He thought about what Jo Murchie and Debbie Houghton had said, but kept silent.

"I can see that they don't want it to happen. It's going to be a hard thing to solve. A lot of people don't want to take the hard cases so their solved case numbers look better."

"But you know what I'm like. I'm playing a hunch. I just know that he's connected somehow. I can just feel it. There is something that connects Tŷ Bwncath, Leo Davidson and those three sets of bones with Sean Barnes. If nothing else he's the right age." Farida frowned at him. "If you track it back, he was in care and growing up at the right time to be sent to Tŷ Bwncath."

"That might be true," Farida countered. "But that doesn't make him stand out in any way at all. You've seen those filing cabinets – there must be thousands of children who passed through there."

"True." Jonah laid his hands on the table. "But we do

have physical evidence though. Sean Barnes was on that platform at the time of the accidental death. CCTV confirms that." Farida nodded. "And that photo came from somewhere. And the witnesses say that no one else was down that end of the platform, so it's either Mr Davidson or Sean Barnes."

"Or it could've been there longer than you think."

"It didn't seem like it," Jonah said, unaware that he'd shifted away from physical evidence. "Anyway, if we could find him, we could ask him. I know you don't have a case to hang it on, but have you really found no sign whatsoever?"

"We've asked the local community team, the PCSOs, the local intelligence officer – no one has seen him recently. He seems to have dropped completely off the radar." Farida stopped suddenly as a thought occurred to her. She focused all her attention on Jonah. "He has vanished about as completely as Emily has. At about the same time. And you're looking for both of them."

Jonah couldn't meet her gaze and instead looked down into the remnants of his coffee.

"Is there any connection between them apart from you, Jonah?" Farida would not give up easily.

"They did move in the same circles," he said warily. "A few months back she mentioned him in passing."

"And more recently? Like in the time immediately before they both went missing?"

Jonah silently cursed the fact that Farida was such a good detective who trusted her intuition.

"I did ask her if she had Sean's phone number. As they had friends in common, that's all." He felt like a naughty schoolboy who had been cornered by a teacher.

Farida rolled her eyes. "And when did you ask her?"

"In the week before she didn't show up for that meal. I'm

sure it's not connected at all. I just asked if she had the phone number, she said she didn't, that was it."

Farida sighed deeply. "You do know, don't you, that this is all going to have to go into the report. This could be a whole new angle." She could see him looking despondent. "And it'll add new weight to your search for Sean Barnes. This will make it more official which will allow us to bring more resources in." Then she gave voice to the fears that plagued Jonah late at night when he couldn't sleep. "What if Emily bumped into Sean somewhere and asked for his number? If he knows you're police that could've spooked him? Or he might actually know something about Tŷ Bwncath and persuaded the two of them to go all Scooby Doo and solve the mystery themselves. There's any number of possibilities but they do have to be looked into."

"And what if I get carpeted for ignoring all requests to cease investigating Tŷ Bwncath? Not only did I push ahead but I dragged my own daughter into it too."

"You only asked her for the number?" Jonah nodded. "You didn't tell her to go and look for a suspect on her own?"

"No! If anything I played it down. I thought it'd be a shortcut to finding Sean, if we could get his number. Then I could have put that through the channels to track him down."

"And now he's vanished," Farida said flatly. "It certainly does put a new spin on it. How far did you get with identifying the bones before the coroner shut it down?"

Jonah had already lain awake wondering how much to tell Farida about the conspiracy of good that he was now on the fringes of. In the end he'd decided that he was a junior member and so it wasn't up to him to tell anyone else or bring them in. With a start he realised that he felt like a prospect in a bike gang – the language had ingrained itself into him.

"In all likelihood, they were looked after children from sometime in the eighties or even early nineties. Given how long ago it happened, there are almost certainly still living relatives. But we'd be looking for the black sheep of the families – gymslip babies, kids who've gone off the rails, that kind of thing. And it's a bit early for anyone to think of keeping DNA. This all means that it'll be unlikely that they'll be reported missing. On top of all this, records are going to be hard, if not impossible to get to. There is one possible avenue though. Not to be too prejudiced, but there is a chance that one of them had a half-sibling or other relative who went on to get in trouble with the law."

"So, we could do a DNA match then?"

"In theory yes. In practice, that takes a lot of time and money. It's not the sort of thing you can just run through a computer and wait until it lists all the relatives. Any close matches need to be looked at by an expert to reach an opinion."

"An expensive expert?" Farida asked, and Jonah nodded. "And then that opinion will need to be backed up by more expensive footwork I suppose. Tracking down whoever the match was and asking if they have long-lost relatives." She shook her head. "If they're anything like the scrotes I get to deal with they'd be more likely to spit on the police than talk to them. And they might not even know if they've got a half-sibling somewhere."

Jonah nodded glumly. It really was chasing down a long shot. On the other hand, he would not stop until every single avenue had been explored. He hated the thought that three children could die and be buried with no one to mourn or even miss them. He would do whatever it took to put a name to them.

"It's still worth doing. I feel like those children had been failed all their lives by the system. Maybe we can do something for them now."

Farida nodded in agreement. "But, when we're not righting the wrongs of the world, we need to find your daughter. I'll write up what you told me and link it all together. I won't make you look too bad either. It'll be okay. This might be the break we need."

Jonah nodded glumly. He knew that no matter how good Farida was with words, he had messed up and soon everyone would know.

CHAPTER 22

Jonah sat down at his desk and started to plough through his outstanding paperwork. He'd been warned off working on Emily's case but he couldn't stop his mind wandering. He knew the process and had to resist the temptation to meddle and check that CID were following all the leads.

He knew, even if they should treat everyone the same, that his case would get more attention, simply because he was a colleague.

He pushed himself back from his desk and went to the window. He wasn't really paying attention to his work and needed to take his mind off the search for Emily. He suddenly remembered the weird meeting he'd had the lunchtime before he'd opened the official missing person report.

In the clear light of day, he could see that he'd been overwhelmed by their personalities and arguments. Obviously there wasn't some big conspiracy to protect paedophiles operating across the country. It might have existed back in the seventies and eighties, but the modern world was different. This was now the era of the Police and

Criminal Evidence Act, digital recording of interviews, everything to do with a case entered onto one central database. There was nowhere left to hide now.

As he had nothing better to do, he thought he'd take them at their word and prove that all their theories were just paranoia with no basis in reality. Even better, he could check up on the evidence chain from his desk. No wasting time or money driving to Merthyr, nothing to excite the coroner as Jonah was just doing his job.

Feeling frustrated he angrily attacked the keyboard and brought up the case file on the three bodies at Tŷ Bwncath. Quickly he navigated through the scant details until he found the report from the pathologist. In dry, unambiguous words, he read how she had removed the soft core of three molars, one from each skull. These three samples had then been labelled and entered on to the police evidence system.

Jonah switched over to that system to find where the samples had gone next and read that they'd been removed twelve days ago, properly signed out with a warrant card, name and number recorded. He frowned when he realised that the notes didn't say which lab they were destined for.

Reaching for the phone, he thought he'd better get hold of this PC Carter who'd signed out the samples. His feeling of unease deepened when the phone was answered by someone at traffic division.

"I'm looking for PC Carter," he explained. "Just a routine follow-up. He signed out some evidence and we need to check what he did with it."

"Are you sure? We're traffic, we don't generally investigate and we don't tend to sign evidence in and out. When was it exactly? I'm his sergeant and I have the rota here."

"Nearly two weeks ago, twelve days to be precise."

"See, I told you. He was in France. Only thing he's

talked about for the last month. He's back now and out on patrol but I can get him to call you if you want."

"No need, I must have made a mistake." Jonah couldn't wait to get off the phone now. "Don't worry about it, I was just following an audit trail. Like I said, it's probably my mistake. I'll go back and double-check."

Jonah hung up with a horrible feeling that he'd just stirred up a hornets' nest. He pulled a blank sheet of paper out of the printer and made notes.

The three samples from the teeth were missing. That was definite. He could make it official and see if PC Carter had lost his warrant card, but he decided not to. It wasn't in his nature to cause trouble for a fellow officer. And he wasn't sure now who to trust or who he might alert by raising a formal complaint.

His head was spinning, trying to work out who he could or could not tell. He wasn't even sure that the missing tooth samples meant that they were right about a conspiracy.

He knew how the evidence system worked. When evidence was retrieved, a warrant card should be checked and a form filled out. But, Jonah considered, it depended on the diligence of the officer who had the job of signing people in and out. You could probably wave a warrant card in front of them and then sign whatever name you wanted in the book. Anyone with a uniform and some confidence could do it if they picked a busy time. It could easily happen. He corrected himself – it had happened.

Even though he was unwilling to believe their theories of a grand conspiracy, he could see no other choice. He had to get back in touch with the group. As she was in the job, he chose to call Debbie Houghton. Once they'd exchanged pleasantries, he got right down to it.

"So, I did a quick check of the audit trail on those

samples needed to identify the bones found at Tŷ
Bwncath."

"And, what did you find?" Debbie's tone of voice told
Jonah that she knew already what he'd find.

"It appears that an administrative error has occurred
and the samples never reached a lab for testing."

"Hmmm." Without words she communicated how she
felt. "Do you know where those samples are now?"

"We have to assume they've been irretrievably lost. If
not lost, certainly compromised."

"You're the coroner's officer, aren't you? Could you take
a personal interest in this? Secure new samples and then
walk them through the process until they're at the lab?"

"That is one of my duties." Jonah said carefully. "To
enable the identification of deceased in my area." He
thought privately that he'd been subtly warned that this
should be a background case. So what, he thought. This
needs to be done and done right. "Are the labs all safe?"

"Personally, I've never had a problem with BioCheck
out towards Swansea."

"Noted."

"Thanks for doing this, Jonah. It means a lot to us."

"Not a problem. If we can get identities on even one of
those children, it'll give us something to move forward with."

He hung up and wondered what to do next. Whatever
he did might be challenged years down the line in a court,
so it had to be watertight. He suddenly remembered Debbie
Houghton's list and found it crumpled in his pocket. Scanning through it, he found a name that he recognised. Earlier
in the year, he'd dealt with a brutal murder in Aberdare and
this officer had been the evidence officer for the MIT. There
had been no problem with his work and his presence on the
list meant he was the right man for the job.

Once he had a plan, Jonah went to make his case to Timothy Carlton. His days of rushing off around the country unannounced were over. He explained that he wasn't looking to go up to Llandavy and Tŷ Bwncath to unravel the truth behind the abuse claims. Instead he was carrying out one of the core duties of a coroner – identifying the deceased. He also neatly skated around the issue of what could have happened to the original samples and why he'd chosen to follow up the integrity of the evidence. Timothy for his part made sympathetic enquiries as to whether Jonah had heard from Emily. When he agreed that Jonah could spend the next day escorting the evidence, he wasn't sure whether it was sympathy or not, but he'd got the result he needed.

The next day he made a series of phone calls and then picked up DC Rob Turnbull before going to the morgue. The pathologist was confused as to why they needed another set of samples. Jonah tried to dissemble but had to admit they'd lost them. In the end however, the pathologist's main concern was to do right by the three children, so she happily supplied new samples.

Then, with Turnbull present, they were bagged, labelled and entered onto the system. The final part of the day was a long run out to an industrial estate on the outskirts of Swansea. DC Turnbull turned out to be good, if unimaginative company. The important thing was the that evidence had been accompanied by two officers at all times and signed in and out in accordance with procedure.

The staff at BioCheck were a bit suspicious when he insisted both on the most expensive series of tests to include relatives and also that they should send the results to no one but him. In the end, all his credentials checked out and they grudgingly made notes of all his requests.

It would take weeks for the results to come back but he was happy that he had scored a minor victory. He had caught the pathologist before the bodies had been committed for an anonymous, council-arranged burial. Once that had happened, without any relatives to approve an exhumation, getting a further sample would have been impossible.

That was presumably the plan. Without any forewarning, Jonah would have waited a couple of months before realising that the evidence had been lost. Now he couldn't wait to see what that evidence would reveal.

JONAH RETURNED HOME from his day shepherding DNA samples around feeling better. Having some actual concrete work to do helped take his mind off the search for Emily. He did still call through to CID when he returned to the office, just to make sure that he hadn't missed anything. There had been no progress on the search at all, though there was some good news.

Reasoning that it couldn't possibly affect the case, Jonah had checked as many coroners' databases around the country as he could get to and as far as he could tell there had been no bodies that were even close to Emily's description. He still stood by his original gut feeling that she was alive, but each day made that prospect less likely.

This feeling was further supported when Farida got hold of Emily's housemate. After a thorough search of her room, they reported that not only were her mobile and wallet missing, but she might have gone on a trip. There was a large holdall missing, together with an assortment of clean clothes and toiletries. She hadn't completely cleared out her belongings, so it wasn't as if she had moved out.

All this information had been quietly reported to Jonah. He was aware of the danger that Farida was putting herself in, and he appreciated the information. He knew from being on the other side of it that any information gave families hope, and often hope was all that they had even if it could be dangerous.

But, with each day that passed, Jonah found himself asking why she would go on holiday without telling anyone. And why wouldn't she then get in touch with her parents, or her brother on his birthday? If something had happened to her, then he would have to find her. He spent every night before sleep trying to remember any plans she might have mentioned for holidays, the names of any friends he hadn't checked, any places she wanted to visit.

Back from his trip to Swansea, Jonah came through the door, flung off his coat and collapsed on the sofa. Alex didn't even move her eyes from the TV.

"Good day? You're home late."

"Yes." Jonah paused. He still wasn't sure how much of the conspiracy theory he believed but he knew better than to share it with Alex. "Yes, feel like I finally got something achieved."

Her head snapped round to stare at him. "Emily? Have they heard anything yet?" Unable to concentrate, she'd taken a few days off work to spend her days waiting at home for the phone to ring.

"No. Not to do with that. They won't let me near any of the operational parts of the case."

"Oh." Alex slumped back down on the sofa.

"They are doing all they can," Jonah said.

"Oh, spare me your stock phrases. I'm not some grieving

mother you can pat back into shape. I know what the odds are. It just feels like they're doing nothing. Like I'm doing nothing, just sitting here waiting for the phone!"

"I know what it's like. We just have to let them do their job. At least I'm one of them so they'll probably try that bit harder. It will work out!"

"That's easy enough for you to say. You have something to do. You've been out all day, leaving me all alone, rattling around here. Trying to think if I've missed anything or not."

Jonah's mind filled with the usual platitudes but he quickly dismissed them all. Alex was in the mood to fight and wouldn't be calmed.

"What do you want for dinner?" He was already reaching for the menus.

"I dunno, I'll have what you choose."

Jonah chose and ordered a Chinese takeaway. While they were waiting, Alex picked up the thread again.

"Where were you anyway? I couldn't get hold of you."

"I had to go get some evidence from the Heath and run it over to a lab in Swansea. It was from those three sets of bones they found up by Merthyr."

"I thought that was all done. Don't see what you can do with bones anyway."

"They're not just bones, once they were children. They were born somewhere, they had mothers." He deliberately pushed aside the feeling he had that they were children from care and probably chosen because no one cared about them. At some point they must have had a mother. "I thought you, of all people, would have cared about that."

Jonah cursed himself. He had thought about the bones and whether a long time down the line that might be how they learned of Emily's fate.

Alex didn't reply but just started weeping. Jonah felt

horrible and confused. Now that she was falling apart, Jonah was starting to realise how much he relied on her being there.

He remembered the trouble they had been through in the past. How she had an unrealistic image of him. Maybe, against everything his therapist had told him, he needed to go backwards. With Emily missing, the pair of them were in limbo.

He went over to Alex and perched awkwardly on the arm of her chair. To his relief she snuggled into him.

"Listen, you remember I had that case earlier this year? The homeless guy, Patrick Kinsale?" He felt, rather than saw, Alex nod. "Well, he was a stranger to me, just some homeless man who froze to death. I didn't give up then. And now, it's my own daughter, so there's no way on earth I'm walking away. I may not be officially allowed to help, but she is my family. If there's anything I can do to bring her home, then I'll do it."

"Oh, I know you will." Alex stopped crying. "It's just the uncertainty, not knowing if she's alive or not." She clapped her hand over her mouth. "I didn't mean that. I don't want her dead. But I do want to know. If she's in trouble, I want to help. If she's lost, I want to find her. It's just this in-between state, this not knowing that I can't stand!"

Jonah told her that she had most likely left of her own accord and had mobile, clothes and toiletries with her. He knew that it could be dangerous to inspire hope in Alex, but he had to do something and she had to know.

They lapsed into silence – Jonah holding her until the Chinese takeaway arrived. While they were eating, he asked a question that had been on his mind.

"How's Gareth coping with all of this?"

"Well, we've agreed that he phones every day at four

pm." Jonah frowned at her. "We're both watching our phones, and if one of us phones the other we assume it's news, so it's easier this way. He's offered to move back in for a few days."

"Do you think he will? Do you want him to?"

"I think it might be nice. I'll see what happens in the next few days, but it'd be nice to have someone here with me all the time."

Jonah nodded and felt guilty that he was still going to work. But work was where he picked up all the gossip and felt closest to the search for his daughter. There was nothing else that he could do.

CHAPTER 23

JONAH SAT at his desk and massaged his temples. He was not just hungover, but felt rough from the stress and lack of sleep. He nursed his coffee and looked around to find something to distract himself from what was going on with his family.

Looking through his desk, he came across his notes from his meeting with the coroner about the death in the ambulance. He was already in enough trouble and he didn't need to drop this ball.

He went through the notes he'd made and saw that the first responding officer from traffic should be on shift now. He had a start when he saw that the officer's name was PC Carter – the same officer who was on leave at the time the evidence had been signed out. He needed to pin down the timeline, but he could also quietly feel the man out and see what had been going on.

He looked out of the window and decided to go out, so he made contact with PC Carter and arranged to meet in Cardiff Gate services.

Soon they had coffees and got down to business. PC

Carter read from his pocketbook. "So, I was waiting here at Cardiff Gate when I got the call from control. They'd seen the accident on the cameras and called me at sixteen thirty-nine. We arrived on scene at sixteen forty-three, it's always good to beat the Highway Agency Officers. After that it was all the usual chaos. We started closing the motorway, directing the traffic, showing the firefighters where to go, all that stuff."

"Is there anything in your pocketbook about when Ms Fletcher was loaded into the ambulance."

"Yeah, that would be at seventeen thirty-four." There was an awkward silence. "Listen, you could have done this by email, is there any reason why you came out here to talk to me." The silence went on a bit longer. "You're DS Greene from the coroner's office, aren't you? My sergeant said you phoned me about some evidence or something?"

"Yeah." Jonah desperately scrabbled around to think of something to say to explain this. "There was a mix-up with the evidence log. I was just chasing an audit trail and..." He trailed off.

"And what? My name came up? I checked out evidence while I was in France? How can that happen? We're traffic. We occasionally seize evidence, drugs or weapons if they're on view in a vehicle, but that's about it. What was it anyway?"

"Medical samples." Jonah could see that it wasn't enough. "Cores taken from the teeth of three unidentified bodies. It contains DNA for testing."

PC Carter frowned. "Well at least it's not drugs or cash. I'd be proper screwed then. What do you think happened?"

Jonah looked around. He didn't really want to get into this but couldn't see a way around it. "There is an outside chance that there's something corrupt going on. Someone goes to the evidence room, flashes a warrant card, but when they fill out the form, they put your details down. If it's busy, there's a chance the guy on the desk won't notice. Or, he could be the one removing the evidence."

"Listen, I'm just trying to do my job. I don't want to get into all this weird political nonsense. I want to drive my car, nick people for speeding, and sleep well at night."

"Thing is, you ought to know, your name and number is down on that form."

"Crap!" He stopped and stared off into the distance.

"What were you doing in France anyway? Package holiday?" Jonah had an idea how to help this man. He felt bad that he'd been dragged into all the weirdness.

"I should be so lucky! That's probably how they heard about it, because I was complaining. My father-in-law died and my wife inherited his holiday home. Or rather his ramshackle farmhouse that's meant to be a holiday home. It was his retirement project, except he never finished it. We tried hiring some local builders but without us there they just did other jobs, sloped off and sat around having three-hour lunch breaks with bottles of wine!" After an awkward pause caused by him oversharing, he continued. "We went over there to try and sort it out before the winter but it's a right mess. Why did you ask anyway?"

"It's a long shot, but you might need insurance. If I was in your shoes, I'd keep hold of all the ferry tickets, anything you paid for out there. Stuff it all in an envelope and put it at the back of your sock drawer. I doubt anyone will ever look for those samples. But you know, it never hurts to have insurance."

"What the hell was in them anyway that anyone went to this much trouble?"

"I don't know. We found three bodies buried up on the Beacons. Children."

"Now this is why I just don't get involved. Cold case child murders and corrupt police losing evidence. Far better off out of it." He stood up to go. "Thanks for the advice about the sock drawer though."

Jonah sat there and stared out the window at the car park with its rubbish curling under the sun. When he started this case, he was horrified that there could be children who were forgotten. Who could be abused, ignored, moved around, even killed and no one would ever complain. Now he could see the wider picture. Whenever he'd thought of corruption, he'd imagined police officers being given brown envelopes of cash or drinking in secret clubs with crime lords.

Now he saw things more clearly, it was a spider's web of contacts and influence. It reached out in the form of favours owed and rules bent. And wherever it touched, it tainted careers. He thought of PC Steve Carter, certain he was an honest officer who just wanted to go about his job, keep the traffic flowing and not be bothered with any of the politics. Now his name was down on a form where it shouldn't be and he'd be worrying about what was going on.

CHAPTER 24

JONAH WAS BACK in the office, scrolling through his emails, not properly reading them, just skimming the subject lines. He was letting his brain idle and mull over several issues. What might or might not have happened to Emily, what had happened to the tooth samples and was it really part of a big conspiracy?

He blinked and stopped scrolling. 'Cofiwch Dŷ Bwncath' was a subject line. With a frown and some disbelief he clicked through to the email. It was a round-robin email sent out to all the Welsh coroners asking if they had any idea what this meant.

Jonah phoned the number on the bottom and after introductions found himself talking to his opposite number in Bristol.

"The words were found on the back of a photo?"

"Yes, ripped into four pieces and tossed in the rubbish."

"Was it like a really old holiday snap?" Jonah tried to keep the excitement out of his voice. "Of a child maybe? From the eighties?"

"What do you know? Have you seen one before?" There was definite suspicion now from the Bristol coroner's officer.

Jonah gave a brief outline of the Davidson case. Then he asked what had led the Bristol police to find their photo.

"Our case was far more clear cut. David Caesaris was found dead at his home. Hanged, with the stool there where he'd kicked it away and a note. No sign of coercion or anyone else involved at all. As open and shut as a suicide can be. He lived alone and his cleaning lady found him."

"And the photo?"

"One of our scene of crimes techs found it in the rubbish bin. It's probably nothing to do with anything but there was a ripped-up envelope with it, postmarked that same day so it might have a bearing. Do you have any idea?"

"Well, Tŷ Bwncath was an outdoor activity centre on the edge of the Brecon Beacons that closed down in the mid-nineties. There are persistent rumours that there was a paedophile group who worked with the owner to abuse some of the children who went there for holidays. Is there any way your victim Caesaris could be connected?"

"I don't know." There was a pause as he considered. "Off the record, to be a bit prejudiced, he does kind of fit. He was an odd sort really. In his sixties, always lived alone. Came from old money had his own house out in the woods. Never married. Our local society pages run an article on him now and again. Used to throw these parties up at his place – lots of people down from London, whole weekend affair, that kind of thing. Bit of a local celebrity in that he doesn't have to work for his living but had a big old house with large grounds."

"So he could travel up to Wales whenever he wanted?"

"From here, easily." Another awkward pause. "He was kind of a patron of a private school near here. Used to sponsor concerts, helped them employ a good music teacher, equipped their music room, that sort of thing."

"And no one questioned that a man with no wife and no children gave so much attention to a school?"

"He was an old boy. The school have an alumni society and he was paying for all their amenities. This was all before child protection and stuff so he probably had free access to the property."

"Let me guess, he dialled back from the school when all the checking started in the noughties?"

"No, we've never actually arrested him, not even a parking ticket, so he's never been on a register. He could pass any DBS check in the country. He just came across as a creep. Someone we should keep an eye on."

"Well it looks like someone did," Jonah said bleakly. "The envelope arrived in the post, he ripped it up and then topped himself? Is that how you read it?"

"More or less, yes. And if the rumours are right about Tŷ Bwncath then that gives him more than enough motive."

"Well, you've got rumours about Caesaris and I've got rumours about Tŷ Bwncath. If both of them are true, it does explain a lot." Jonah paused. "I mean, it ties up both loose ends, doesn't it, but it doesn't really move us forward."

"No. You can't arrest a dead man."

"And even if you could, I can't give you the evidence to do that. It's all a long time ago and mainly circumstantial."

"Well, at least I can tidy this case up and close it. Definitely suicide. Another verdict, another case closed. Do you need anything more from our end?"

"If you could send over a file on David Caesaris that would help. Any photos, both recent and from the eighties and nineties would be especially useful. If we track down some survivors it might help to corroborate the details.

Also, did you get a forensic work-up on the photo from the bin?"

"No, we collected it and entered it into evidence but that was it. Did you want to do that?"

There was a pause. Jonah knew the other man was working out what would be more work, using their own forensics or transferring the evidence between forces.

"We had our photo examined, we could get the same people to check this one, see if they're connected?" Jonah offered. I'll give him a way to shift it to our budget, Jonah thought.

"Okay then. Give me a couple of days to process it and I'll get it over to you."

"Thanks."

When he'd hung up, Jonah went back to scanning through his emails. Debbie Houghton's name came up, so he clicked through to view it. It was one simple line asking Jonah to call as soon as possible.

Once pleasantries were exchanged, Debbie got straight down to business. "Can you still access the computer files related to your daughter's abduction?"

"On the quiet, yes. I'm not to act on any information received and certainly not to go and question any witnesses or gather any evidence." He tried, unsuccessfully, to hide his bitterness.

"Right, well, you need to go into the phone log. There's a tip line. Anyway, look at yesterday, around eight forty in the evening."

"Why? It's usually just nutters."

"No, I think this one is good."

"Fair enough." Jonah absent-mindedly hung up the phone as he navigated through the awkward menu system.

Finally he came across it and his heart leapt when he saw the word 'Sean' as the caller.

Even reading his words on the screen, he could tell that the caller was agitated.

"This is a message for the people who are looking for Emily, a message from Sean. You need to join things up, with all the photos, it's all real. I've done what I can, started things rolling, but you need to make arrests, pick them up."

That was it. Jonah sent an email to bring it to Farida's attention. He trusted her to see the significance without getting him in trouble.

He reread the short message, then checked the notes underneath. The number was recorded – a phone box on the outskirts of Merthyr Tydfil. Of course it was, he thought bitterly. I'm always being drawn back to that town, nestled above Cardiff, up in the Beacons.

CHAPTER 25

"So, why did you summon me up here? Have you found anything about Emily yet?" Jonah looked around the meeting room. It was just him and Farida but it was odd. They usually met informally in the park or canteen. She perched on the edge of a table, and got up when he entered. But she didn't come to him, she went halfway before going back to where she'd been seated. Jonah could feel the tension.

"No, nothing yet. It's early days. The good news is that it's gone through case review and been assigned as a live case. That means access to all the resources to find her. And thank you for highlighting that call from Sean. If that is Sean Barnes, then it gives us a definite lead. For the moment we're running with the scenario where we assume it is." She stopped and saw the look on Jonah's face. "Sorry, I'm sure you know all that. It's just that I don't really know how to ask this." She paused again. "You know I passed my FLO training recently? Well I could be assigned to this case. But the thing is that I'd be working with Alex and Gareth. It's been decided they could use an FLO as an impartial contact with the police."

Jonah opened his mouth to speak and then closed it again. He was going to protest that he could keep his family in the loop. But he had enough experience to know that often families don't survive this kind of event. And to know that sooner or later the shadow of suspicion would fall across him and Alex, either together or separately.

"If I accept the role, then my first focus will be to look after Alex and Gareth, keep them up to date. I also have a responsibility to the police and the case. Like all the other officers on this case, my job is to bring Emily home safe. That does mean though that you'll come at least third on my list of priorities for a while. I know you'll want to know everything as soon as it happens, but there will be things that I just can't tell you, especially things that Alex wants kept private as well as operational matters."

Jonah nodded and considered the implications. He would take comfort from having Farida involved in the case. He trusted her implicitly – she had saved his life based on her intuition after all. But on the other hand, she could even end up working against him if that's what her job required. In the final analysis, he was grateful that she had given him the chance to decide before she accepted the posting.

He took a deep breath. No matter what his personal feelings were, Farida would be the best FLO he could hope for. He knew she was a good detective. And having her on the case as FLO would mean a greater chance of finding Emily.

"Yes, you should do it. You'll do a brilliant job and anything that helps find Emily is fine by me."

"Do you really mean it?" Farida looked hopeful. "And we'd be all right? Our friendship?"

"Yes. Just bring Emily back to us."

Farida nodded grimly. She had started to relax once she got past the awkward question. "We will," she assured Jonah.

"Thank you for asking though. I'm sure you'll be the best person for the job." He wondered how his life would be with his best friend and wife essentially working together. He thought it would be a good thing – he knew that Alex was feeling left out of the loop and being at home alone wasn't doing her any favours.

"You're welcome," she said, breaking Jonah's introspective mood. "But my boss is waiting for the answer so we can get all of this in place." She gave an apologetic half shrug before letting herself out of the room.

JONAH WENT HOME at eight thirty that evening. Even though their meeting had only been that morning, he was still surprised when he entered and found Farida was there, putting on her coat in his hall. She'd obviously started straight away. She seemed a bit tense when she nodded and said "Goodnight."

Jonah couldn't miss the atmosphere in the house.

"What's up then?"

"What?" Alex replied.

"Well, is everything all right with you and Farida?"

"Yes, she's great. I can see why you're friends." There was an awkward pause. "I spoke to Gareth today. He says Emily was excited to be looking for someone for you. That wouldn't be connected to her disappearance would it?"

Jonah could hear that her tone was dangerously flat and calm. He also wondered whether Alex knew that Emily had been looking for the same person that was now the main suspect in her disappearance.

"I just asked Em if she had a phone number for someone. I actually told her not to go looking for him!"

"And how exactly did you come around to the idea that sending our daughter off after a killer was a good idea?"

"He's not a killer! He just," Jonah was lost for words. He wanted to say that Sean was there when someone died, but that didn't sound reassuring at all. He remembered the phone call from Bristol and wondered how much he really did know about Sean Barnes. "He's a person of interest. Emily knows him, or knew him. I saw him months ago when I met Emily at a launderette. I just thought it'd be quicker to ask her for his phone number."

"Did you put this in your notes? Update your systems at work?"

"No, I went for lunch with my own daughter. I don't need to put that on the system!"

"You do when you're treating her like a confidential informant!"

"She's not--"

"You're cutting corners and putting my family at risk!"

"We don't even know if it's connected, Alex!"

"Oh no! It's probably a complete coincidence. You're looking for someone connected with a death. You mention that person's name to our daughter. Our impulsive daughter who's always willing to help. Who always feels that she's a bit of a disappointment to us and wants to prove herself. Then, out of the blue, she disappears and you still haven't found your man!"

Jonah put his head in his hands. There was no defence he could give. Alex had put into words everything he was fearing but did not dare to think. He had spent ages trying to hide from it by working too hard and drinking too much. But to have Alex shout it directly at him gave him nowhere to hide.

Had he really contributed to his daughter's death? Or was she alive somewhere and just missing? He thought back to their conversation about ghosting. Was that what had happened? Would they become one of those families on TV with the presenter saying ten years ago Emily vanished?

Jonah realised a dangerous silence had fallen between them and searched in vain for the words to break the deadlock. Alex mumbled something and Jonah looked up and frowned.

"I think you should move out." Alex spoke quietly but clearly and forcefully. Jonah opened his mouth to speak but Alex held up a hand. "No. Let me explain. First of all, you might have endangered my baby and I can't look at you right now. All the time you're living here we'll be having a row."

"But ..."

"I know you. I know what you're going to say. You hate yourself more than I do, and I believe you. We need to get past this, get some answers, know what we're dealing with. This brings me to my second point." She paused and looked out of the kitchen window at the garden beyond and the deepening gloom. Still not facing him, she carried on speaking. "I know you're a bloody good policeman, for all your self-doubt. But if something does happen to Emily, I don't want the guilt of thinking that maybe I distracted you, that you couldn't concentrate. I don't want you rushing home to make sure I'm okay, or avoiding home because we're arguing. I want you to do one thing, focus on one thing and only one thing. Bring my child home."

She finally turned to face him, tears rolling down her cheeks. "Our child," Jonah said simply. "So, you want me gone? To live a hermit-like existence til I've atoned for my sins?"

"Oh don't play the bloody martyr with me! I want Emily back! That's all! I don't care about you, or the job or any of it!" She turned back to the sink. Jonah could see her knuckles white on the edge of the worktop. Her shoulders were tense but she didn't turn around.

Jonah knew that she wouldn't hear anything he had to say and that nothing he could say would make it better. Or rather, there was only one thing he could do to fix this. He went upstairs to pack.

PART THREE

CHAPTER 26

Jonah leaned against his car and took a deep breath. He had been a combination of stupid and unlucky. He now wondered what the price would be for his mistake.

Sitting alone in his bedsit, he had gone back over everything. He remembered, more vividly than ever before, that fateful evening in the launderette, the first time he'd seen Sean Barnes. Somehow the idea had formed in his head that he hadn't properly checked it out.

Maybe, just maybe, if he drove past there again, he might see where Sean had been going that night. He might find the place he'd left and where he went. Even though it was months ago, he might pick up the trail. It was the first place he'd seen Sean Barnes so it might reveal a clue.

But when he got to the car, he forgot that he'd left it parked in gear, so it leapt forward into the car in front. Luckily, no damage had been done but the car alarm had gone off. Jonah had let the car roll back before a large Asian man had come rushing out of his house to see what had happened.

There was much shouting, but Jonah heard little of it. He was fighting off the rising panic caused by a flashback to Mike Khan. He knew this man was shorter, had a full beard, but that didn't stop his subconscious seizing control of his body.

In the middle of all this, with the man getting more irate because Jonah wasn't answering his questions, a uniform turned up. He saw the keys in the ignition, smelt the whisky on Jonah's breath and reached just one conclusion.

Jonah's panic attack did little to convince the officer of his sobriety. Eventually he fumbled in his pocket and dropped his warrant card on the pavement. It landed open, the South Wales Police logo glinting under the street lights.

The officer picked it up slowly. "Shit!" He gingerly handed it back to Jonah while he went off to talk into his radio. When that was done, he led the other man aside and tried to calm him down.

Jonah knew from his experience that the officer would be solely concerned with the other man. If he tried to intervene now he'd call for backup and all sorts of trouble would descend on him. He shook his head – all sorts of trouble was already here. He tried to sit on the wing of his car but his suit trousers were too slippery and it was just the wrong height to be comfortable.

He looked up and down, the scene made flat by the sodium glare of the street lights. He wondered how he'd got here, to some anonymous road in the suburbs of Cardiff, waiting patiently with his head spinning while other people decided if he still had a career. To him it all felt far away and unreal.

He nearly fell over when someone gave him a playful shove on the shoulder. When he looked around he saw Farida but she was looking anything but playful.

"You idiot!" She shoved his car keys at him. "I took these out of the ignition and locked it up. No point in leaving evidence lying around."

Jonah fumbled the keys into his pocket.

"What were you thinking? Were you really going out driving in your state?"

"Well, I just thought. You know, the launderette and Emily. Sean might be there, or you know, walking past?"

Farida shook her head. "You're not making a huge amount of sense. Let me see what the score is over here." She headed over to where the officer and the other man were chatting.

Jonah felt wretched. He'd had a single thought – a new direction to look for Emily. From that it had spiralled to the bump which had summoned the Asian man. And that altercation had escalated to drag in first the uniforms and then Farida. He could feel his whole life unravelling, everything coming apart starting from that one point.

Eventually, Farida came back over. "Right, there's no damage done. Seems you just knocked it hard enough to set the alarm off. Steve has the guy calmed down and I've assured him that I'll take care of you." She frowned at him. "By rights I should take your keys home with me, but that means I'd have to come back in the morning. Is this where you're living now?"

Jonah nodded miserably.

"You've had a big shock so I'll leave you with your keys. But really, stay home tonight, sleep it off." She stopped to see if he was properly listening. "And sort yourself out. I know you, this isn't like you. This isn't why I saved your life."

Jonah could think of no sensible answer to this so he shrugged and turned to go back to his room. He heard Farida's exasperated sigh behind him but didn't stop. Back in the room he fell onto his bed fully clothed and slept fitfully in the sticky heat.

CHAPTER 27

JONAH WOKE UP FEELING AWFUL. At first he was just hungover – his mouth was dry and his head pounding. But as he lay there suffering, fragments of the previous evening came back to him.

Had Farida been there? And he'd tried to drive out to the laundrette, but something had gone wrong. He shivered when he remembered the angry Asian man who he supposed was now one of his neighbours.

He remembered Farida being pissed off at him and looking around the bedsit he could see her point. The building was advertised as a residential hotel but that was overselling itself. He had got a discount for signing up for a week and in return he had a room that had an uncomfortable bed, en suite bathroom and a worktop which served as a rudimentary kitchen. As Jonah surveyed the sink, kettle, microwave and fridge grouped around three cupboards, he thought that kitchen was overstating things a bit.

He managed to get up out of bed and staggered to the shower. Wrapped in a towel, he found some clothes in the holdall that he had hurriedly packed the night before last.

They weren't his best clothes, but they were clean which was a start. He found a jar of coffee but no milk or sugar.

He phoned in sick to work, knowing from experience that the story of what happened last night would have spread all over the station. He made the call as short as he could. Timothy Carlton wanted him to take time off anyway so there was no problem.

He needed to get his life back on track. He still didn't trust himself to drive so he walked to the nearest greasy spoon.

He walked in, ordered and sat down with his second coffee of the day. He looked around and felt different somehow. Then he realised – the change wasn't in himself, it was in the people around him. There was no fear or suspicion. He caught sight of himself in the window – he wasn't wearing a tie and he hadn't shaved. He'd just come straight here from his room after getting dressed.

Did that mean he wasn't a policeman? He didn't feel like one. He felt like one of the people who lived around here – by definition they were all a bit lost. Canton was the place where he'd come because he had nowhere else to go. How many people around him were here for similar reasons?

When his food arrived – a full cooked breakfast – he watched for the owner's attitude. He was wary as Jonah was basically a stranger in this small community but on the other hand, he didn't present a threat.

With another start, he realised that he'd left his warrant card on the side at the bedsit. He felt strangely exposed without it, yet at the same time free. He pushed all these thoughts aside and concentrated on eating some good food. He couldn't remember the last time he'd sat down and eaten a cooked meal from a plate. The last few days had been sandwiches and takeaways.

Feeling much better, he returned to pick up his warrant card. With no real purpose he drove over to the laundrette. Without Emily the place was empty and depressing. He looked through the same window from the same chair but he didn't succeed in conjuring Sean Barnes out of thin air. He even tried wandering up and down the street outside but to no avail.

There were no clues. He could remember the burning conviction he'd felt last night that this place held all the answers. Now he just saw a plain Cardiff street, a few closed-up shops and a bit of graffiti but no Sean. He shook his head and went morosely back to his car.

All too soon, Jonah was back at his flat. He saw his holdall spilling clothes over the floor and decided to unpack. Last night he hadn't wanted to admit this might be more than temporary. But there had been no word from Alex so he might as well accept it.

Soon he finished. His stomach was full and he hadn't had a drink. And he was bored. He couldn't go back into work and he couldn't stay here and stare at the same four walls until it got dark and the whisky bottle would tempt him again.

He decided he would just get in his car and drive around, thinking and looking for Emily. But he was fooling himself – soon he was on the A470 heading north out of Cardiff. North towards Merthyr Tydfil, and beyond that to the Beacons.

He found the phone box mentioned on the report for the call. It was on the main road, right by the junction with the B road that lead to Llandavy.

He couldn't face the hostile and inward looking Llandavy so he drove straight through. He planned to park in the car park of Tŷ Bwncath and go for a walk, up past the now empty graves and see where his feet took him. Fresh air and exercise, he thought, imagining himself giving an account of his movements to Farida.

He pulled himself up short. He should be accountable to Alex surely, not Farida. Although, it was a police matter and she had the necessary contacts to be able to sort it all out. And, he reasoned to himself, it was Alex who had put him in that position. If she hadn't kicked him out, he wouldn't have found himself there at that time of night. By all rights he should've been tucked up in his own bed in his home.

By now he was approaching the thirty-mph sign on the outskirts of Llandavy. He had been careful to keep his speed below the speed limit, aware that not only was he out of favours with his own force, South Wales Police, but he was also out of his area. Even on the derestricted country lane, he kept his speed to a reasonable level. Somehow even passing through the town brought out the worst in him.

He felt angry and resentful, towards Alex, and towards Sean, without whom none of this would've happened. But mostly he burned with a hatred of himself. Why had he tried to take shortcuts? He should've known that Emily would take off on her own to track down Sean. She was every bit as strong willed as her mother.

He accepted now that he was heading towards Tŷ Bwncath. The house seemed to be the centre of everything so he supposed it would be a good place to start looking for Emily. His anger had dissipated a little and he was now prepared to be honest with himself.

When he approached Tŷ Bwncath he was so lost in his own thoughts that at first he didn't register the change. He stopped the car in the road and stared. The big old house had no roof. Wisps of smoke were curling from the remains. The walls were no longer dirty white in colour – now they had black soot streaks together with water damage.

Gingerly he edged the car up the road and swung into the car park. There was a single red van there, bearing the South Wales Fire and Rescue logo. A tall lanky lad who looked to Jonah like he was fourteen lounged against the bonnet.

Jonah parked next to the van and the lad came over to his window before he got out.

"Are you from the council? Structural engineer?"

"No, police." Jonah said and produced his warrant card. The young man didn't seem interested in the fact that he was out of area.

"Didn't think you lot would be bothered." He waved at the wreckage. "It looks deliberate but it's an empty building in the middle of nowhere."

"It's not the fire I'm interested in. This house is part of an ongoing investigation."

"Well, I hope there wasn't any evidence in there!"

"What happened exactly?"

"Best we can tell, about midnight someone forced open a shutter on one of the windows, broke it and chucked in petrol and set it on fire. Of course, out here no one saw until the farmers noticed the glow from miles away. It was well alight by then." He shrugged expressively. "Even then, they didn't call it in straight away. One of them came over to have a look, then decided to phone us. To be honest, there wasn't a lot we could do by then. Just damp it all down."

Jonah steeled himself to ask the question he'd been dreading. "Were there any casualties?"

"No. I've been here all morning. First of all the dog unit

came out and failed to find any remains at all. Now, I'm waiting for the council structural engineer to come along and say that it's safe, what with it being close to the road. And I expect the arson investigator will be along to check as well. But that'll be a low priority, what with it being an abandoned building with no casualties."

Jonah nodded, relief flooding over him. This was replaced with another concern. What had the young fireman said about evidence? "Can I go a bit closer? Have a look?"

He frowned for a minute. "Don't go in. Don't touch anything. And wear this." He got two hard hats out of the back of the van. "I'll come with you."

Soon they were stood in the garden, peering through a broken window. The smell of damped down smoke hung in the air and even in the summer heat, the ground was damp in the shadows. "That's the window that was put in," the fireman explained. He then turned and pointed to a pile of twisted metal in the corner of the car park. "And those are the shutters that we took off to check the building."

Jonah looked in. As he feared, the window that had been chosen to start the fire looked straight into the office. Throughout the room, there were mounds of rubble with bits of broken, charred wood sticking up out of them like black bones.

Above all this, on the walls, were the ghostly outlines of the shelves that had held rows of box files. These were now all gone, presumably into the detritus below. Jonah could make out the rectangular shapes of several filing cabinets sticking up. However they were not only blackened by the fire, but also buckled with the heat. And they'd been soaked by the firefighters.

Looking further in, across the width of the building,

Jonah could see that the destruction was centred here. All that paper had been the first thing to catch fire, then the ceiling of the room above had fallen into it. While the records had been a mess before, now they were irretrievably lost.

He moved carefully around the flattened garden, trying to look through the windows from different angles. He remembered the layout of the place, but with the interior walls and ceiling mostly missing, it was impossible to make anything out of the piles of rubble. Over on the left was a large open area with less debris – this was where the dining room had been.

He shook his head and backed away from the wreckage. Somehow he had relied on this place being here. He had thought that it always would be, waiting for him to find the final bit of evidence before he could unlock its secrets. Now those secrets were lost forever.

———

JONAH STOPPED at a Wetherspoon's on the outskirts of Merthyr. His current mood meant that he wanted a pub that was part of a chain as an antithesis to the Prince of Wales in Llandavy. At least here he'd be able to get an ordinary, reliable meal. He looked at the rows of beer pumps and the optics hanging behind the barman's head and felt nothing.

He didn't want a drink, he wanted a clear head. He felt closer to solving this case than he had for a long time. Closer to finding Emily, to finding Sean, maybe even to finding some sort of truth.

He ordered a meal of beef and ale pie and an orange juice and lemonade before sitting down at his table.

His mind was whirling now. Had Tŷ Bwncath been burnt to hide the secrets in those files, to destroy any evidence that might have lingered? Or was it one of the survivors striking out at the place where they'd been hurt?

Except, he thought to himself, no one had really been hurt there. They'd been taken from there, probably to the Prince of Wales. He looked around the pub and sipped his orange juice and lemonade. This place was a world away from the inn in Llandavy. This was twenty-first century corporate dining, with its laminated menu and carefully chosen look and feel. The inn by contrast had always been dour and inward looking, almost designed to keep strangers away.

On the drive back into Cardiff, he resolved to clean up his act and get back into work tomorrow. There would still be gossip but he needed to face the music. Even when he slept fitfully in his lumpy bed in the bedsit and found himself awake at three in the morning, he managed to resist the pull of the whisky bottle.

He forced himself to wake early, shave and put on an ironed shirt, knowing that his every move and every aspect of his appearance would be judged. Annoyed that he hadn't slept properly and kept yawning at work, he was relying on coffee to keep going. When he went back over the same file three times without understanding it, he got up for another cup of coffee as Farida appeared in Jonah's doorway with an odd expression on her face.

She frowned. "Are you okay?"

"I'm fine. Haven't had a drop since... well, you know." There was an awkward silence. "Thank you for the other night. And sorry." He stared down at his desk.

"I don't mind getting you out of trouble. But I'm not your mother, you don't have to tell me that you've been good. You just need to get your act together." There was an awkward pause. "Anyway, it's good to see you back at work. I brought you something odd. Whatever else is happening, you might be onto something with Tŷ Bwncath."

"I'm not sure. There actually isn't much of Tŷ Bwncath left any more." He briefly filled her in on what he'd learnt over the last twenty-four hours.

"So, the records...?" Farida didn't need to finish the question.

"It looks like the office is where the fire started. Whether that was deliberately to destroy the records, or chosen because it was full of paper, or just luck is anyone's guess. What's certain is nothing survived. It was hot enough to buckle the filing cabinets before everything was soaked in water."

"So, that's it, you're just giving up?"

"Sometimes I feel like I never started. It was just a few odd facts held together with guesswork and supposition." He shook his head as if freeing it from his negative thoughts. "Anyway, what brings you down here?"

"I've got another photo." She handed over the picture in a clear plastic wallet. It was a picture of a girl, around ten years old, in a simple sundress. Behind her anonymous green grass rose in a bank. Jonah didn't need to turn it over to know that written on the back was "Cofiwch Dŷ Bwncath".

"Where did this come from?"

"A woman came in and dropped it off. She's the wife of an Assembly Member. According to her they arrived in a plain brown envelope. He husband was visibly shaken and chucked it straight in the bin. But she's made of sterner stuff and wanted to know if it was some kind of coded death threat so she brought it in."

"How did you get hold of it?"

"Well I sent the second photo from Bristol over the tech guys and then this one turned up. We were lucky that the same tech worked on it and assumed that I'd sent it through so he phoned me with the preliminary results. Once we'd got over the confusion, he let me have a look so I could confirm if it was part of a series or not. All it took was one digital photo of what they had and I was sure. When they finished, they sent the original to me." She took it back and studied it. "They are a bit weird, aren't they? I mean on the one hand, it's just a photo. But on the other, these are people. This person here she would be a woman in her thirties, maybe even forties."

"If she's even still alive."

"That's a bit bleak."

"No, think about it. We've got three bodies and three photos. Doesn't it seem a bit weird?"

"So, we could get the skulls and do a reconstruction and then make a comparison to the photos?"

"No, I don't think so." Jonah frowned while he went through his pile of files, looking for the Tŷ Bwncath one. He found the piece of paper he was looking for and ran his finger down it. "They don't match," he said slowly. "Neither the sexes nor the ages. It's something more complicated." He picked up the photo to stare hard at it. "What do you think though? Could they scan these in and look at the background?"

"What for? It's just hills and grass and trees."

"No, they might be recognisable you know. Some of the hills like the Sugarloaf and Pen Y Fan are really distinctive."

"I think you're grasping at straws. You know it's already been through document analysis. They've tried everything."

"I know." Jonah sighed. "I just feel like every step we

take forwards then something pops up and we're taken three steps back. This case is a web of half-truths and suppositions and guesswork."

"You know what police work's like though. You just keep slogging away, adding evidence, bit by bit and then one day you'll have enough for it to make sense."

"Or not. We don't solve every single case. Some get away."

"You mustn't think that about..." Farida couldn't bring herself to finish the sentence.

"Emily? I know, as a father, that I won't give up on her. But as a policeman I know that we've lost the first twenty-four hours. We've had no contact from her for nearly a week. No one who knows where she is. There's nothing."

"But you know it's connected to this case." Farida tapped the photo on the desk in front of them.

"Do I? Because Sean was the right age, right area and in care we assumed that he was a victim of abuse at Tŷ Bwncath. But these people didn't keep lists with names and dates of birth! All I know is that I asked Emily for Sean's phone number and she vanished along with him. There might be a third person in this case. Someone who's trying to keep it all quiet, doesn't like people asking questions."

"Okay, but what about the photos? They're what's pushing this forward, dragging this out into the light. The lab boys say it's reasonably likely to be the same handwriting and they're from the same stock of film, roughly the same age, which is confirmed by the clothing and other details in the photos. So it looks like Sean sent them all."

"Or," Jonah argued, "it might not all be Sean. We already know that they form networks on the Internet. Maybe this is a concerted campaign. One person sending one photo. All pre-arranged."

"Maybe, but the handwriting matches. And if we use the CCTV to link Sean Barnes and Leo Davidson with the first photo, then it follows that the rest are Sean as well. That's one thing I can understand about this case. If he is a victim, then I can see Sean handing out these photos to his abusers, try to prompt them into doing something. Admitting their guilt maybe. What we need to focus on is where Emily fits into this, to understand what happened when she met Sean."

"And that is the problem! Emily! I can start to understand where all the corruption and corner cutting comes from." Farida frowned at him so he continued. "Well, if someone turned up right now, like Mayweather, and offered to bring Emily home, I'd be tempted to look the other way on all the Tŷ Bwncath stuff."

"You can't mean that!"

"I don't know!" Jonah sat back down at the desk and looked down. "I don't know. If I was offered the chance I honestly do not know what I would do." He took a deep breath and levered himself up. "This is getting us nowhere. Thank you for bringing in the photo. I'm going out for lunch, try to gather my thoughts."

He left, leaving the door open and Farida wondering if she should follow him or not.

JONAH WANTED to get away from the station, his job and his responsibilities. He cut down past the national museum and dodged around the lines of foreign school children earnestly being shuttled from one site to another with their worried teachers and matching backpacks. It was hot and sticky as it was nearly noon.

Cathays Park itself was similarly crowded with a mix of local sunbathers and tourists. Needing a break and a chance to think, Jonah turned his back on all of them and found his way to a side street with long rows of terraces and shops that were never seen by visitors.

On a whim, he stopped outside a pub that advertised 'Food served all day'. It was a proper old Cardiff pub, Victorian with heavy enamelled tiles and stained glass in the windows. Inside, the building didn't disappoint either. It hadn't been modernised or snapped up in the expanding wave of chain pubs.

He sat at the bar and ordered a lager, mainly because the walk and the sun had given him a thirst. He vaguely thought of his promise to Farida, in fact to his boss as well, that he'd clean his act up.

But the arrival of the third photograph had knocked the wind out of his sails. This was a mystery where he simply didn't have enough of the pieces. Worse than that, someone else did hold them all and was handing them out carefully, one at a time. He hated the feeling of not being in control. Now, with Tŷ Bwncath and its associated evidence destroyed, he didn't know if he even had a case any more.

And he found himself caring less and less. The abstract good of bringing peace and closure to victims of long-ago crimes was outweighed by the real good of finding his daughter.

Of course, he thought, sipping on his beer, it was all academic. Both goals were so far away as to be nearly impossible. He felt that he was missing some big piece of the puzzle, one fact that would make everything else fall into place.

He ate a moderately disappointing pie and chips with his second pint, then sat back and considered his options.

He didn't really want to go back to work. His job was tied up with finding people. But the one person he desperately needed to find, he wasn't allowed to look for.

He looked at the end of his pint, stood next to his empty plate, the suds slowly sliding down the inside of the glass. Everything swirled in his mind, the loss of Tŷ Bwncath, the fact that he was searching for both Emily and Sean with no success. Every turn he made, he was blocked.

If he went back to the office, he'd be shuffling paper around and trying not to think about Emily. He was tired from his fitful sleep and aware that he had been making mistakes at work. The office would also remind him of his many failures. What he really needed was time to think.

He left the pub and walked in the general direction of his bedsit, the route taking him past several pubs and an off-licence and he wasn't in the mood to be resisting temptation.

By evening, Jonah was slouched on his bed watching the sun set between the buildings through the grimy kitchen window. On the bedside table was the remains a bottle of whisky that Jonah was slowly working on finishing off.

CHAPTER 28

JONAH OPENED his eyes and for a second wondered where he was. Then it came crashing back in on him. Together with his memory of the last conversation he'd had with Emily.

Unlike her drifting, rootless friends, he'd simply dug into his savings and paid out for a week in a dodgy residential hotel in Canton. He hadn't even properly looked around and tried to choose a nice place.

Subconsciously he didn't want somewhere good. A flat with an entry intercom and lots of chrome and pale wood would mean that he'd made a permanent change. He wanted somewhere shabby because that would prove to himself that this was all temporary.

He felt awful and when he saw the level of whisky in the bottle on the coffee table he remembered why. The ice in his glass had melted into the tail end of his last drink. He picked up the glass and downed the sour liquid as he carried it to the sink.

Slowly he got himself together, had a strong tea and burnt some toast. It was late so he threw on yesterday's clothes and made his way over to work, eating his toast on the way.

He was settled in with a coffee and about to see if he could face his emails when he was summoned in front of the coroner, Timothy Carlton.

"There was a death in custody today, just after five in the morning. You know all about the paperwork that's needed. Statements, mandatory inquest, the whole lot. Anyway, as I couldn't raise you on your mobile, I got one of the new DCs from upstairs to sort out our side of it."

"Sorry, must've slept deeply, not heard the phone. Only got my mobile at the moment..." Jonah trailed off when he saw the pitying look on the coroner's face. He reached into his pocket and turned his mobile over in his fingers. He remembered waking up this morning and finding it out of charge. He had forgotten to plug it in and had meant to do it when he got to work. Self-consciously he rubbed his cheek and realised he hadn't shaved this morning. "It's just a bit difficult, right now," he said weakly.

"I know and there's yesterday afternoon. I know you've been given a lot of leeway with your current situation. We know you want to do some background research but we still need to know where you are when you're on duty."

Jonah took a deep breath and prepared to make up a story about doing further research into Tŷ Bwncath. But his heart wasn't in it. Unless it lead to Emily, he wasn't interested.

"It doesn't really matter. We all understand, both here and in CID. You've been put in an intolerable position. If you take a few days off now we can keep it all from being official and away from HR. Just some compassionate leave. Nothing like before. No problem whenever you feel like you're able to come back to work."

Jonah opened his mouth to say that he didn't want to go, never mind thinking about when he'd be back. Then he realised how far short he'd fallen. Drinking on a work night, not charging up his phone, rolling into work late and unshaven. The only thing was that he'd be at home with nothing to do. He honestly didn't know what to say.

"Right, so that's agreed then. We'll go back to the old way, before you started. Rota in a few DCs from upstairs. I'm sure they can hold the fort til you're back."

Jonah felt dazed. He didn't want to be floating around at home, watching daytime TV while the action all passed him by then a thought brought him up so short that he actually paused halfway back to his office. He wouldn't be loitering at home. He would be at the room that he'd rented. He'd taken the place because he believed it would just be a place to sleep between shifts. Now he faced the thought of sitting on that lumpy bed with nothing to do but brood over all the ways his family had pulled itself apart.

He stayed in the middle of the reception area and considered going straight back in. He would offer to take a couple of days off then come back to work. He would straighten his act up, live like a monk in his cell, come in fresh shaved and early every morning. He had just worked up his resolve when he caught sight of Farida through the window of the door to the stairs. She wasn't coming in but waiting to catch his eye.

Curious, he went over to her.

"Fancy a coffee in the canteen?" She turned and led the way before he could ask what she was up to.

He followed, his previous resolve to challenge his time off forgotten. When they were sitting in a far corner with drinks and biscuits, Farida launched into her pitch.

"I've come with an olive branch," she said, patting the beige folder she'd brought with her.

"Do you need one?"

"Well, I do feel I've been siding with Alex and the police a bit during all of this." She paused and looked sympathetic. "I know that you agreed to move out because it's what Alex wanted. I couldn't say anything even though I wanted to. It's my job to stay neutral and respect her wishes."

"It's okay," Jonah waved away her apologies. "Alex will always do what she wants. She'd have made up her mind long before you heard about it. It's put me in a tricky spot though. I've got a grotty room and I've been put on leave. Last time it was bad enough being at home and pottering in the garden. Twenty-four hours in that place and I'll go mad!" He was keen to change the subject. "What have you got there anyway?"

"It might be the answer to your prayers. I've spoken to Linwood." Jonah gave a snort and got a reproachful look. "He's more human than you think. Him and some of the others on the case, well they've all got family. So I've got some background on Sean Barnes and Jeremy White here. You've still got your warrant card haven't you?" Jonah nodded. "So, work through this. Go deep into the background. If you have to go out and about, Linwood will have your back."

Jonah reached for the file, but she curled her fingers around it. "There are conditions though. Firstly, anything you find, no matter how insignificant you think it is gets logged onto the system. The search is being co-ordinated from room three twelve so you can pop in there and update the computer whenever you need to. More importantly, if you get close, like if you see Sean, or if you definitely know where Emily is, hold back. Follow at a distance and call in the cavalry. No one wants to see this get chucked out by the CPS because you were involved." Jonah nodded slowly. "Do you agree?"

"Yes," he said resignedly. "I'll log everything and if I get any sniff of where she is, or if I find Sean, I'll call it in. After Mike Khan, I've lost my appetite for solo heroics."

She released the file, and he slid it across to his side of the table. He still didn't open it for the minute. He wanted to do it properly, at home. Or rather, back at his room.

JONAH DIDN'T GO STRAIGHT BACK, INSTEAD he diverted via the shops. He came back with a stack of notepads, a noticeboard and various other items of stationery. Still feeling insecure he took the file with him everywhere he went, but he didn't want to read it yet.

Back at his room, he set up a proper workspace. He moved the tiny table over by the wall and managed to fix the board to the wall. Not wanting to waste time cooking he grabbed a makeshift ploughman's from items he'd bought in a drunken haze the previous day together with a can of beer. Once he was settled, he set up one column for Chalky White and another for Sean Barnes.

Farida had tasked him with deep background, so he decided to start right at the beginning. Chalky was born in the suburbs of Manchester and spent most of his life in care before arriving in Merthyr Tydfil. Sean had a remarkably similar upbringing, starting in a sink estate in London and then going swiftly into care. Once again he had a fairly uneventful life until he also arrived in Merthyr.

It would have been easy to say that they fell into the same circles in school, except for one inconvenient fact. Chalky White was just over seven years older than Sean

Barnes. There was no conceivable way that Jonah could stretch the facts to see the pair of them at school together. Chalky didn't seem the type to stay around for sixth form, and even if he did, there was still no reason to think he'd associate with a boy who'd just started.

He looked at their work history. Chalky had worked at various factories and distribution centres around Cardiff. He flicked through the list and saw that it was mainly unskilled labour although he did have a fork lift license. There was nothing really to report, he seemed to be mostly working in the warehouse, loading and unloading lorries, and other similar manual jobs.

Sean had a much spottier employment record. There was a suggestion that he was a low-level drug dealer although he'd only been cautioned a couple of times for possession. There had never been enough evidence to make intent to supply stick. Jonah was forcibly reminded of his last conversation with Emily. It seemed now that Sean was working in shops and had an Uber account. He had disappeared into the zero-hours contract and gig economy which Jonah guessed would mainly be cash in hand and not on any records anywhere.

At the bottom of the pile, came a single sheet of paper. It was a report from the phone line. Someone called Kirsty Price had called in and said that she had lent her car to Sean Barnes.

As he scanned through the details, his excitement increased. She had given her car to Sean just days after he had last seen Emily and the day after the missed birthday meal. Could this be the car used to abduct his daughter? It made sense as Sean didn't have a DVLA vehicle record in his name.

Even better, the exchange had taken place in the car

park of the council offices, in full view of CCTV. That was all he needed. He shoved in the last mouthful of bread and washed it down with the dregs of his beer.

Soon he was walking back into work. He chose his route through the building carefully so he could get to the offices on the third floor without meeting anyone he knew.

As he hoped, the report on Kirsty Price had been logged and the relevant slice of CCTV had been uploaded to the system. He sent up a silent prayer. This was very quick work and it meant that everyone working on the case was taking it seriously. They obviously felt that he was one of their own and were pulling out all the stops.

In the darkened meeting room he replayed the footage five times. Sean waited in the car park, looking nervous and glancing at his mobile. Kirsty appeared, dressed in smart business wear and greeted him warmly. There was a brief conversation while she led him over to her rather battered looking Ford Fiesta. The number plate was clearly visible. They exchanged a few more words, Kirsty gesturing at the car. Then she handed him the keys, they had a brief hug, and Sean let himself into the car. As Kirsty Price left the shot to go back to work, her expression was clear. She was concerned.

Jonah leant back in his chair and rubbed his eyes. Who is Ms Kirsty Price? What do they know about her? She appeared to be mid-thirties, so she could be the link between Chalky and Sean. He ran her name through the computer but didn't come up with anything. Unlike both Sean Barnes and Chalky White she hadn't come to police attention.

But she knew Sean and could have helped him abduct Emily although there was no sign of her on the video. The fifth time he watched it, Jonah ignored the two main players and focused on the margins, the edges of the shot. He didn't see even a strand of blonde hair or a shadow out of place. As far as he could tell, Emily was not there.

He tried to work it through in his head. Emily found Sean Barnes, because she thought it would help her father out. Once she'd made contact, somehow he'd managed to come away on his own to borrow a car. Did that mean he'd planned to abduct Emily? Had he left her somewhere he could find her? Or simply agreed to pick her up later?

Woven through all this was the nebulous relationship between Sean Barnes, Chalky White and now Kirsty Price. Did it have anything to do with Tŷ Bwncath, Jonah wondered bleakly. The more he uncovered, the more questions he seemed to have.

Looking back at the footage, he estimated that Kirsty must be somewhere in her thirties. So, she might be a little older than Sean and younger than Chalky. He rewound the tape and watched the hug. Friends, he thought to himself. That ruled out one theory – she didn't act like Sean Barnes' girlfriend, but he couldn't see her going out with a biker like Chalky either. Also, he especially couldn't see Sean asking a favour of and hugging Chalky's girlfriend.

Jonah spent a couple of minutes flicking through the various DVLA databases, making notes. From the number plate he was able to get her address, which gave him access to her driving record. As he'd thought she was right between Chalky and Sean in age. Even if she too had gone to Merthyr, he couldn't see her being friends with a couple of boys like Sean and Chalky, one four years below her, the other four years above. Neither of them had much ambition, yet here was Kirsty working in an office, living in a nice area, building a normal life.

He rubbed his eyes. Then he went back into the databases. Sean Barnes seemed to have a charmed life. While he drifted around Cardiff, buying and selling and doing whatever he needed to do to survive, he managed to keep out of trouble. Every time something brought him to the attention of the police, somehow he seemed to evade charges. Reports from social services, cross service committees, charities and quangos all arrived to clear up the mess. Until now, when he had disappeared along with Jonah's daughter, Emily.

Jonah needed to escape from his claustrophobic room and feel like he was achieving something – anything. So he made one call to set up a meeting, then got into his car. It was time to find out more about the trio of Sean, Kirsty and Chalky.

SOON HE WAS DRIVING, as he always seemed to be, north out of Cardiff. He bleakly wondered if he should have got a flat in Merthyr Tydfil and been done with it. This time he knew where he was going and who would be waiting for him.

He went into the reception of Merthyr Tydfil High School and Mrs Williams was waiting for him. In spite of her imposing appearance, there was the hint of a smile this time.

"Here I am, ready for more detective work!"

"It's not that exciting." Jonah smiled back at her. "It'll be more trawling through dusty files. I've got two more names to look for this time."

Soon they were back in the dim, stifling records room. This time, they had details for Kirsty Price and Sean Barnes to look for. When Jonah opened Kirsty's record and found the emergency contact form, a chill went through him. He took it over to Mrs Williams.

"Look at this. Gwen Price, also in Llandavy."

"You won't build a case based on two people in the same village being called Gwen. Not around here."

Jonah didn't want to reveal what he was thinking until he was certain. "Can you pull Jeremy White's record again? I need to know if they were neighbours. Maybe if they grew up together it might prove something."

"Sure. 1993 wasn't it?" There was a breathless moment for Jonah before she brought the second file over to the low table they were working at. Jonah pulled out the emergency contact form for White and laid it next to Kirsty Price's form.

They had not only precisely the same address, but they were filled out in what was unmistakably the same handwriting. Even the vague scrawl of a signature at the bottom was the same.

"What the hell?" Jonah was shocked. "They had the same mother?"

"The surname's different, she could have remarried?"

"No, because both Kirsty and Jeremy grew up in care in other parts of the country." Jonah spoke automatically, careless of the personal information that he was dispensing.

"So, they were fostered?"

"I guess so." Jonah thought that something deeply wrong was going on but he didn't want to arouse Mrs Williams' suspicions. "Can we pull Sean Barnes as well? Just to see if there's a pattern."

Soon, there was a third form laid beside the first two. Although they spanned nearly ten years, it was clear that the same hand had written each one. Just the surname of the mother had changed, presumably to avoid suspicion.

Jonah looked around at the rows of filing cabinets. How many more would there be? Although they'd be impossible to find as they'd all be filed under different surnames and from any year in a fifteen to twenty-year span. All they'd have to go on would be the address and the handwriting.

He knew an impossible task when he saw one, so he simply gathered up the three forms he had found. "Can I photocopy these? I need to go back and see if I can persuade the council to release fostering information."

"Of course." Mrs Williams still seemed to be excited to be part of the discovery.

Jonah tried as hard as he could to be polite, but all he wanted to do was get back to his makeshift office in the B&B and see if he could fit the new information onto his chart.

Once he was there, he made three columns and put the emergency contact forms at the top of each column. After doing that, he considered the most logical assumption. That all the Gwen's, including Gwen Davies, were the same person. That in turn implied that all the figures in this case would have grown up together in the same house.

He looked back over all the puzzling events and viewed them through the lens of this new information. Sean Barnes left the scene of Davidson's death and crossed the car park to get a lift from his elder brother. In fact, Jonah had often seen them together and this now made sense.

He replayed the CCTV from the council in his head and again saw that it made sense. Kirsty was his elder sister, protective towards him while also being concerned.

It all made sense apart from one thing. How did Gwen Davies, an uneducated cleaner and housekeeper manage to adopt three children from three separate care systems?

CHAPTER 29

JONAH CHECKED the time and realised that it was too late to go into work and check out more details for Kirsty Price. He was wondering if he should go and get a takeaway or have a drink first when his phone buzzed in his hand. Gareth was downstairs, unexpectedly. Jonah was unwilling to let him see the room, both because it was dingy and also because he had operational details all over the walls.

He texted back and soon they were in the Red Lion, the nearest pub to the B&B. Jonah was shocked when Gareth fetched the drinks and passed him an orange juice and lemonade.

"What's this? Has your mother been complaining about my drinking?"

"No, nothing like that," Gareth said, but he did look shifty.

"I can tell by the look on your face that something's up."

"Well, I did have a row with Mum actually. She had a message for you and I wanted to make sure you got it."

"Who from?"

"Apparently there's this bloke she knows, called Big Tony even though he's only five foot six. Anyway, he's the one who knows everyone in the biker scene." Jonah leant forward with interest. "Anyway, he passed a message to Mum saying that you should go to this pub, tonight." He passed a bit of paper across.

Jonah took it without reading it. "Did she say who told Big Tony?"

"Some guy called Chalky? For some reason he can't talk to the police, so it was all a bit hush-hush."

Jonah merely nodded. Chalky was one of the three people he was now very interested in talking to about Emily and he had now requested a meeting.

A silence had fallen between them, finally broken by Gareth. "Why don't you come back? Mum's acting all weird as if you're to blame for Emily disappearing." When Jonah didn't respond, Gareth looked shocked.

Eventually, more to stop his son thinking the worst, he briefly outlined how he had tried to get Sean's phone number from Emily and since then neither had been heard of. He didn't mention the phone call from outside Merthyr which suggested that Sean was holding Emily.

When the conversation got too awkward for Jonah, he said, "Well, I'd better see what's waiting at this pub then," tapping the piece of paper.

He walked back to the B&B, and changed. He didn't have a huge range of clothes so settled on his only pair of jeans, a polo shirt and a brown leather jacket. He was glad that he hadn't had a drink and drove to the pub, which was a short way outside Cardiff, quite isolated in the countryside and

pulled into the car park. Rather ominously there was a crude hand-painted sign that directed cars from the car park into a nearby field. The proper tarmac car park was filled with rows of bikes.

The sky was just darkening and the heat lay heavy over everything. Seeing the number of bikes here and hearing the pounding music, he did wonder what he'd been set up for. Still, he knew the message had come from Alex through Gareth so he needed to follow it up. He'd been given a chance to prove himself. If this meeting was a step on the road to finding Emily and repairing his marriage, then it was something he had to do.

Still – it was a daunting thing to get out of the car and head towards the pub. His jeans and jacket were the only vaguely biker style clothing he owned, yet the weather was way too hot so he held the jacket over one shoulder feeling more out of place than ever.

As he neared the pub, he could see that just beyond the back of it a field sloped down and a temporary stage had been set up at the bottom. A band was playing and the whole area was decorated with temporary lights, emphasising the deepening gloom.

He decided to get the lay of the land, so he crossed in front of the pub, then went down the side, to come at the bar from the quieter end.

He was ignored by all the patrons and could see that the whole back of the pub had been opened up and that was where the customers were being served. Jonah decided to have one pint and then clear out. He didn't think that a group of bikers would actually assault a serving police officer, but he didn't feel welcome and didn't want to test his theory too far.

After a few uncomfortable minutes on the edge of the crowd, he caught a barman's eye and got himself a pint. He moved over to the side of a patio and leant on a door frame to get a better look at proceedings while he sipped his drink.

The air was thick with heat and humidity and he could hear the noise of people talking over the band. At first he concentrated on the performance on the stage. The group wasn't bad, certainly the drummer could keep the beat and the singer was in tune. But there was no real spark there. He had never before realised what the difference was between a professional band that made the big time and all the others, the hundreds who played local pubs and clubs. Now, watching this group on stage, he realised. They were musically proficient, hitting all the right notes, there was just something missing.

He turned his attention from the stage to the audience. In some ways it was as if the seventies had never ended. Women tottered past in high heels, thick make-up and short skirts. Hair was big and everything was on display. The men were a mixed bunch, some had hair in ponytails, others cut short, some with dreadlocks even though the crowd was predominately white. Jeans were an almost universal uniform, with the only exceptions being armoured leather trousers – these he recognised because Alex had a pair.

In the heat, there were no leather jackets being worn, but he could see that groups had marked out their territories with piles of coats and helmets dotted about. Some people had commandeered picnic tables, the others just stood around.

With the knowledge gleaned from both Alex and the police gangs unit, he could start to identify them. This was made easier as many of them wore leather waistcoats over T-shirts or bare chests. Mentally Jonah practised the correct vocabulary. Those waistcoats were called cuts, abbreviated from cut-offs, a hangover from when they'd just take the sleeves off a jacket. Now you could buy them from eBay, probably made in China. There were some three-part patches evident, mostly from the Riders of Annwn, but other groups were present. That would be their colours, Jonah thought. The colours were a vital part of their identity. He watched closely and saw that while there was no friction, the different groups all kept to themselves.

Among the Riders, there were several chapters present, their location shown by the lowest patch on their back – the bottom rocker. He saw at least one member of West Wales getting big hugs and backslaps from the Cardiff members.

Aside from those groups, there were others like the friends that Alex rode with. Obviously all together, chatting and drinking, but with no patch to link them.

On the grade in between the two extremes, were a variety of other patches. Not the formal three-part patch with an MC, but still recognisable groups.

Jonah felt like the narrator on a TV wildlife special. He could see that some of the men there were clearly more important. Faces were turned towards them, stories listened to. When they walked around, no one got in their way.

Similarly, now that he was tuning himself in to the different scenes, he could identify the lower order members of the groups. He saw one young lad with just a centre patch, the Hell Hound and a bottom rocker identifying him as Cardiff. A prospect, Jonah thought. He would be the bottom of the food chain, doing what he was told and hoping to get voted in as a full member. When that happened he'd be patched in with a party.

When Jonah looked closer, he could see that some other bikers were buying drinks and chatting to the Hell Hounds, but without patches at all. According to the gangs unit these were actually the lowest rung on the ladder – the hangarounds, hoping to move up to being prospects and from there to full members.

With a start, he realised that it was like being at a big police social gathering. Even without uniforms, you'd always know who had rank on who. The different areas, and specialities – forensics, CID, traffic – would all drink together. This realisation managed to make Jonah feel that the scene was both familiar and completely alien at the same time.

He was at a big tribal gathering, with its own rules, alliances, feuds, and structures. And now Jonah was well aware that here he didn't have a tribe.

He was paying most attention the Riders of Annwn as he was supposedly here to meet Chalky.

A SUDDEN, dark thought crossed his mind. Had he been called here to be warned off? He checked his phone and was relieved to find that he had signal. He had no compunction about running from trouble, then calling it in. He looked at the groups around him and wondered what would happen if the police arrived in force. Probably a small riot, he thought. Which wouldn't make him popular with either the force or Chalky or his wife.

Jonah resolved to de-escalate any situation he found himself in, but also to keep safe. And find out anything he could about Sean Barnes and where Emily might be. He was just despairing of how tricky this would be when he caught sight of Chalky.

He was standing with a group of Riders, with his back to them. But he could see his cut, with the usual patches and the thick thatch of dark hair above it.

As if he could feel Jonah's stare, Chalky turned around

and gave a brief nod of recognition. Jonah waited for anything else, but Chalky turned his back to him.

Jonah was annoyed now. He had no idea what game was being played but he had better things to do than hang around watching a second-rate band work through rock classics and be ignored by the person who had summoned him to a meeting. He had about a third of his pint left and swigged it down in large gulps.

Not really caring who he upset, this time he walked across the back of the audience as it was the quickest way back to his car.

He was halfway across the car park when he was stopped by a shouted "Oi!" from behind. He paused and tensed up as one hand reached for his phone. Had he broken some unwritten rule by walking too close to the rows of bikes?

He turned slowly and saw Chalky walking towards him. He was relieved to see his hands were empty, held loosely at his sides. Like most people there, he was in jeans, T-shirt and his cut. Jonah noticed that even facing him, he still had patches on the front of his waistcoat. He had a small RoA Cardiff patch and one reached around his left side, looping from front to back. For a second, Jonah had a vision of the patches encircling Chalky's chest, binding him, holding him back from talking to the police.

The biker waited until he was close before speaking softly. "Leaving so soon?"

"Yes, it wasn't really my..." Jonah paused, unsure what to say. He looked at Chalky, and saw a young man who seemed eager for something, approval maybe. "...type of music," he finished lamely.

"You came though," Chalky said with a nod. "You've got front."

"Front?"

"Balls. Coming here even though you're, well, you know. One of them."

"Well, it's my family. I got the idea that you might be able to help. With Emily."

A silence hung between them. Jonah didn't want to tell him what he knew about his relationship with Sean Barnes. Chalky's eyes darted around the deserted car park. Finally he nodded. "Not here though."

"Well, when?" Jonah felt conflicted. Despite the fact that Chalky had invited him here as some kind of challenge or test, he actually liked the man. There was some basic honesty about him that he valued. Also, he now knew that Chalky held some information about Emily.

"I've got some things to sort out. Club business. Give me a couple of days, I'll get back to you." Something flickered across his face, a mixture of emotions as if he couldn't quite make his mind up what to say next. Then he dropped his head and spoke while looking at the floor. "It's crap though. What happened with Emily. It's not right. Family should always be together."

Jonah was itching to ask what he knew but the words had been barely mumbled as if they cost Chalky a great deal to say. And he had the promise of more help in the future. So he waited as yet another bike rumbled into the car park. When the engine was cut a silence fell between them.

"Chalky!" A yell came from behind him. A look of fear flashed across Chalky's face and he turned on his heel and went back to meet his friend without a word to Jonah.

Jonah decided to make himself scarce. He walked off, barely hearing the greetings and chatter behind him. He tried to decipher what had just happened. Whatever this evening was, he had passed the test. He had started down a road that might well lead him to Emily.

Jonah realised that Chalky had been in more danger than he had. Common sense might prevent the crowd from handing out a beating to a serving police officer – it would bring a world of trouble down on their heads. But one of their own? Who'd invited the enemy into the heart of their camp? And who would take a beating and never report it to the police? They would be in big trouble.

He found, to his surprise, that he was warming towards Chalky. He'd called him here at great personal risk and seemed genuinely upset that his family was threatened. He wasn't expecting to become best friends, but he did feel he'd made an unlikely ally.

CHAPTER 30

"I KNOW you aren't an organised group, but you seem to be the head of your little gang, so I thought we could do with a meeting."

"Of course." Jo motioned to the seat next to her. "And you got the message about the car?"

"Yes. That came from you? Because Kirsty is in your department?" Jonah leaned forward and peered at her, trying to figure out how much she knew. She was as guarded as him – they were like a pair of high stakes poker players. He had gone into the station in the morning to see what he could find out about Kirsty Price. He wasn't very surprised to see that her boss was Jo Murchie but was extremely fed up with the extent to which Murchie and her cronies were withholding information. Two can play at that game, he thought, resolving not to tell her that he'd figured out the link between Sean, Kirsty and Chalky.

"Yes, partly."

"What exactly is your connection with Kirsty and Sean Barnes?" Jonah asked. How honest would she be?

"I don't mean to be rude, but that is kind of a need to know basis."

"And I don't need to know?" A dangerous edge crept into Jonah's voice. "He's the main suspect in kidnapping my daughter and you think that I don't need to know?"

"Well, that is to say, we have been aware of him for a long while now."

"You can say that again! Everywhere I look there is a multi-specialist team this and a cross-agency report that. The guy has had more breaks than I can count and it seems that he's pissed all of them away." He paused for effect. "Trust me, if he has abducted my Emily, then you are not going to be able to protect him."

Jo held her hands up. "He's never done anything this serious before."

"Maybe you'd better start at the beginning." Jo Murchie just stared at him. He took a deep breath. "Look. Because it involves a family member, I'm not officially allowed on the investigation. It would compromise all sorts of evidence and be a bastard to get to court. But," he looked left and right theatrically, "I have been given some background work. They knew that if I sat at home doing nothing then I would go properly stir crazy. So, at the moment, I'm reading everything I can about Sean Barnes. Starting at the beginning. His mother was already known to social services so he hardly stood a chance. In care before he could walk. What's really odd is the gap between about eleven and thirteen when the records aren't there. Next thing we know, he's moved from Birmingham social services and enrolled in Merthyr High School. Once he's on our patch he soon came to our attention and started building quite the file. As I said, nothing much came of it because of you lot submitting reports and committees and teams."

"Look, I'm just not sure how much I can say. This is bigger than just Sean and me and you. There are other careers, other lives at stake here."

Jonah pushed back from the table. He wanted to storm out knocking chairs over on his way. But he also wanted to get the answers, find his daughter. He stood, towering over Jo Murchie. To her credit, she just sat there, unmoved.

"I will find Emily. And if Sean has anything to do with it, anything at all, then I'll be coming after you." He paused and gripped the back of the chair as he leaned in closer to her. "In fact, I'm going back to the office right now and the first thing I'll look up is if you have a professional body. Maybe an ombudsman or something. I'll have all of this raked over to see if somewhere you overstepped your bounds."

This did have an effect on Jo. Her face went white and she clasped her hands in her lap. When she didn't speak however, Jonah flicked his hands, sending the chair skittering across the floor and stalked from the coffee shop.

Before he reached the door, Jo called out. "Wait!" He stopped but didn't turn. Eventually she added, "I'll tell you everything."

Slowly Jonah turned and made his way back to the table. He picked up the chair and sat down as if it was the most natural thing in the world.

Jo spoke in a low, urgent voice. "I will tell you everything but give it a minute." Jonah looked around and saw that the coffee shop had fallen quiet. Those without headphones and the baristas were obviously waiting for the next instalment.

Somehow it broke the tense mood and Jonah chuckled quietly. "I guess that's the most excitement they've had in here for a while."

Just then an extended family bustled in. They rearranged chairs, parked pushchairs and talked loudly. One woman approached the counter and the others called orders over to her while she was ordering.

"Right, like I said I'm guessing that Sean was a victim of Tŷ Bwncath – with the timeline and the behaviour it all fits."

"We prefer survivor," Jo murmured. "But, yes, you are right. He did come through Tŷ Bwncath and was unlucky enough be there on a week when an event was scheduled. So we made a bit more of an effort to look after him."

"But how could you do that? We estimate that the operation was running for over ten years. With about three or four events per year, that could be hundreds of survivors. And that's just one dodgy operation. Surely you must know thousands of adults who need a hand to deal with their past."

"That is the hardest thing about what we do. We have to choose. We can't help all of them."

Jonah tried to suppress his excitement. So Jo Murchie knew what had gone on as well. Just how involved was she? "How did you choose?"

"Well in this case, Gwen made the final choice."

"Gwen? How does she fit into all of this?"

"You know how you told her that she should report it?" Jonah nodded and filed away the fact that Gwen had reported their conversation to Jo. "Well, she did report it. Bless her, she was still trying to protect me, right up to the end. I was a junior social worker then, just started, so it was down to me to answer the phones. Sort through the calls and do a first pass on what would be followed up."

"So it was you who told her not to report it? You made the decision?"

"It was the hardest decision I had to make. It was very early days – over thirty years ago now. So difficult to see the right thing to do. But you won't be able to understand the decision unless you're able to see it in context.

"It was the late eighties. Some of us knew, or at least we'd heard the rumours about Jimmy Savile. But, while we were hearing the rumours, we were watching him on TV. He was everywhere, with Margaret Thatcher, the royal family. Opening hospitals, running marathons, giving millions to charity. If half, hell, if even ten per cent of what we heard was true then we knew he was a monster. But the world loved him!" She stopped to run a hand through her hair. "The whole eighties was a bit of a minefield for us. I was a young, idealistic social worker, thought I could change the world. I travelled around a bit, met other members of socialist groups, people who ran underground newspapers, all that kind of stuff. There was a real network of people trying to oppose Thatcher.

"But everywhere I went, I heard the same story. Paedophiles. They were in the government, at the BBC, high ranking judges and police officers." She paused and gathered her strength to make a fresh admission. "Listen for every heart-warming tale that makes it to Hollywood, for every hero who fights the system and wins, there are at least ten, if not a hundred who just don't make it. We knew the truth, we had the moral superiority, but we couldn't get anything to go public. Some people tried, but they got nowhere and their careers stalled, they were chucked out of their jobs." Jonah looked sceptical. "Even now, look at the case in Rochdale. Social workers put everything on the line to bring a case that no one wanted any part of. And that was in a post-Savile world. Back in the eighties, I was just starting out, we all were. We had families to provide for, careers to start and mortgages to pay. We weren't prepared to risk everything. Don't forget that was a time when the police would break the unions, would get dressed up in riot gear and charge down students. It was us versus them and they had all the power."

She stopped again and looked at Jonah as if she had just remembered that he was there. "Sorry. I guess that it's always weighed on my mind. We were young and inexperienced and made decisions. So yes, we let Tŷ Bwncath carry on. We supported Gwen as best we could, helped her collect evidence where she could. And we got a few children out, like Sean and Chalky."

"How did that work exactly? How could you get them out?"

"Well, Gwen came to us after the first disappearance. Must have been mid-eighties by then. Instead of making a report I persuaded her to play the long game. It really was the beginning of our little organisation. We had a meeting in a pub. But Gwen had no idea if the child had been abducted or killed. If they were dead, we had half the Brecon Beacons as a possible grave site. It was impossible. In the months that followed the disappearance, there were no repercussions. We, in social services, kept an ear to the ground but heard nothing. That was when Gwen saw one ray of light. So, about six months later, towards the end of the season, she took a child home with her."

"What? Just like that?"

"Yep. Actually stood up to Bryn, challenged him. The whole relationship was built on brinkmanship. Gwen had figured out that Bryn had a contact in the councils that sent the children. If one disappeared, then they could cover it up. So she took a child to be her daughter and they had to cover it up."

"Because they were afraid of what she knew?"

"Precisely. Brinkmanship. And of course, we were embedded within the local council so we could get a copy birth certificate, enrol the child in a local school, sign up for housing benefit and register with a doctor. After that everything else just follows."

"But they must've realised that she wasn't their mother? Surely someone checked?"

Jo chuckled softly. "I expect your wife registered your children. It's not something you'd remember. But if an adult turns up with a child and a story about having moved to the area, who's going to think they've basically abducted that child? Especially if the child in question doesn't complain and appears settled with their new family."

"But surely, the police, or social services or someone?"

"What would they do? In fact, what would you do?" When Jonah didn't answer, she continued. "You, like the all the police, only respond when someone raises a case. If a complaint was ever made it wouldn't have taken you more than half a day to find the missing records and the fudges we put in place to make it all look official. You've already mentioned that you found a gap in the records.

"But that initial complaint never happened. From our end we were determined to keep quiet and the authority that the children came from worked some magic to make the children disappear. So, provided they kept their heads down, it was all fine."

"But Sean didn't keep his head down? We've got a file on him."

"Yes, but he said he was adopted, Gwen took responsibility for him, so who would ever challenge it?"

"You're right. I mean if the original mother turned up claiming that it was their child, then maybe CID would look into it, especially if it got violent. But I suppose that never happened?"

"That is the saddest part of our job. I mean, some of the placements are temporary and the children go back to their families. But so many of them have drug problems, or mental health issues and just never reach a place where they can have their children back. Or they do recover, make a new family and then don't want to be reminded of their gymslip children. To be honest, I think the rather grim truth is that the predators had already selected those with the weakest links and the lowest chance of families coming back to collect them. So when we rescued them, they were already lost children."

An awkward silence fell across the table as Jonah considered the difficult job that she'd had. Then the familiar mixture of worry and anger came back to him. Emily. He had to remember what he was doing here, and it was not reminiscing with a colleague. "So Chalky, Sean and Kirsty really were like siblings?"

"Yeah, Chalky was one of the first, kind of like a big brother to all those who came after. Including Sean Barnes."

"All of them? You mean it wasn't just the three of them?"

"Lord no! That woman was on a mission. She'd have opened her own children's home and run it properly given half a chance. As it was, she took in nine children over the years, all difficult and all at different ages."

"Blinding! And any of these could be helping Sean hide my daughter?"

"No! You don't understand them! They never had a family unit until Gwen took them in. Then it became the most important thing to them." Jonah started to protest but she held up a hand and continued speaking. "I know what you're going to say. We have no idea why Sean has done what you claim he's done. And any of his adopted siblings would only help him out if they didn't know what he was doing. That's why Kirsty leant him the car. She knew nothing about what he was doing or where he would go next."

"That doesn't help me much."

"It does. We've already told you about the car. As soon as we figured out that he was wanted by you lot then we handed over the details. Kirsty acted in good faith, you've got to believe me on that."

Jonah grunted, not trusting himself to speak.

Jo picked up on his frustration. "I don't know what you want from me."

"I want to know where my daughter is!"

"We don't know. Sean's dropped off our radar as well. I've been honest with you. More honest than I've ever been with anyone else." She slumped back into her chair, completely spent.

Jonah ran his hands through his hair. "Yes, I know. I've got some more deep background on Sean, I'm just not sure how it helps me. I know about Sean, Chalky and Kirsty, what about the other six who Gwen adopted? I could track them down. See what they know."

"No! I've shared with you but that's where I draw the line! They've had a bad start in life and now they're trying to make a good life and I won't have you disrupt all of that!"

"But they might know where my daughter is!"

They stared at each other in silence for a few seconds. Jo blinked first. She looked away and then back to Jonah. "Sorry. I know you're hurting. We know who they are and I'll go round them. As I've said they all value family and will want to help bring yours back together."

"Even at the expense of Sean?"

"Yes. He's gone beyond the pale." When Jonah still seemed not to be mollified, she continued. "Listen I've got a relationship with these people. I've helped them out, got them jobs, I've had their backs. Don't you think they'll be more likely to talk to me? To tell me something. And I do promise, anything I find that would help with locating Emily, I'll pass on, either through official channels or straight to you."

And you'll still be able to protect Sean by editing the information, Jonah thought. On the other hand, he didn't see that he had a lot of choice. His only other option was to go official and raise complaints. But if he did that, firstly he wouldn't find Emily and secondly he would hurt who knows how many other survivors. No matter what his reservations, he did believe that overall the conspiracy was doing good work. And he was loath to disrupt the life that the survivors had built.

"I suppose I've got to take it," he conceded. "But be quick, please. It's tearing my family apart, not knowing where Emily is."

Jo Murchie gave a curt nod. She'd seen enough families in distress to know what she was seeing. "I will try. But don't hold out too much hope. Chalky and Sean were always a bit different. The others tried to leave the chaos behind, mostly they got decent jobs, tried to blend in. I just don't think those two could manage it so they always lived on the margins." She saw Jonah's face fall a bit. "But don't worry. We've got Gwen's funeral tomorrow, and while they won't all be there, I'll be able to get in touch with the rest over the next few days. Anything I do know I'll pass on to you."

It wasn't enough but it was all Jonah could get.

CHAPTER 31

UNSURE OF HIS STATUS, Jonah chose to wait at the back of the church and observe the funeral of Gwen Davies. It turned out to be a good choice as he could see everyone coming in. He saw Kirsty Price sitting by her boss, and Jo Murchie, unsurprisingly joined by Debbie Houghton.

He was still trying to work out how he felt about all of them and the part they may have played, however unwittingly, in Emily's disappearance. The one thing he definitely did not want to do was to approach them and offer an olive branch.

Looking around the church he wondered how many of Mrs Davies' foundlings were there. He could understand the competing desires to be at their adoptive mother's funeral and to keep her secret, even now after her death.

Sticking out like a sore thumb, among all the suits and formal dresses, Chalky was easy to spot. Despite the sweltering day, he was wearing a T-shirt and his waistcoat with his colours on it. He seemed oblivious to the looks he was getting. Jonah was starting to understand the mindset – in his own way Chalky was wearing his best clothes, honouring the only woman who had mothered him.

He felt comfortably anonymous on the last bench, in his proper suit and black tie. He loosened his tie a bit to undo his top button and wondered when he could remove his jacket. He stood to sing the few hymns and did his best to blend in. When everybody left, he tagged along and an usher told him the name of a pub on the outskirts of Merthyr where the wake would be held. He now understood why Gwen would not be returning to Llandavy and why the wake would not be at the Prince of Wales inn.

He decided to go to the pub. A whole upper floor of a modern pub had been commandeered and, being a weekday morning, the rest of the building was empty. Jonah decided to mingle and gather what information he could. If someone wanted to tell him where Emily was or pass on any information, now might be the best time.

The first person to come up to him was a short woman in a smart business suit. She was large, with blonde hair cut in a bob and as she got closer, Jonah noted that she was close to his age.

"Jonah Greene?" She held out a hand to shake.

"Yes, DS Greene," he confirmed.

"Ah, right. This is a bit irregular, you see. I am, well was, Mrs Davies' solicitor. She knew she was dying so I was helping her with her will and to sort everything out." Jonah looked at her quizzically. He had no idea what was going on but suspected Gwen Davies was still pulling the strings even after her death. "Anyway I have very strict instructions from my client. I tried to tell her that it isn't usually in my remit, but she was a good client. If I'm honest I got a bit fond of her. Anyway, I've been instructed to hand this over to you. In person, not through the post or anything." She held out a plain white envelope with his name on it.

Jonah frowned as he took the envelope. It was light, probably only containing a single sheet of paper. Without saying a word, he slit it open and removed a sheet of headed Golden Valleys' notepaper. On it was written:

THE TREASURE IS in the middle of the vegetable patch.

JONAH TURNED IT OVER – the reverse was blank – then back to the front. There were only ten words, in shaky handwriting, obviously written by Gwen towards the end.

Jonah showed it to the solicitor who shook her head. "I have no idea. Like I said it was more of an indulgence than official duty." She lowered her voice and leaned in closer. "I think she might have got a bit funny towards the end. Kept insisting that I hand deliver it, didn't trust the post system or the internal mail in the police station." She shook her head. "Still, mustn't speak ill."

"Thank you," Jonah said absentmindedly. He made his excuses and moved away, his mind turning over what the message might mean. As he was thinking, Chalky caught his eye and signalled that he was going for a cigarette.

———

THEY MET outside in the smoking area. The pub owners had done their best to make it nice with wooden benches and some wooden slats that offered precious little shelter from the sun. Jonah guessed they'd be just as useless in the rain.

Fortunately no one else was there, so they sat side by side, an improbable couple. Chalky in his colours, Jonah in his funeral suit and black tie.

Chalky started rolling a cigarette, balancing a tin on his knee and carefully selecting the required elements. Jonah tried his hardest not to look at what Chalky was doing. The last thing he needed to see was a lump of cannabis resin or a small bag of green leaves.

"How come you're talking to me? What happened to article eight?" Jonah wanted everything out in the open. He was fed up of being lied to and messed around.

Chalky calmly clamped his finished cigarette in his lips and pocketed the tin. Then he stood up and turned his back. Jonah heard him lighting his cigarette but he didn't turn back around. Jonah finally realised that he was being shown something so he concentrated on the jacket.

His cut-off had changed, where the bottom rocker should be was a curved darker patch of leather – he'd removed the word Cardiff.

"So? You removed one your patches." He paused briefly to be sure he got the terminology right. "You've lost your bottom rocker."

"It's more than that. I've gone nomad." Chalky turned back around, puffing on his cigarette. Jonah still looked confused, so he continued. "The club is very organised, every member is sworn in by their chapter, in my case Cardiff. Once you're patched in, then you owe everything to them. Any other full member says jump, you ask how high. If you break the rules, the sergeant-at--arms imposes punishment. If it's serious, he meets with the president and vice president to decide what to do.

"But, every chapter is also part of the club as a whole.

The chapters all get their charters from the mother chapter, Aberystwyth. If you go nomad then you leave your chapter but remain as a member of the club as a whole." He paused looking thoughtful. "I think I'll get a bottom rocker that says nomad – it doesn't feel right not having the three-part patch. I ain't no prospect."

Jonah tried to decipher what he was saying and remember what Alex and the gang unit had taught him. "So, you're now a nomad, still in the Riders of Annwn, but not in your local chapter, or any chapter?" A prospect, Jonah remembered, would often be awarded his three-part patch in stages.

"Yeah, that's right, I'm in the club but not in a chapter."

"Okay. How does that help me?"

"Well, I spoke to Jez, our president and explained the problem. We worked this out, and it's a bit of a fudge. Now that I've left the chapter, they have no call on me. So Rotty can't have me if I bend the rules."

"Rotty?"

"He's our sergeant-at-arms. Sorry, he was my sergeant-at-arms. Now I'm under the mother chapter if I do anything wrong. It's been said, off the record, that I can talk to you about the past and my family. That's about loyalty and doing the right thing, which is another part of the club code. But I'm not at liberty to discuss any member of the club, or anything that they or the club may or may not be doing." This last part was recited by rote. Jonah wondered exactly how informal and off the record Chalky's discussions had been. "So, how far did you get with Mrs Davies?"

"Well, we know she worked at Tŷ Bwncath, even that she knew what was going on there. I think she used various aliases but we're still trying to untangle that." Jonah remembered looking around the congregation at the funeral he'd just left. He wasn't quite sure how much to say about his furious row with Jo Murchie. "We know she kind of adopted you and Kirsty and Sean, along with others that we don't know yet."

"She was a good woman, one of the best I've ever known," Chalky said decisively. "She was like a mother to me. Better than my real mam or any of the care placements, that's for sure. I gave her all kinds of shit and she just wouldn't stop looking out for me." He took a moment to look away and Jonah left him to it. "That's part of the reason to go nomad. I want to spend some time in Liverpool. She had family up there. They might want to talk about her. Anyway, they should know what a good woman she was." He paused and looked bereft. "Also, I was partly staying here because I wanted to be close to her, in case she needed anything. Now, I can go anywhere so I don't need to belong to the Cardiff chapter."

Jonah's mind was spinning. He'd tried and failed to understand all there was to Gwen Davies. Cautiously, he picked out the right words to say to Chalky. "Did you meet her when you went to Tŷ Bwncath?"

"Yes."

"How did she do it? We've found no record of any adoptions?"

"Yeah, that's as maybe. When she took a shine to one of us, she took us. Simple as that. Lemme tell you what happened to me. I was in care in Birmingham when I came out here on a holiday." His voice had gone quieter and he was staring into the distance as he spoke. "Fair play to him, Bryn Bancroft was a monster, but for the first part of the week everything was great. We played games, sat round the fire, explored the Brecon Beacons. But then Friday night came. I guess I just got unlucky – I've met with other survivors and it seems there were four parties a year. They drugged our hot chocolate you know. Friday evening Mr Bancroft made it himself and handed it out. So he knew who to come back for and take to the hotel."

"Do you have any memories of what happened?" Jonah hated himself for always being a policeman.

Chalky shook his head. "That was the beauty of their scheme. You woke up in the morning with the mother of all hangovers. Several of us were sick. I could only just keep down toast for breakfast. No idea what had happened except where we were sore. But your body remembers even if your mind doesn't. Even now if I see a bushy beard or smell a particular aftershave or even hear someone breathing in a particular way, I want to stab them." He stopped, weighing his options. "Or run and hide," he added quietly.

"But you escaped?"

"Not escaped. Mrs Davies got me to one side and told me to wait. I was like a zombie that morning – so bloody tired and ill. When the minibus left she just told me I was going home with her. Took me the best part of a week to realise I'd never be going back into care in Birmingham. And more than a year to realise how lucky I was."

"I don't mean to be harsh or unfeeling, but how does this help me find my daughter?"

"Well, that's the thing you see. It's all about family. If it is Sean who's got your daughter, then he must be doing it for the strongest of reasons. It's all any of us ever wanted was a proper family."

"We did have a message, Chalky, probably from Sean. I

think he wants the story to come out, everything to be publicised. But I've spoken to our PR officer, there's no guarantee that it'd become a national story and even then it could take months. I don't know where she is, but Emily can't wait that long."

"That does make sense." Chalky nodded. "He'd want this exposed. It's all he's talked about forever. Whenever he could get access he was on that bloody website, sharing stories, stirring up trouble. Some of us survivors try to put it all behind us, carry on like normal. Pretend it never happened like. But there are some, like Sean who get obsessed. He just couldn't believe that it had all been swept under the carpet. If he wanted anything, any demand to release your Emily, it would be to have the story told. The guilty locked up. I just never thought he'd go this far."

Jonah's heart sank. The whole thing was impossible. Even with his connections he was being led down blind alleys and finding it impossible to make people listen. And now Tŷ Bwncath itself had burnt out, taking its secrets with it. Sean's demands were impossible to meet.

"Suppose it couldn't be done. Even after Savile and all that, it might just not be possible. Where would Sean take a hostage?" Chalky stared pointedly off into the distance. "Come on, he's not in the club. You can't hide behind article eight on this one!" He was answered with more silence. "If you're going to condemn my daughter, at least tell me why!"

"It's not that easy. I had no loyalty growing up, no one fighting my corner til I found Mrs Davies. All we've got is each other. Me and the club, me and the family that Mrs Davies made. If I turn him in, then what have I got left?"

"But if you don't you could be breaking up another family? Don't we deserve a chance to get it right?"

Chalky turned back to Jonah, pain and indecision etched on his face. "Tŷ Bwncath. It's where it started and it's where it will end. Despite everything that happened there, he couldn't leave the place alone. He's always stayed around there, it's where he goes when he's stressed. He has hidden camps in the woods, little valleys. He took me to some of them. But I know he's always moving, finding new places, getting rid of old camps. Even if he was still at an old one, I couldn't find them. If he's anywhere, he'll be up there."

"I could do it," Jonah said, almost to himself. "Get the dog handlers out, helicopter with infrared cameras and a line of officers across the landscape. Flush him out."

"Nah," Chalky shook his head. "You start moving vans and stuff up there, there's only about three roads in and out of Llandavy. He'd be long gone before you even assigned people into teams."

"How? He won't outrun a helicopter on foot."

"He's got the Fiesta. Probably hidden out of sight. He'd be long gone. Trust me. I know Sean."

"All right then, you know him. What should I do? Even if I do what he wants, expose people, make arrests and news stories, that won't happen for months. And he's not exactly somewhere he can keep up on the news is he?"

Chalky looked away again, lost in thought. "Go up there," he said finally. "Up to Tŷ Bwncath. Walk around it in a big circle. Stand on ridges, don't try to hide. When he sees you're alone, he might come out and talk."

"That's it? Go for a walk in the sodding country? And hope that he deigns to come down and talk to me?"

Jonah thought of the card from the solicitor. He hadn't wanted to go near the place again. But if he did go there and see if he could decipher the card, maybe he would get to meet Sean as well. And then what? "What should I say to Sean, assuming your plan works?"

"Tell him you have contacts. You're identifying the children who've died, uncovering stuff that happened decades ago. Could you get a journalist interested? Maybe get him an interview to tell his story?"

"I could do," Jonah said uncertainly. The truth was that if Sean Barnes was holding Emily hostage, then he was in a world of trouble. Kidnapping, plus involvement in two deaths, meant that he was looking at a lot of jail time. But then Jonah's natural instinct as a father reared its head. He must do whatever was necessary to get Emily back, even lie to Sean.

Jonah still didn't wholly trust Chalky. Maybe he was still in touch with Sean, maybe he even knew where Emily was. But still, he was sending Jonah signals, so he had to respond. He tried to sound confident. "I do know some journalists, I could find on who does feature work – long term projects. There's every chance this could take off and be blown up into something big."

"That'd be good. I know I don't agree with Sean, but maybe if this was in the press it'd be a good thing. Let them know they can't do this and get away with it."

"Yeah," Jonah said, as if he was already forming a plan. "I'm sure it can be done." He gestured with his empty pint glass towards the bar. "Do you want another?"

"No, I'd better head off. I don't think I'm very welcome here." He paused. "Had to see Mrs Davies off though. The world won't be the same without her."

With these words he slipped through a gate in the fence. As Jonah reached the door back into the pub, he heard the familiar bark of Chalky's bike being fired up.

He stood at the bar with another pint and tried to make

sense of what had happened so far. As he neared the bottom of the glass he realised that he'd have to go back up to Tŷ Bwncath. Being outside Merthyr Tydfil, he was closer to Llandavy than Cardiff and there was nothing waiting for him in the city.

CHAPTER 32

JONAH STOPPED his car in the car park of Tŷ Bwncath. Not much had changed since he was last here. There was still a gaping hole in the roof towards the rear. He walked over for a minute and peered in the broken window. Mr Collingsworth had done nothing to secure the place. He presumed that the council had deemed it safe and not a threat to the road. He looked up to the sky showing through the roof. The hole was fringed with tiles like broken teeth. They looked ready to fall on anyone stupid enough to venture inside. There were still piles of rubble in the middle of the floor, still filing cabinets sticking up. Some of the lighter scraps of paper had blown around the yard. There was still an incongruous poster beside the hole where the hatch used to be.

He stepped back out of the shadow the house and the heat beat down on him. The sky was a bowl of pure blue, undisturbed by clouds. He was already sweating, just standing here looking around.

Carefully he surveyed the garden between the house and the car park. It was a patch of dusty earth, still marked by boots from the firefighters. The middle of the vegetable garden, he thought. Was there even a vegetable plot here? And if there was, would he recognise it? He started pacing, carefully studying the ground, occasionally looking around at the gardens.

He used to garden a lot, and now thought wistfully of his patch back home. Since long before Alex had thrown him out he had neglected it. He had a sudden longing to be back there fixing it up, the memory triggering his brain – he knew what he was doing!

A vegetable garden should face south, be close to both the kitchen and the water butt. He looked to see what fit the criteria. There was a rectangular plot, right by the kitchen window, with paths all the way around and the water butt in the corner. That was where he'd site a vegetable plot.

Everything there was overgrown, and the leaves were all wilting now in the heat. He started to half-heartedly pull up some plants, pushing aside the earth with his foot.

To his surprise he found himself holding a long, crooked carrot. This must be the vegetable plot. And, he frowned, someone had been growing plants here recently. He didn't think the carrots had survived for twenty years. He looked at it and then cast around for any tools at all.

To his surprise, he saw a ramshackle shed, more of a lean-to, tucked into the corner between the main house and the dormitory. It was blackened by smoke but appeared to be undamaged. As the rest of the house had been abandoned, he was hopeful as he approached it. Opening it up flooded him with a wave of nostalgia – the sight and smell of all the tools took him straight back to his garden at home. Or at the house where Alex lived. He wasn't sure which.

In no time he had fastened string from corner to corner of the plot to crudely mark out the centre. With the spade he made an initial blow into the hard, dusty earth. As he attempted to fling it out of the way of his eventual hole, half of it slid from the spade and after a couple more attempts he leant back and wiped the sweat from his eyes.

It was just after noon and the sun was on this side of the house offering no shade anywhere. He squinted at the sky and looked around. He could feel his shirt sticking to his back. He wondered if the water was still connected and if he could find an outside tap. Even if it was, would he want to drink the water from here? Although he was a rational man, the house had a bad feeling and he wasn't sure he'd want to take water from there into his body.

He took a careful swig from the water bottle he'd brought with him then soon lost himself in the work. He put his foot on the spade, pushed into the earth, shifted his grip and lifted out the soil. He tipped it out and re-positioned the spade to repeat the sequence. He fell into a happy rhythm, remembering to keep sipping his drink.

The work was what he needed. The physical labour pushed the thoughts out of his head. Losing his daughter, the state of his marriage and his career, dodgy police and politicians, secret conspiracies – all of them were set aside by the task. His back twinged and his hands burned but he kept going. It was a moving meditation.

His reverie was broken when his spade jarred onto metal. He had lulled himself into believing that he was on a fool's errand and decided he was only going to dig for an hour or so, just to calm himself down. Now, improbably, he had found the treasure at the bottom of the hole.

Awkwardly he wielded the spade to clear off the top of the box. Every time he tried to clear it, he knocked more earth back into the hole. He remembered seeing a trowel in the shed so he straightened up and stretched.

Before walking to the shed he looked around and took a drink of water. When he brought his head back down, a movement on the ridge high above caught his eye.

Sean Barnes! Standing there, in silhouette, waiting to be noticed. With Farida's warnings still clear in his mind, he pulled his phone from his jacket. One signal bar should be enough, he thought. He called through to Farida with one eye on the figure on the ridge who wasn't moving. Farida answered on the second ring but was immediately cut off when the signal dropped.

Jonah stared stupidly at his phone for a second before stuffing it in his pocket. If he went up on the ridge, he'd have better signal and a chance of catching Sean. He wasted precious seconds trying to figure out how to get through the outbuildings and onto the farmland beyond. When he was in the clear field, he struggled up the slope to the now deserted ridgeline.

His face prickled as the sweat broke out. The air felt like treacle being sucked into his lungs. He longed for another drink from his bottle, but held off, knowing that he might have to chase further into the Beacons to find Sean.

When he'd gained the ridge, Jonah leant with his hands on his thighs, gasping for breath. His scalp tingled as the sun beat down. Finally he straightened, shielded his eyes, and cast around for his quarry.

Down the other side of the ridge, at the bottom of a small valley, was a copse. He saw a flicker of white as a figure moved deeper into the trees, following a path down from where he stood.

Relieved that he'd soon be in shade, Jonah jogged down to the trees. It was easier going downhill and he was pleased with his progress.

Inside the wood it appeared dark until his eyes adapted.

There was still mottled light and here the heat was trapped by the trees. Although the sun no longer beat down on him, the foliage made a humid tunnel of heat and moisture.

He allowed himself one sip to take his bottle to halfway and then plunged on into the wood. At the heart, there was a narrow stream, bridged by a simple wooden plank. Beyond this, paths led up and downstream as well as straight ahead.

Jonah stopped. He couldn't afford to wait and think for long. The path ahead was short – he could see the light of the open moor from here. He would take that one, cast around, and still be able to backtrack if he was wrong.

He crashed down the path and straight out into the sun again. He blinked the sweat out of his eyes and cast around for his quarry. There! Diagonally across the field was the line of a faint path. It ended in a stile, and just beyond there was something. Heat haze made everything shimmer but Jonah was sure he'd just seen the back of Sean's head and not one of the spots that were floating in front of his eyes.

Labouring now, he climbed up the next hill, his bad left knee starting to ache, reminding Jonah of all the physio-therapy appointments that he'd missed. Although there was a path, the tufts of grass seemed to catch at his feet and he struggled to make the steps. At least the stile would be a high vantage point from which he could get his bearings, check his phone, and hopefully keep Sean in sight.

When he finally made it there, he stood, one foot each side and surveyed the countryside. There was no sign of Tŷ Bwncath now. There were a couple of other copses of trees and an ancient hedgerow snaking over the fields.

He took a mouthful of water, then retrieved his phone. If he had signal, then they could bracket the area, seal it off, find Emily and arrest Sean.

The battery had dropped alarmingly and the signal bar was empty. He held it up and moved it around experimentally. If he could just get one bar, at least he could text Farida.

Something stung his hand. He dropped the phone, and stuck his finger in his mouth, causing him to lose his balance from the stile. Landing heavily on his shoulder he rolled towards some nettles. He lunged away and ended up on his front on the dusty ground.

He realised he was looking at a puddle. With a sinking heart he saw that he'd dropped his water bottle and the lid hadn't been secured.

Feeling a bit stupid, he got to his feet. His hand was swelling and a bruise was appearing on the back of one finger. It was red and angry, but he couldn't see a bite mark. Experimentally he flexed his fingers – nothing broken.

He retrieved his phone and saw that the screen was cracked and dark. Looking closer he saw that the case was dented on the edge. He was trying to figure out what had happened when there was a crack from next to him as a smooth pebble bounced off the fence post – Sean must've brought a catapult or sling with him.

Jonah ducked down below the level of the foliage. I'm hiding from a bloody schoolboy weapon, he thought. Although the throbbing in his hand reminded him that he still had to be careful.

Crouching in the dirt, he slowly moved from feeling dejected to angry. Why was he letting Sean run rings around him? He abandoned the cover of the stile and charged recklessly up the hill. But there were no more stones fired at him.

When he reached the top, Sean had already fled. He stopped to catch his breath and look for his quarry. He turned around in a complete circle but all he could see were the Beacons stretching away to the haze.

He was still gasping for breath and now his stomach was lurching. He bent over and retched but kept his lunch down. Straightening, he was alarmed at how much the world appeared to sway and spin. Still the sun beat down and he was sure now that his scalp was burning. He could feel every part of his body prickling with sweat, sticking his shirt to his back.

With a rising panic, he realised that he couldn't work out which direction he had just come from. He looked in vain for the stile, or was it a wood, that he had just left. All around the landscape looked the same.

He saw a flicker of movement dead ahead. Squinting, he saw there was a false rise and his quarry must've disappeared over that.

Plunging off again, he aimed at a short tree that was just below the summit. As he neared it he decided to pass it to the left to benefit from a little shade.

He had a moment of incomprehension as his foot wouldn't respond and take a step. He looked down and saw a root over his foot. Then he fell. He saw sky, grass, sun and dirt, spiralling over and over again, tasting dirt as he kicked up plumes of dust. He came to a halt and everything went black.

CHAPTER 33

THE FIRST THING Jonah was aware of was the dark red of the inside of his eyelids. From the heat and light he knew he was lying on his back in the fierce sun even though his forehead felt cold. Experimentally he turned his head to the side and cracked his eyes open a little.

He was looking at dried grass and someone's leg, clad in green trousers. Squinting against the brightness he looked up at Sean Barnes, his quarry. Sean was sat on the grass, with his arms loosely held around his knees, looking comfortable.

Jonah levered himself upright – he felt at a disadvantage lying down. The sun was so bright it hurt his eyes and his throat felt parched. His head swam. He looked over more carefully now. That was definitely Sean, the thin face and straggly hair although in this heat he wasn't wearing his army coat. He had a loose, long-sleeved white top instead.

A brief burst of ecstasy coursed through Jonah eclipsing his physical discomfort. He had caught his prey. Sean Barnes was right here, in touching distance. He'd been caught.

The other man held out a bottle of water. "Gently though, small sips at first."

Jonah did what he was told, letting the cool water work its way through his body. After a few mouthfuls he could feel a headache starting and his stomach cramped. He held the half empty bottle on his knee and took a breath.

"Sean Barnes, I am..."

"No! I know you're a policeman and your instinct is to arrest me." Jonah chewed his lip, trying not to interrupt and finish the caution. "Before you charge ahead and get yourself somewhere you can't get out of, answer me one question." Jonah looked at him mutinously. "Where is your car?"

"What do you mean? It's parked at Tŷ Bwncath, in the car park."

"Okay then. Which direction is that? Just point which way you would go."

Jonah cast his mind back. He'd seen Sean on the ridge above the house and given chase. There had been a copse, then the stile where he'd lost his water bottle and phone. Then what? Another field, ridge, hedgerow, it all blurred together. He craned around behind him and saw the final tree that he had tripped over before rolling down to this spot.

He had no idea. He could easily have circled around. Tŷ Bwncath might be in front of him, or behind him. He looked around at Sean who smiled slowly. He pulled a hat out of his pocket, unfolded it and placed it calmly on his head. It was a floppy canvas hat in beige, the sort of thing an elderly man might wear.

He had still made no move to escape and a horrible truth was starting to dawn on Jonah. Had he really caught his quarry? He looked around and all he could see in any direction were heather coated hills, dry stone walls and hedges. No indication of any landmarks that he could use, even if he did have a map or a compass.

"You see, you might be able to say the words but you can't actually arrest me. You have no handcuffs. You can't really drag me to your car if you don't even know where it is. Meanwhile I've got my lovely hat, and somewhere near here I've hidden a bag with spare water and snacks. Or I might go back to my campsite, wait up in the shade and then move on in the evening when it's cooler."

Jonah looked around helplessly. He was lost and felt weak after the ordeal of the chase. More to play for time than anything, he carried on talking. "So, why do you come back here then? Surely the whole area has bad memories?"

"Memories. That reminds me!" Sean reached into a satchel and brought out a plain brown envelope which he passed to Jonah. He opened it and peered inside to find fifteen or so photographs. They were all of children in the Beacons, from sometime in the eighties or nineties. All they needed was Sean to write Cofiwch Dŷ Bwncath on the back. "I took them from Mrs Davies before I moved out. I kind of felt bad about taking them, but she had loads. Always taking photos she was." He paused looking around at the landscape. "This was our playground growing up. Some days we'd go and perch on a ridge and watch them playing games in the fields around Tŷ Bwncath. Always careful never to get too close. I felt bad about that too. Even the kids who were lucky, who avoided one of those weeks, I felt bad for them. They got one week out here then back to their shitty lives."

"So, you were happy here, even despite...?"

Sean frowned as if he was trying to work out a complex

problem. "It's not that simple. You have no idea really. I was an inner-city kid brought up in care. Passed around from foster family to children's' homes, social workers, the whole lot. This place was a paradise for the first six days. I know he was a monster, but Mr Bancroft was good at his job. We got to play outside, some fresh air, plenty of exercise, team games, all of that good stuff. The last night..." He paused to stare off into the distance. "I've spoken to other survivors. Put the pieces together. He was a canny old sod. There were only three or four parties a year." He spat into the dust. "Parties! That's what they called them! The worst fucking night of my life and for them it was a party! It was always the last night of the week, and we were drugged. Next day, they'd be on a minibus home with a hangover." He paused to fix Jonah with a stare. "You know what you should be doing? Instead of chasing me and hassling bike gangs? You should look into how come the minute a group got home, they were all split up. Look at the accounts on the website. The month after a party, the group involved was broken up and sent all over the country. Stops us comparing stories, doesn't it?

"Anyway, there was all that, but there was also Mrs Davies. I take it you've put all this together? Best thing that ever happened to me. I don't know how she managed it but she gave me the closest thing I've ever had to a family. Of course, I was too old, too damaged to know what I'd got. I acted out, but she was always there for me. So, yes, this is where it happened. But it's also where I found a family."

A long pause stretched out between them.

"What do you want?" Jonah asked cautiously.

"Well, I was going to hold Emily to force you to expose everything that went on here. You know, get the story out there like Rotherham or Savile or something. A nice

Channel 4 documentary and a big spread in the Sunday papers."

"But?"

"Well, I kept checking my phone when I could. Mrs Davies always said that when she'd gone, it would all come out. But I got a message from Chalky and nothing happened."

"She did leave me something, but I've only just found it," Jonah said.

"Anyway, I've been speaking to Emily and she told me about that case earlier this year. The homeless guy? I figure if you risked everything to do the right thing by someone homeless who you didn't even know, then maybe you'd do the same thing for the survivors?"

Jonah saw a ray of hope. His chance to get Emily back. "Of course. That's what I will do. I've got a good relationship with our press officer. I can work with her to find sympathetic journalists, we will get the story out."

"I have trouble trusting people but I do believe you."

"So, what do you want now?"

"Oh, it's not about what I want. It's about what will happen. The first thing is that I'm not going back."

"Back? Back to where?"

"Back to anywhere that is run by a civil servant. I've had enough of light green painted brickwork and fire safety doors with their windows crisscrossed with reinforcing wires. The same bloody smell whether it's a foster home or a probation centre. The low sofas, tables with carefully placed tissue boxes and professionals with concerned smiles." He stood up and started pacing. "I've spent half my life in bloody institutions! But no more! I'm done with that crap!"

"Okay, calm down." Jonah needed to redirect him before he got too excited. "What about Emily? Is she safe?"

"Emily? Oh yes, she's safe, for now. You know, I was so disappointed in her." Jonah's stomach clenched at these words. "She had it all, I was entranced. She had a family that loved her, a home to go back to if she needed to, everything I always wanted. And then, she threw it all away. There was that birthday party that she forgot to go to. She laughed it off. Laughed! I'd have given anything, everything to be invited to a family meal and she just couldn't be bothered."

"But is she safe?"

"Yes! She's very safe! This is the whole point. I need to know that families still exist, that you can make the right decisions."

"What are you talking about? My daughter is missing and you know something! Start making sense!"

Sean took a deep breath and put his head in his hands then looked up, now a lot calmer. "Right. Yes. Come on, stand up next to me."

When the two were stood side by side, Sean stretched his arm out to point at a gate in a far corner of the field. "See that gate down there. That opens onto a lane. On top of the gatepost is a key and there's another bottle of water in the shade there too. If you turn right, a few hundred yards down the road you'll find Emily handcuffed to a gate. Once you've freed her, continue until the crossroads, then turn left. After a mile or so you'll come to a pub. The landlord should let you use the phone, get out of the sun, all that good stuff."

Jonah frowned. "And what will you be doing?"

"Me? I'm going that way." He turned round and pointed

to the ridge behind him. "I'll find my camp and get out of here. A whole different country. Somewhere English-speaking where I can work cash in hand. Or maybe I'll spend the summer on the Med. I never had a holiday so now would be a good time. You'll never see me again, I'll make sure of that."

"And I can trust you?"

"I'm not lying about your daughter." He paused. "I want you to make the right decision. Not for myself, not so I can get away. But so that I know that family still exists, that someone still puts their family above their job, their passions – above everything."

Jonah stood there, frozen by indecision. He turned to go after Emily, then stopped again. He might be choosing family over his police duties but he had a case to solve. Sean was still in earshot so he called out. "Wait! I've got one question."

Sean turned and looked down on him from higher up on the ridge, a questioning look on his face.

"What happened? With Leo Davidson? At the railway station?" There was a pause, so Jonah continued. "I'm not going to see you again but I have to know."

"I recognised him, you know, from the parties." He scowled as he said the word. "My whole life is a mess and there he was on the platform, nice suit, just exuding this air of having succeeded, you know. Everything worked out just fucking peachy for him and his friends. I couldn't bloody believe it. It was an insult to me, you know, to see him like that, not a care in the world. Anyway, I figured a man like that probably had a routine, so I went back the next week, same time, hung around the station, watched him go in. The third time, I'd already broken the camera and I actually went to confront him. I wanted to give him a photograph. Try to burst to his bubble."

"And then what?" Jonah was torn. He knew that his daughter was down there, chained up. But this was also the end of his chase. The answer.

"We argued. I know what you're waiting to hear but I can't give it to you. I tried to give him the photo but he wouldn't take it. I was shouting and he pushed me back. I stepped forward and well, he went back. I don't know if I pushed him or he tripped, but he just vanished. One minute a man, next a train. It was just a blur after that."

"So..." Jonah didn't know what to ask.

"So there's no answer. No neat box you can put this one in. I don't know. Maybe I'm a killer or maybe it was an accident?" He shrugged and carried on up the hill.

Jonah knew what he had to do. He had family. Before he was a policeman and after he retired, he would still be a father. But when he turned away and started towards the gate, it wasn't without cost. He felt the wrench. He felt the failure. He couldn't even properly label Sean as a suspect. Once Emily gave her statement, there would be a warrant put out for his arrest for kidnapping.

Walking towards the gate, he turned over the rest of it in his mind. Sean Barnes had set events in motion that led to the death of Leo Davidson, but he doubted that death would be added to the warrant. And there was the matter of Davidson's guilt too. Sean was the only witness who claimed to be able to identify him and now he was in the process of disappearing. He was still trying to plait fog.

He reached the bottom of the field by the gate and found that so far Sean was as good as his word. He had a fresh bottle of water and a key in his hand. Soon the rest of the puzzle fell into place.

It was good to walk to the pub with Emily. It gave them a chance to talk before the whole circus of paramedics and police descended on them. Jonah learnt that Sean had suggested a camping trip up in the Brecon Beacons, only to drive there in the dark so she had no way of getting home. He also confiscated her phone, leaving her totally trapped.

CHAPTER 34

By the end of the afternoon, Jonah was back at Tŷ Bwncath. Now his car wasn't alone in the car park. It had been joined by other vehicles – paramedics, police and Alex. She had come straight from home. She wouldn't be separated from Emily and her daughter needed her there.

Before too long, the official vehicles started peeling out of the car park.

"Back together again," Alex said. "You should come back with us. I've called Gareth, I'll cook dinner for all of us."

Jonah frowned. He felt pulled around. He was the dog that was alternately offered treats and a kick and now he didn't know which way to go. He looked over to the brooding shell of the house and felt drawn. Then his eye fell on his shovel, sticking out of the earth with his jacket over the handle.

"Not right away. I've still got work to do."

"Jonah! You nearly died up there! Surely you can take one day off. You're not the only person in the police force. If there's anything needs doing, get someone else in."

"No. This is a job that I've got to finish." He stopped, his mind whirling. He was completely exhausted. He thought about corrupt officers, cover-ups, the missing teeth in the DNA lab and wondered who he could trust. As if his thoughts has summoned it, a red BMW arrived on the lane and stopped where the driver had a view of the whole scene. This strengthened Jonah's resolve. "I'll only be an hour or so. I've got more water now than I know what to do with. I'll be okay."

"Well, take my phone then." Alex held it out and didn't move until Jonah took it. "It seems to have good signal up here. And come round tonight, to bring it back."

Jonah watched them go back to the car and when he was alone walked back to the veg patch. His limbs felt heavy and when he got to the hole, he stopped to gather his breath. The shadows were longer and the air a bit cooler so he thought he should make a start.

He was summoning the energy to look for a trowel in the shed, not even thinking about how he would manage to lift the box and carry it to his car. Then he heard a familiar sound, the bark of a motorbike on short exhaust pipes. He was cheered by the thought that Chalky had come to help. The biker leant his bike over onto its side stand and came over to where Jonah was standing.

"I felt bad about sending you up here and then leaving you to it. How did it go? Did you find Sean?"

Jonah gave him a brief recap of his afternoon, fortunately remembering that he was talking to someone who was basically a brother to Sean so he made sure to colour his account to paint him in a better light.

"So Sean's gone then? I'll probably never see him again?" Chalky looked downcast.

"Yes. If he comes back here, you know we'll have to

arrest him." Jonah shrugged apologetically. "He's committed a whole list of crimes."

Chalky nodded. "He'll never let you do that."

"I figured." There was a pause which was surprisingly companionable.

"I saw this thing on Facebook." Chalky broke the silence. "The best revenge is a life lived well. Made me think, you know. How far did it get Sean? Being all eaten up inside about this?" He turned to indicate the ruins of Tŷ Bwncath. "Some days I wonder if Kirsty Price didn't get it right. She'll have a normal life, probably get married, have kids, grow old surrounded by her family and love. Maybe she'll have the best revenge."

Jonah had no answer for that.

"So, what are you doing here then?" Chalky indicated the hole.

"I'm meant to get that box out," Jonah said. "But I had heatstroke or something up there. Now I can barely stand. But it's Mrs Davies' last request so, you know."

Chalky squinted. "Doesn't look that heavy."

"There's a trowel in the shed," Jonah offered. "If we could just get the handles clear."

"There's no we about it, old man. You sit down and drink your water. I've never shied away from hard work and especially not if it's for Mrs Davies."

Jonah felt bad but pretty soon Chalky had hefted the box out by its handles. It was a dull green metal box. Less than two feet across, it was narrow and secured with metal clips.

"Here it is, what do you want to do with it?"

"Can you put in the boot of my car?" He remembered all the problems in the past. "I'll have a look inside and decide what to do. I need to preserve the evidence."

Chalky carefully carried it to the boot of the car. On the way Jonah realised it was an old army ammunition box.

When it was laid in the boot Jonah carefully put on latex gloves and once the clips were open, he found a sealed plastic bag in the box. Aware that he could be compromising evidence, he peeled the old tape away from the bag. It was a heavy-duty garden waste bin liner, rolled down and taped.

He held the bag open and peered inside. There were three books, hard-backed, old-fashioned ledgers. They had dark red covers and he knew the end pages would be marbled. He thought he could see the edges of photographs and newspaper clippings, but he'd seen enough. He folded the bag over, put it back in the box and reapplied the clips over the lid.

A shadow fell across him, so he turned. As he did so he protectively slammed the boot down on his car. His other hand found his key fob in his pocket and he locked his car.

The figure of ex-ACC Mayweather loomed over him. In the background, he saw Chalky drift back towards his bike. "What have you got there, Greene?" The tone was that of a senior officer expecting to be obeyed.

"Nothing."

"Don't play games with me! I saw your friend get that box out of the earth and carry it to the car. Now, what's in the box!"

"That's not your business." Jonah had to bite his tongue to stop himself adding sir to the end of his answer.

"This is Dyfed Powys force area so we're both off our home turf." Somehow Mayweather managed to make this sound like a threat.

"Not really," Jonah countered. "I'm working with Dyfed Powys police, assisting them with their enquiries. That assistance extends to executing a search warrant at these premises." He stopped to stare down Mayweather. "That's why I have lawful authority to be here on private land. What about you?"

Mayweather looked completely unconcerned. "It's not private land, the gate to the road was open. I just came in to keep an eye on things for my friends." He stopped as if considering his next words. "It's good to have friends." He turned to look pointedly at Chalky who was watching from where he stood by his bike. "But you must pick the right friends. You might want to think on that, Greene."

With that he turned on his heel and stalked off before Jonah could think of a response. He leant back against his car and took yet another swig of water. When Mayweather's car had left, Chalky came over.

Wordlessly, he gave Jonah a fierce, backslapping hug. Then he let him go, and turned back to his bike. Soon the echo of the exhaust note had died away and Jonah was left alone. The shadow of Tŷ Bwncath stretched over the car park. He watched the sun sink down below the horizon but the day showed no sign of cooling down yet.

It was time for him to leave Tŷ Bwncath.

———

DRIVING AWAY FROM THE HOUSE, Jonah couldn't stop thinking about Mayweather and the box in the boot. He was reminded of the missing DNA samples from the children's teeth and wondered how safe the evidence system really was. He saw a lay-by coming up and pulled in. Flicking through his phone, he called up DC Rob Turnbull's number.

Soon, he was on his way back to Cardiff but he wasn't

going home or back to his station. Instead, he went to disturb the evidence officer at his home. Once they were on their way into Cardiff Bay, he outlined the problem, Mayweather's constant interference, the missing tooth samples and the box full of evidence now in the boot of his car.

DC Turnbull took over the process of entering the evidence into the system. When the box was all booked in and they were walking back to the car, he spoke to Jonah in low tones.

"Right. Here's all the reference numbers. But I've made a mistake. It's actually filed as if it went into evidence on this date but three years earlier. I can find it, you can find it but anyone else will have a devil of a job. I'd still rather you came through me when you need it back though."

Jonah nodded and gave his thanks to the detective whose evening he had interrupted. Soon he had him back home, and feeling that he'd done the best he could, he headed off to his own home.

Soon Jonah was sat around the table with his whole family. Everyone was subdued after all the excitement, grateful to be together again. In all the running around he'd had a chance to think. He had been pushed and pulled around by everyone from Jo Murchie to Sean Barnes, and by everything from his family to the demands of his job.

When the meal was over he returned Alex's phone and told her that he was going back to his room in Canton.

"Why? This is your home, you should be here."

"We haven't really sat down and talked things over yet, though. We need to sort things out between us. Find out where we are and what's going on with us. And me. And before I do that, I need to clear my head. Know what I'm thinking. At the moment I'm so tired I can't really think straight. Give me a few days."

"Are you sure? You're welcome here."

Jonah felt uneasy that Alex had ordered him out of his home and then summoned him back. He needed to find himself before he could repair his relationship.

He also needed to make peace with the mistakes he'd made and being back in his room gave him a chance to do things right.

CHAPTER 35

AFTER HIS ORDEAL on the Beacons, Jonah was under strict orders to take a couple of days sick leave to get his strength back. He had planned to go on long walks around the city and cook himself proper food. In the end, he was still exhausted so he ate takeaway and alternated between long nights asleep and dozing on the sofa.

When he felt himself in danger of sinking into a stupor, he started flicking through his case notes, looking for things he had missed. He knew that there were loose ends to be tied up and realised that now he knew the truth about Gwen and her children, he could move forward with identifying the bodies.

He made the call and arranged to meet Jo Murchie in coffee shop about five minutes' walk from his flat. Another bloody chain coffee shop, Jonah thought. When had they started popping up on the high streets across the country? When he was growing up, there had been a few cafés here and there, but nothing like the espresso machine equipped barista bars that were everywhere now.

Soon he was sitting with an over large coffee in front of Jo Murchie.

"Firstly, thank you for all your hard work on this case. We got a good result. I'm intrigued as to why you wanted to talk me but I also wanted to talk to you anyway."

"Okay, what did you want to say?" Jonah wanted to clear the air before he launched into his pitch.

"It's nothing bad. I've pulled some strings to get you in on a meeting you'll want to attend."

"What's that then?" Jonah had a sinking feeling. It seemed that Jo was doing him a favour before he launched into his attack.

"Well, we've negotiated a way to enter the journals from the box that you dug up into evidence. It'll involve a set of lawyers contracted by the survivors working with police technical teams."

"Of course, I'd love to be there, to see the end."

Jo Murchie gave a low chuckle. "This is not the end. This is just the beginning." There was an awkward pause. Both of them knew that Jonah had called this meeting for some difficult reason.

Jonah jumped straight in with both feet. "I need a list of all the names of children that were unofficially fostered by Gwen Davies." He paused for a moment, then added. "Actually any children that were unofficially fostered out of Tŷ Bwncath."

"That's out of the question."

"Hear me out first. On the one hand I have three bodies buried up on the moor. We know their sexes and have rough age ranges for each of them. On the other hand I have reports from the survivors of around a dozen children who went to Tŷ Bwncath and never came back. If I have that list of unofficial adoptions, then I can reduce my list of missing children down to something manageable. This will enable me to move forward in ways that would otherwise be impossible." Jo nodded slowly, deep in thought, so Jonah pressed on. "I wouldn't contact them. I don't need addresses or phone numbers. Any names they've been known by and date of birth will be enough. I just need to exclude them from my list of missing children."

Jo paused a little longer. "I suppose that I could give you a list of first names and birth years. That should be enough for you to eliminate them from your enquiries, shouldn't it?"

"No, actually it is not enough." Something deep inside Jonah snapped. "Either I'm inside your grubby little conspiracy or I'm not. I'm done with living on the edges. I've risked my life up on the Beacons – hell, I put my own bloody daughter in danger. And then, after all that I brought back the prize. I did everything you wanted and now you don't fucking trust me? You expect me to work with one hand tied behind my back? Work through your half-arsed redacted list and come back to you begging for more information if I get stuck. Well, fuck that and fuck you! Either I'm in on equal terms or I'm not."

Jonah had no intention of waiting for a response; he stormed out of the coffee shop and was halfway back to the station before his head cleared. And once he was thinking straight, he found he had few regrets though he recognised that a good half of his anger towards Jo should maybe have been directed at Alex, and maybe even himself.

CHAPTER 36

JONAH SWUNG by the office before his meeting about the buried diaries. He needed to access the computers and bring himself up to date on the latest progress in the whole Tŷ Bwncath case. He was surprised to see a plain buff envelope on his desk.

Inside was a single sheet of A4, with a typed list of names and dates of birth. It also gave also known as names and even suggestions as to which council they had been in care with. At the bottom was a pink Post-it note which read simply, 'Welcome to the team'. Jonah smiled and thought that maybe he ought to shout and swear at more people.

The meeting Jo Murchie had arranged took place in an anonymous meeting room in an office on a business park on the outskirts of Cardiff. In a room was a desk with a laptop that had a host of wires snaking away from it. One went to a scanner and a further two went to external hard drives.

When Jonah went into the room he was introduced to a solicitor, the senior partner in a firm that was assembling a class action suit. Also present was a civilian from the police's forensic documents unit. Jonah was there as the police presence, and Jo Murchie had somehow got herself an invite too.

The muddy, rusty ammunition case that Jonah had dug up looked strangely out of place among all the high-tech equipment. The three books that had been buried for decades were laid on the table in pride of place.

Jonah asked if he could have a quick look through before they started technically logging them. There were glances and nods between the technical person and the solicitor.

Jonah put on his latex gloves and opened the ledgers. They were heavy, old-fashioned leather books with marbled end papers. He started skimming the contents.

Initially, Gwen had written a diary for each day that a party had taken place. She'd listed who she knew to have attended, both the adults and the children. After two or three however, it either got too distressing to write it like a diary or the same names kept turning up.

Whatever the reason, she had become more formal. The other two books were used as a cross-reference from this point on. One was a list of every adult, numbered with a reference starting A. Each one was given half a page and it looked as if Gwen had kept them updated over time. The other was a list of children, starting with C1 and going up to C279.

From this point on the diary of parties became a more functional list of dates and attendees. Jonah couldn't help himself – he started looking for ex ACC Mayweather. He found him and had a quick check through the list of events. It did not surprise him when he found that Mayweather had only visited one party. He'd always struck Jonah as the sort of person who didn't get involved.

Davidson and the other two recipients of Sean's photos

were also listed, as far more active participants. It looked like his information was spot on.

Every single page would be scanned and then the data would be cross-referenced to build up a complete picture. The two hard discs were for the solicitors and the police and every single page had to be saved to both.

The process was slow and laborious. It was made even more so by the fact that various photos and newspaper cuttings had been taped in. By now the tape had gone yellow and brittle so the forensic technician had to make a best guess as to which photo went where. He also had a digital camera and took many photos to record the process.

Jonah found his mind wandering back to the conversations he'd initially had when the diaries came to light. Naively, he'd initially thought that as soon as someone was named, then the police would swoop round and arrest them.

Now he was more cynical. It had been explained to him that Mayweather would make a good guess as to what had been found. Hopefully this would spread throughout the network and drive some of the guilty to resign or retire. Jonah still wanted formal justice in court but he knew the reality. And he remembered the mantra – what was best for the children? At least this way, the network would be splintered and people would be removed from positions of power.

In a dark corner of his soul, he wondered if the discovery of these three books would lead to more suicides. And if it did, would it be a bad thing?

He realised that he'd been thinking like a father. If someone messed with one of his children, his first thought would be to push them under a train. But he was also a policeman. Should his first thought be about preserving evidence and bringing the guilty to justice? When he had been alone on the Beacons, without any support or oversight, he had acted firstly like a father. Could he now find his way back to behaving like a policeman?

He shook his head, causing Jo to look at him questioningly. He shrugged and rubbed his eyes as if something external was bothering him.

Not that he shouldn't be bothered, he thought. He was sat in a room with a detailed account of the abuse of a great many children by a large number of adults, stretching over twelve years.

When the first day was over and two uniformed officers took the ledgers back into evidence, Jo Murchie nervously approached Jonah. "If you're still talking to me, I've got someone I'd like you to meet."

Jonah didn't know what to say. He had no regrets and no intention of apologising. He nodded. "Thank you for sending over the list. It'll be a big help when it comes to identifying the bones."

"You're welcome. And don't feel bad about your outburst. This case has put you through the wringer. Now, there's someone I want you to meet." She held up her hands. "Don't worry, I won't hang around and make things awkward."

Soon he was at the motorway services and sat opposite a slightly overweight man with iron grey hair and square glasses.

Jo made the introductions. "This is Steve Gregg. He was a senior officer in North Wales Police and on retirement has served a term as police and crime commissioner. My sources tell me that he's at the top of the list to be heading up a public enquiry into events at Tŷ Bwncath."

"Thank you for that potted CV, Jo. You do flatter me and make me sound more important than I am." He had a definite Welsh lilt to his voice that made his words sound soft but Jonah made a mental note not to underestimate him.

Jo made her apologies and left the two men to it.

"I wanted to meet you to thank you for what you've done so far. And I wanted to talk over with you what will happen next."

"Me? I'm a DS and coroner's officer in South Wales Police. It's nothing to do with me."

"You've earned this. And when I was serving I always wanted to see a case through to the end. I know you should pass everything over to the CPS but I never saw a case as closed until someone was behind bars." He paused to assess Jonah. "What do you make of the evidence that you found in the vegetable patch?"

"Well, the ledgers are good and the chain of evidence is secure. On the other hand they are basically hearsay from a dead person so they could be ruled out. If I was pushed I'd say that they could form a good part of a case. But you'd need something else."

Gregg nodded slowly. "We're thinking the same thing. The first thing we've done is to arrest Alan Cooper."

Jonah frowned, trying to remember where he fit in the investigation. "The landlord of the Prince of Wales?"

"Yes, it was important to get him out of there before he got wind of this. We secured his office and currently have forensic document officers going through and logging all the paperwork from over thirty years of running the pub and hotel."

"But surely he wouldn't have kept anything incriminating? No one's that stupid!"

"I don't know what kind of criminals you get in the south, but everywhere I've been, criminals always make mistakes. Besides, nothing has happened for twenty years, and his knowledge of what went on is his power. It's very likely he kept something back for blackmail. We think he knew Bancroft and they both bought their properties as part of a plan."

"You mean, they set it up from the beginning?"

"It's something we're investigating. It certainly makes sense. If there ever had been an investigation, it kept the evidence away from Tŷ Bwncath."

"And the other location is a hotel, so there won't be any useful evidence there either – it's a place with multiple occupants and regular cleaning." Gregg nodded soberly before Jonah continued. "So, why are we spending so much effort on the ledgers then?"

"Well, we're going to keep them under wraps for a bit. When we've digitised everything, we'll put the information into a database. Then we can go back and talk to the victims." Survivors, Jonah thought to himself, but he didn't interrupt Gregg. "We'll get stories from them in as much detail as possible, properly recorded as interviews." He started to get excited as he spoke. "I'm planning to get pictures of the alleged perpetrators named in the diaries, as they would have looked back in the nineties. With more photos from the nineties, we can do a virtual identity parade. As soon as we get even one account that matches up on the dates and the people present, then the ledgers start to become corroborated. The more accounts we gather, the harder it'll be to discount them.

"On top of all that, we'll be processing the Prince of Wales' documents. I suspect that a creep like Cooper didn't just stop when Bancroft died. With a bit of luck we'll catch him with something naughty on his computer. Might even be able to turn him, get him talking."

Jonah nodded. He could see the logic of what the other man was saying. "But that'll take..."

"Months? Years? Maybe. But it's what we do. Doesn't matter if I'm in uniform or not. It's about catching the bad guys. The main point is that you brought the diaries back and we were able to enter them into evidence. Do you think they're real?"

Jonah frowned at the other man. "I'm certain they are. Have you flicked through them? They are well aged and the inks used are all different. Besides, why would Gwen invent them? All they do is blacken her name once she's gone."

"No, no, I'm with you. I just wanted to check. My gut feeling is that they are a record of the events that happened, written at the time. That's what I'm going to do, put that at the centre of my investigation. Everything else will just feed into that."

"Okay, thank you. I'm really grateful to you for taking the time to let me know what's going on."

The other man slid a business card across the table. "Like I said, you've earned it. Without your relationship with Gwen, and your pursuit of the truth we wouldn't have an enquiry. You should be able to follow our progress in the papers but if you want to know anything, give me a ring and we can have another chat."

CHAPTER 37

Jonah had got up early and caught the train to Manchester. It was the quickest, cheapest option and allowed him to doze on the train.

He got off at Manchester Piccadilly feeling gritty and horrible. The weather hadn't yet broken, so it was already hot and sticky. He was thankful that his contact in Greater Manchester Police was waiting for him on the platform.

"Hi, Greg Smith." The man shook his hand warmly. Jonah was dwarfed, he was well over six foot though he wasn't built like a weightlifter, it was more like he had run to seed. He certainly wasn't skinny. He had a worn face and short-cropped hair.

When they had made their introductions, Jonah was led back to a standard issue unmarked police car. When they were standing each side, Jonah waiting for the door to be unlocked, DC Smith asked,

"You sure you want to do this?"

"Yes, of course, why wouldn't I?"

"You haven't met Maggie North, have you?" Jonah shook his head. "She's a bit of a legend, certainly among uniform.

She's bitten more than one of them. If there's a call for someone shoplifting, or drunk and disorderly, odds are that it'll be her."

"What's her story?" Jonah asked. It was obvious he was set on this course so Smith unlocked the door.

"Same old, same old. She was born to a waster of a mother, no father on the scene. Soon the prostitution and drugs came home to roost and little Maggie went into care." He stopped to look at Jonah. "I know some of the kids go into care, get a good foster, good adoption, but Maggie wasn't one of those. Shuffled around, no consistency. Wasn't long before she followed her mother's footsteps."

He started the engine and they pulled away from the kerb, expertly merging into the traffic.

"Have you ever heard of a brother on the scene?"

"Yeah, I know that's what you're doing up here. We're not social workers, we just try to keep her from scaring the locals. Lock her up when she's too drunk. I did have a quick chat with her case worker, nope not a thing. She ran it through the computer, but it's needle in a haystack time. If he'd been adopted separate from here then he could easily have a different name. Or he could've been transferred out of area. Or sent to a secure unit. Those records would be sealed. Without a date of birth you're pissing in the wind." There was a pause as he considered his next words. "If you really want to know, asking her will be the quickest way."

Jonah caught the odd tone in his colleague's voice. "What's with the attitude? Surely she'll want to know if she had family, what happened to them?"

"The problem is," Smith gestured with one hand while driving, "not the telling her. I'm sure she might want to know. The problem lies in the bit between when we show up and she finally understands we're not there to give her grief."

They lapsed into silence, driving deeper into an estate near the centre of Manchester. Finally they pulled up outside a long, low block of flats.

"You sure?"

Jonah nodded and they prepared to go in.

They went down a hallway that was fairly clean and only smelt faintly of urine until Smith stopped and indicated a blue door.

"Looks all right," Jonah commented.

"Yeah, council property. Not too shabby." He knocked on the door.

After a pause, they heard a voice through the closed door. "What do you want? Do you know what time it is?"

"It's the police. We just want to talk, a minute of your time." Smith rolled his eyes.

"Fuck off! You know I don't talk to no filth! Was that why you woke me up?"

"If you don't want to talk, will you listen?"

There was a longer silence, then the door opened a crack, held on a security chain. A face appeared, framed by a straight black fringe. Suspicious eyes squinted through the gap. "Who are you? You ain't the usual filth. What do you want?"

"I've come all the way from South Wales to talk to you. Just want five minutes of your time."

"South Wales? Ain't they got no phones down there?" She chuckled at her own joke, then got more serious. "So, you're not on your own turf? You can't arrest me?"

"I'm not here to arrest anyone." Jonah fought to keep the frustration out of his voice. "I've found out something about your family. Thought you might want to know." He was prepared to leave, sure that curiosity would lead her to call him back.

"Ha! Shows what you know. I ain't got no family. Me mam died years ago."

Jonah decided to wait her out. Eventually she said, sulkily, "Well, what's this message then? That you've come all this way to give me. Couldn't be done over the phone."

Aware of the houses to either side, and certain that they were being watched, Jonah stalled. "It's a bit personal. Not the kind of thing we should be talking about on the doorstep."

"Well, I ain't inviting no coppers into my house. I know better than that." She thought for a second, her brow creasing under the fringe. "We can get a coffee down in the community centre." As she withdrew to get ready to go out, she muttered under her breath. "Might get an adviser to sit in."

Soon they were in the community centre café. Maggie had insisted on buying her own coffee – "Never took nothing from the police and not starting now" – and an adviser was sat with them. He was a young man, in his twenties, with oversize glasses and a wispy beard. He looked bored by the whole proceedings.

Maggie sat opposite them in leggings, vest top and rather oddly considering the weather, an oversize parka. She had cheap tattoos showing on her neck and hands.

"So, go on then." She was still confrontational.

"You said you had no family," Jonah started. "But did you know about a younger brother you might have had? Maybe a half-brother?"

Maggie's eyes suddenly shone as she fought back tears. She quickly turned to stare out of the window. When she had herself under control, she spoke. "I thought I did. I mean, Mam said I did. Bobby. I was in care about thirteen or fourteen and she said this kid, Bobby was my half-brother. I was meant to look out for him as we were in the same children's home." She paused as if deciding what to reveal. "I didn't do a good job. Fucked it up like I do everything in my life. I was more interested in stealing booze and fags than looking after a snotty eight-year-old I never even met before." She stopped and stared at the two policemen, chin jutting out, daring them to criticise her.

"When did you last see or hear about him?" Jonah asked gently.

"After a couple of years I pretty much gave up on being in care. I was hanging around with older kids and they all said that you just get cut loose at eighteen so I thought I might as well just leave early, strike out on my own, you know. Around that time me mam died as well. I guess maybe she knew her time was up and wanted to me to watch out for Bobby." Her face creased as she worked something out. "I last saw him when I was sixteen, a few weeks after me birthday. Would've been the middle of 1992, I reckon."

"Do you know if he ever went on holiday to South Wales?"

"What the fuck is going on?" Maggie pushed back from the table and looked around, ready to flee. The adviser leant forward and put a hand on her arm. She took a deep breath, then leaned forward to peer at Jonah. "Who the hell are you?"

"I'm DS Greene from South Wales Police and I might know what happened to your brother. But before I tell you, could you tell me what you remember?" There was a pause, during which Maggie watched him suspiciously. "It would help me to hear what you can remember before I tell you what I know. That way what you say won't be coloured by what I'm about to say."

She nodded reluctantly and fished a battered pack of cigarettes out of her pocket with a cheap lighter. The adviser started to say something, then stopped when she glared at him. "There was this big holiday thing, down in Wales. All sorts of lame stuff like canoeing and climbing." She lit her cigarette defiantly. "We were all meant to go but I was in trouble for stealing fags and breaking curfew so I didn't. It was pretty much when I stopped going back to the home anyway. I went back a couple of weeks later, just to check in and I hardly recognised anyone. They'd made a load of moves and transfers. What was a home with fifteen kids in suddenly had half a dozen. Place closed down six months later."

"And your brother?"

"Never saw him again. Every now and again, one of them social workers asks me what I want. You know, what I'd be aiming for. They always say that if you want to get clean, you've got to have a goal, a vision of a future without drugs." She waved her cigarette dismissively. "And I used to say to them, I want to find my brother. I tell 'em his name and my mam's name and that he must've been born in 1982. And nothing. No records, nothing in the system." She shook her head. "Over the last few years, I started thinking either I made it up or me mam did. She was a bit of a mess, most of the time. Maybe she got confused or I did."

"No, Maggie. I'm really sorry but it looks as if your brother died in Wales."

"Was there an accident on the holiday?"

"No, I'm sorry to tell you that there was a ring of paedophiles operating out of Tŷ Bwncath, the holiday centre. When we investigated, we found bones buried on the site. The DNA from one of them was a partial match to your own DNA, taken from one of your arrests. Like I say, I'm sorry to be the bearer of bad news."

Maggie shook her head, confused. "So it was all true? What me mam said, that boy I knew for a couple of years. But the records? I don't understand."

"We haven't really pieced it together yet. But it looks as if some people who worked for social services deleted records, broke up the children so they couldn't talk, closed down the children's home."

There was nothing more to say, so Jonah took a couple of photos from his pocket. One was the reconstruction from Bobby's skull, the other was a copy of the photo from Gwen Davies' ledgers that looked to be the closest match.

"I don't know if these would be any use to you?" He slid them across the table.

"Yeah, that's him. It's not right, you know. What happened." She let her fingers trail over the photos, then stopped and swallowed hard. "I suppose I should thank you. You didn't have to come out here, do this."

"I think he should be remembered. He shouldn't just be an unmarked grave on a lonely hillside." Jonah paused, reading the look on Maggie's face that she wasn't able to even travel down to Llandavy, never mind arrange something. "I've got some friends in the area. They've suggested a simple stone where the bodies were, with his name and dates on it."

"That'd be nice." Maggie couldn't say any more. She pushed back from the table and was out of the door before anyone could say anything.

CHAPTER 38

"So..." Jonah was unsure of how to broach the subject with Alex. "I've spoken to HR and because I had sick leave and such I've got a lot of leave accrued, both from this year and carried over from last." Alex watched him closely, waiting for him to get to the point. "Anyway, I have a contact, who has a house in France. He needs a caretaker, someone to make it safe for the winter, talk to local builders, stuff like that." He trailed off uncertainly.

"And you want to go? Alone?"

"At first. But once I've got the place secure and comfortable I'd love you to come out for a holiday. And the children if they can. But first of all I need a bit of time on my own. To recover a bit. Good honest physical work is what I really need right now."

"You've already made your mind up, haven't you?" Alex sounded forlorn.

"I have made the arrangements provisionally." Jonah thought of his phone call with PC Carter when he'd offered. "I could stay, if you think you'll need me. Or the kids?"

Alex shook her head. "It pains me to say so, but I think

you're right. A break would give us time to figure it out. And a free place to stay in France for a month or two? We'll definitely take you up on that offer."

Jonah nodded. He knew it was for the best but it was also a leap into the unknown.

ACKNOWLEDGEMENTS

Thank you for reading this book, especially if we've never met. As a writer, selling my books to strangers, is the best feeling. (Obviously, if you're friends or family, thank you for supporting me!) This was a book I really wanted to write and I hope it deals with the subject matter sensitively. As well as my readers, I have other people to thank who turn a first draft into a published book.

Melanie Underwood is my editor who finds and fixes my mistakes with endless grace and patience. The beautiful cover was designed by the talented team at Ebook Launch. Thank you to my wife Ellie who has always supported me and believed in my work, especially when I didn't. And Barry Blackmore and Anne Miller checked over the text for accuracy and typos. All surviving mistakes are mine.

Please consider leaving a review on Amazon. You can also sign up for my newsletter and learn about my other books by visiting my website GrahamHMiller.com. Jonah Greene is currently having a rest while I write another series, but I hope to return to his world soon.

Printed in Great Britain
by Amazon